Historical fiction
Bath 2026

THEA

A NOVEL

GENEVIEVE MORRISSEY

Copyright © 2025 by Genevieve Morrissey.

The right of Genevieve Morrissey to be identified as the author of this work has been asserted.

All rights reserved.

No part of this book may be reproduced, stored in a retrieval system, or transmitted, in any form, or by any means (electronic, mechanical, photocopying, recording or otherwise) without the prior written permission of the author, except in cases of brief quotations embodied in reviews or articles. It may not be edited, amended, lent, resold, hired out, distributed or otherwise circulated, without the publisher's written permission.

Permission can be obtained from www.antlands.com

This book is a work of fiction. Except in the case of historical fact, names, characters, places, and incidents either are products of the author's imagination or are used fictitiously. Any resemblance to actual persons, living or dead, events, or locales is entirely coincidental.

Published by Genevieve Morrissey.

ISBN: 979-8-9901192-0-8

Cover design and interior formatting: Mark Thomas / Coverness.com

*To Mark Thomas and Kelly Schaub
for all the mistakes they've stopped me from making,
and to Jim
for all the ones he's just let me go ahead and make*

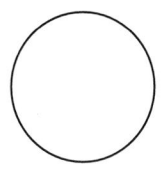

Chapter One

"Up, Ma. Time to get up."

Ma pulled the sheet over her head—as usual. "Five more minutes," she managed to say before her voice trailed off. Mother hated mornings.

I shook her. "No, not even *one* more. It's time to start breakfast. Get up."

The breakfast my mother needed to start cooking wasn't ours. I'd eat whatever I could grab from the kitchen quickest, and Ma would have coffee. Lots and lots of coffee. My mother was employed as a cook-housekeeper to a medical doctor, Dr. Hallam—Edward James Hallam III, according to the framed diploma propped carelessly against a pile of books in his office—and the breakfast she needed to get out of bed to cook was his.

"You start it," Mother mumbled, head still under the sheet. "You can do that, can't you? Please? You get it started, and I'll be along in a minute."

If this were a Saturday, Sunday, or a school holiday, I *would* have gotten it started. In fact, every Saturday, Sunday, and school holiday, I *did* get it started. Doing the cooking myself was much easier than getting my mother out of bed. But this was a school day.

"No," I said firmly. "I've got school. Come on, now. Get up."

I shook her arm and nagged until Ma finally roused enough to say irritably, "All right, all right," and swing her thin legs over the side of the bed. "Stop trying to drag me. Do you think I can't get to the toilet by myself?"

"Wash your face, too," I answered.

"That's what you think, isn't it? That I can't get to the toilet by myself."

I started laying out Ma's uniform: black dress and white apron. Only maids wore caps. I did our laundry (the doctor sent his out), and I was glad I didn't have the extra work of starching and ironing a maid's frilled bandeau. "I don't think anything," I said.

"Yes, you do. You're always thinking bad things about me. My own daughter!"

I knew better than to rise to her bait. If I let on she'd gotten me in a tender spot, she'd escalate, repeating her "point" (in this case, that I was unjust) until she made me cry.

Instead, I glanced at the clock—an ornate walnut bracket model that, like my mother and me, had come down in the world. "If you can get to the toilet by yourself, then get to the toilet," I said in an even tone. "And do it quick, or the doctor's breakfast will be late." I'd be late to school, too. I didn't mention that part. I was fifteen, and my mother hated that I was determined to finish high school instead of getting a full-time job to support us. I was partway through sophomore year now, with two more to go. "How about if I go over to the house and start the coffee while you get dressed?" I offered. "That way, you can have coffee as soon as you get there. That'll help."

Still not moving, Ma said, "I didn't, Thea."

"Didn't what?"

"Didn't— do what you're thinking. I didn't. I swear before God I didn't have a drop."

I knew this was true. I'd have known if she'd been drinking. I always knew.

"Fine," I said. "Get up, then. I have to leave in a minute."

The promise of coffee worked. Ma finally shuffled off toward the bathroom. I waited, listening, until the sounds of her washing became more energetic, then hurried out.

The apartment where Ma and I lived was a single room plus bath above the garage of a house in a new neighborhood on the north side of Oklahoma City. Our apartment was only really big enough to accommodate one person, and had never been fully finished, but it was my seventh "home" in four years, and I wanted to keep it. I'd been the one to spot the doctor's advertisement in the paper and the promise of a separate apartment was the thing that had made me insist Ma apply. I'd watched her lose job after job from being caught drunk and neglecting her duties. She only ever drank at home, so Prohibition notwithstanding, she'd never been arrested, but each job-loss meant starting over, broke, in a new place. I figured a separate apartment to hide her when she was in no condition to be seen greatly increased my chances of finishing a year at the same school I started in.

When I got to the doctor's kitchen, I brought in the milk from the back porch and lit the burner under the percolator for Ma. Then I cut bread for toast, sliced bacon, and set eggs and butter within easy reach of the frying pan I'd left ready on the stove when I washed the dishes the night before, meanwhile stuffing my face with whatever came to hand. After that, I assembled and filled the coffee-making contraption the doctor referred to as a "cafetière," because the doctor would not drink percolated coffee. Mother told me this was because he was "Old Money," an expression I didn't understand as meaning anything beyond that he was very particular about coffee.

The kitchen clock told me I'd miss the beginning of my first class, but luckily this was only geometry. I ranked a solid second in geometry at Central High School, and my teacher usually pretended not to notice if I was tardy.

The bacon was half-done, and I was about to begin frying eggs when my mother finally made her appearance. I'd really be late for class now. I didn't complain about this, though, because Ma looked cheerful and was steady on her feet, which she wasn't always. She felt so good, in fact, that she even offered me her cheek for a kiss.

"Go on," she said. "I'll take over."

I poured her the coffee I'd promised, then ran back up to the apartment both to retrieve my schoolbooks and to ransack it, quickly but thoroughly, for any sign of a bottle or flask. There wasn't one, and even better, my stash of carfare nickels was untouched. Ten nickels a week for the streetcar was my pocket money, and Ma usually left it alone, but if nickels stood between her and a drink she was determined to have, she'd help herself to anything she could find.

Then, schoolbooks under my arm, I ran for the streetcar stop two blocks away.

I saw Dr. Hallam at the window of the front room as I passed. He saw me, too, which was too bad. The doctor knew I existed, of course, but it was my policy to make myself as inconspicuous as possible to maintain the illusion that my mother was the one—the only one—who got his house clean and his food cooked.

I couldn't entirely figure out the doctor. He was youngish, nice looking, and mannerly—things everybody wishes they were, but many aren't. Since he was a doctor, I guessed he must also be very smart and educated. He owned more books than some libraries, and had a car, nice clothes, and a house, so obviously he had plenty of money. He let my mother buy what she needed for housekeeping and paid the bills without even looking at them. Taken altogether, in fact, Dr. Hallam had everything anybody could possibly want in life—and as far as I could see, he didn't notice he had them or care. He didn't seem to care about anything, in fact. He seldom talked, and I never saw him smile.

He didn't have any sweethearts, though if he made half an effort, his looks and money would bring women around in droves, and though he'd lived in Oklahoma City for more than a year, his house was empty beyond a few sticks of dining room furniture, a bed for him to sleep in, and a desk and chair in the library. Aside from a dozen medical books and some stacks of medical magazines, the library's two walls of shelves were empty. The books that should have been on them were still packed up in crates lining the hallway. Lamps in the doctor's bedroom and the front room stood on the floor. The house was always going to be too big for him to live in alone. There was no helping that. It had been built for a large family who ended up not wanting it—there was a story there, but I didn't know it—but I thought if Dr. Hallam brought in at least enough chairs and tables and sofas that he didn't rattle around the rooms like a bean in a boxcar, he might be more comfortable.

The doctor didn't try to be comfortable. He didn't try to be happy. He just—lived. Worked and lived. That was all.

This annoyed me. Personally, I'd have liked to have seen a law passed that said people who had advantages—especially money—and didn't appreciate them were obliged to share their advantages—especially money—with the rest of us. Ma and I quarreled about a lot of things, but we were always in perfect agreement about wanting more money.

At the Central High stop, I jumped off the streetcar before it stopped rolling and ran for school's back door.

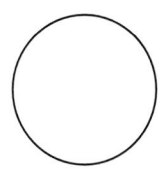

Chapter Two

I was born in 1911 in a small town in southern Oklahoma when my parents were around forty years old and my brother Tom and sister Jane were almost grown. My arrival surprised everyone, apparently including my mother. She always said I was welcome, but I had my doubts. Ma's family were only dirt farmers, but she bragged they were "good stock" and claimed she'd married beneath her. I had doubts about that, too. All Ma meant by "good stock" was literate for several generations back, possessors of a Bible and an almanac, and—most importantly in southern Oklahoma—incontestably White. It didn't mean they had money or any likelihood of ever getting money.

Dad's family, on the other hand, seemed to be climbing in the world. I didn't remember my father well, but I knew he'd had an eighth-grade education and made enough working for the railroad for Ma to live in a nice house, wear pretty dresses, and pay for birthday parties and music lessons for Tom and Janie.

That is, he made *almost* enough money for those things. When Dad died suddenly—I was five years old at the time—it came out that he was in debt, mostly for things Mother'd bought on time payments. Every penny of his railroad life insurance (which was only $250 anyway), along with what my brother Tom raised by selling the piano and some of our furniture, went to settle my father's estate.

With Dad gone, Ma expected Tom to stay on and take over the role of family breadwinner, but Tom had other ideas. He moved to Louisiana to live, and we didn't hear from him much. My sister Jane stayed around for a couple years, but at the time Dad died she was already working at a drugstore in town, and it turned out she wanted to keep the money she made there to buy things for herself. When I was seven, she moved to Pauls Valley, and aside from a bare signature on a card at Christmas, we didn't hear from her, either. Mother was shocked and disappointed by the way her children took care of themselves instead of her.

For a couple of years after that, Ma was able to keep the two of us afloat by selling off most of the rest of our household goods, except for the walnut bracket-clock, which for some reason she loved. After each sale, we lived fine for a while, with new clothes, plenty of food, and bus rides across the border to a town in Texas that had moving picture shows. Each time, as the money ran out, we stayed home more and more and had soda crackers crumbled in milk for dinner, and eventually, just the crackers. Then Ma would sell a few more things, and the good times would come back, although I didn't recognize this as a pattern until much later.

Finally, when there was nothing left to sell but the house itself, Ma wrote begging letters to Tom and Jane. Tom didn't answer, but Janie sent five dollars and offered to take me in. She didn't invite Ma, so I didn't go.

After that, Ma and I moved from one place to another, staying in cheap lodgings or with relatives of Dad's who didn't want us. We ended up in Oklahoma City, where with the very last of the money from the house sale, Ma paid for a business course for herself. Our fortunes had turned, she told me. "Business girls" made good money. We lived in a single room in a boarding house that I entered and left by a window that opened onto an alley to save the money the landlady would have charged for a second tenant, and ate what Ma could smuggle from the table for me.

Ma soon abandoned the business course. She couldn't get the hang of shorthand, she said, and the clacking of a roomful of typewriter keys gave her a headache. We had no family who wanted anything to do with us, and we didn't know a soul in town.

Life after that was just Ma, me, and Ma's faithful friend, liquor. Of the three of us, Mother loved liquor the best, because although it kept her bone-thin and paper-skinned and couldn't solve any of her problems, it reliably, though only briefly, made her troubles seem less.

My comfort was school. I loved it, and I was good at it. I never had real friends. Moving from place to place (not to mention Ma's drinking), made friendships impossible. Books were my companions, and my teachers' praise—not soda crackers—were the meat and drink that fed me. From the time I was ten, my highest ambition in life was to get a high school diploma, and after that the kind of nice job a diploma could get me. Now I was fifteen and resigned to the fact that this meant another three years of keeping my mother employed and reasonably sober.

As I'd anticipated, I was late to geometry class. Although my teacher, Mr. Brody, pretended not to notice me slipping in at the back, some of the students turned around and stared pointedly on purpose to draw his attention to me. Sometimes it seemed like everyone in the class hated me except Homer Escoe, the boy who was always in first place in geometry to my second. Homer was the only student who didn't seem to mind the fact that, though a girl, I was better at math than most boys. He was always very nice to me, in fact.

When geometry was dismissed, I went on to my next class, literature.

Literature was a new subject at Central. Until 1924, the school only offered regular English classes, which had some reading to them, but were mostly grammar drills and diagramming sentences from things like *Poor Richard's Almanack* and the Bible. I didn't have anything against the Bible (or Poor Richard), but I didn't like diagramming sentences.

Our literature books, on the other hand, were brand-new and full of modern stories and poetry, so of course every meeting of the school board ended in fights and demands for a re-vote on whether literature classes were tools of the Devil. Oklahoma was Baptist country (my mother was a Baptist), and Baptists were always on the alert for tools of the Devil. I liked literature class, and I liked my teacher, who was young, pretty, and what passed for stylish in Oklahoma City. Sometimes I suspected the real "tools of the Devil" the Baptists were afraid of were young, pretty, stylish female teachers.

After literature came economics—one long hymn of praise to the free-market system—and then civics, where we learned that the fact that Oklahoma's governors kept getting impeached for corruption meant our justice system was working perfectly, but the fact that corrupt men kept getting elected to the Oklahoma governorship definitely did *not* mean our political system was in any way flawed. I took notes lightly in pencil so that when the notebook was full I could write over them in ink for another class because notebooks cost money.

Then I went to French class. French at Central was taught by an elderly German man with a strong accent—not a French accent—and an annoying denture-whistle. Monsieur Baumann also taught Latin, but the only language he spoke well was German, which he was not allowed to teach. During the Great War, the teaching of German had been banned at Central, and nobody'd bothered to change the rule back since. Monsieur Baumann was funny—sometimes unintentionally—and he never assigned homework. I liked him.

My school day ended with Physical Education, which I dreaded because our P.E. uniform was laced soft shoes, bloomers, and a middy blouse, and mine were all several years old and too small for me. My teacher, a "sporty" kind of woman with a loud voice and a *very* short bob, told me almost daily that I "looked like the rag-picker's daughter"—which was probably true, but I didn't love her for saying so.

I'd always been poor, but for a long time I didn't stand out at school because there were lots of other poor kids there, including Erma, an actual rag-picker's daughter, who in fact was a little better off than me and better dressed. My clothes were all dresses and skirts of my mother's that I'd remade to more or less fit me, but Erma got a brand-new dress every year on her birthday. Erma didn't have to run for the streetcar, either. Her father dropped her off at school every day in his rusty Ford truck before starting on his rounds collecting rags and bones and other scrap he could sell for money. But poor kids mostly left school ("had the good sense to leave school," as my mother put it) after eighth grade. By tenth grade—my present grade—there were still a few poor boys left, but no other poor girls besides me.

After spending an excruciating forty minutes in P.E. doing calisthenics in my too-tight old middy and trying to get the hang of volleyball, which was a newish game nobody but the teacher really understood, I changed back into my street clothes and went home.

At the beginning of the school year, I'd gotten Ma to promise that the three hours between the time I got home from school and the time she (we) had to start the doctor's dinner would be my study time. I reminded her of the agreement frequently. She never remembered for long.

Dr. Hallam was tidy, and being a doctor, he wasn't home much. The only housework my mother had to do most days was the dishes, general sweeping and straightening, sending out the doctor's laundry and dry cleaning, and ordering in his groceries. But sometimes Mother also needed "somebody"—I was Somebody—to run to the nearest market for things she'd forgotten to put in the grocery order, or to make the doctor's bed because her back hurt, or to scrub his bathtub because she didn't like to. Also, since Ma was afraid of heights, jobs like dusting shelves and washing windows high enough to require standing on a ladder to reach were also mine.

I was a fast worker, and I could usually manage to have everything of that nature done within the first hour of my study time. What I couldn't always manage to do was to get Mother to let me be for the two remaining hours.

Typically, as soon as I settled myself on a corner of our bed with a book in my lap, the questions began.

"What are you doing, Thea?"

I let myself read two paragraphs before I answered. "Reading a story. Sort of a story, anyway. A chapter from a novel."

"Just one chapter?"

"Yeah."

"Well, that's silly. Why doesn't your teacher make you read the whole thing? In my day, we read whole books in school."

I tried not to sigh—at least not audibly. "I think the idea is that if we read part we'll get interested and read the rest of the book on our own."

"Oh." A moment's silence, and then, "Will you?"

I let myself have three paragraphs this time. "Will I what?"

"Will you read the whole book?"

"Yeah, I want to. Only it's out at the library right now."

"Don't say 'yeah.' Say, 'Yes, Mother.'"

"Yes, Mother. Gotta read now, okay?"

"Yes, all right. All right, then. If you'd rather do that than talk to me."

For ten minutes, Ma went back to whatever she'd been doing, and then the questions started up again. "What's the book called?"

"Huh?"

"That book you're reading part of. What's the name of it?"

"*Les Misérables.*"

"Gracious me! Is that *French*? Why does your teacher want you to read a French book for *English* class? The children who haven't studied French won't understand a word of it!"

I explained the phenomenon of "translation."

"Oh," Ma said, still appearing dubious. "What's the book about?"

I read another four paragraphs. The story's action was heating up. "It's about a man who steals a loaf of bread and gets in trouble for it. That's not in the part I'm reading, though."

"He *stole*?" Mother thought about this for a few minutes. "I don't think schools should let students read stories about criminals. It might give them ideas about turning criminal themselves."

"Well, he's not being a criminal in this part of the story. He's being very nice, in fact, and buying a doll for a poor child who doesn't have one."

"Oh. That's good, I guess. People should help the poor." The poor Ma wanted most to see helped was herself, of course. "I still don't think it's right for the school to have you reading stories about bad people, though. You should be reading the Bible instead."

I thought about mentioning Judas, but decided the chance to crack wise wasn't worth what would come after it, which would be a long lecture from my mother on the Fifth Commandment.

I finished the story and pulled out my notebook.

"Are you done with your lessons now?" Mother asked hopefully.

"I've finished reading the story, but now I have to answer questions about it. See?" I held up my book to let Mother see a long list of questions without telling her I only had to answer a few of them.

"Oh, all right then. You'd better do that. You know, speaking of dolls, I had a very nice doll when I was a girl. I had several dolls, in fact, but there was one that was always my favorite. Did I ever tell you about the doll my grandmother gave me, Thea?"

I learned long before that "yes, many times" was not an acceptable reply to this or any similar questions. I said something noncommittal instead while uncapping my pen and beginning to write.

Ma talked on about her doll, but as soon as my pen stopped moving, she broke her story off to ask again, "Are you all done with your lessons?"

"Not quite. I've still got to do my Economics. You know what, though? I think I could get it done quicker if I sat outside. Fresh air helps me think."

"You could sit on the stairs. I'll come out with you."

Dear God, no, I thought. "I need to move around a little. Maybe I'll do a quick turn around the park before I get started."

The doctor's neighborhood was so new that the "park" at the center of it was still only a stretch of native prairie, studded with baby trees and mowed so short that in every rainstorm, eroding red earth briefly made the creek that ran through it resemble a river of blood.

Mother immediately brightened. "Well, if you're going over to the park, maybe you could stop in the kitchen on your way and start the roast," she suggested.

"Okay, I'll start the roast. Is it ready to cook?"

"Yes. Well—except that it needs to be trimmed a little. That won't take a minute. Trim it, salt it good, and put it in the roaster with the fat side up, all right? Put some pepper on it, too. And some marjoram. You know where I keep it. And after you do that, maybe you could peel the potatoes for me. I think five should do it. They're big ones. If you peeled the potatoes for me, it would save me a lot of standing."

I got out quick with my economics book before she could suggest I scrub the carrots and shell the peas, too. At the house, I started the roast and peeled the potatoes, then did my economics homework in the park before going back to help Ma finish making the doctor's dinner.

While we were working, the telephone rang. The telephone rang twenty times a day because the house was on a party line, but this time it was our ring—one long and two short ones. The doctor wasn't home yet, so Ma wiped her hands on her apron, and I took over at the stove while she went out to the telephone niche in the hall to answer it, leaving the kitchen door open behind her.

"Dr. Hallam's residence," she said in her fake-cultured "telephone" voice. "No, I'm sorry. He's not at home." Then there was a pause while Ma listened.

She was just turning toward me, eyes wide with surprise, when Dr. Hallam burst in at the back door. I said before he hardly ever smiled. Now he looked positively grim. Without even taking off his hat first, he snapped, "Is that for me?" and snatched the telephone receiver away from my mother, while at the same time with his other hand he gave her a push—not hard—toward the kitchen door.

As the door closed behind Ma, the doctor said, "Yes. Speaking. Go ahead." He sounded excited, but whether in a happy or upset way, I couldn't tell.

Ma stood where she was for a minute, her mouth open. "Gracious me," she whispered, kind of nervous. "I've never known Doctor to act like that before! What do you suppose has gotten into him?"

"Maybe it's some kind of medical emergency," I whispered back.

"I don't think so." Ma came to the stove and took the spoon from my hand. "Always stir custard clockwise, Thea. Otherwise, it'll curdle. Well, maybe it was something medical, though the man didn't say it was."

"It was a man?"

"Yes, and he said he had a message for 'Dr. Hal.' I guessed he meant 'Dr. Hallam,' but what if he didn't? What if it was a wrong number?"

I pointed out that the doctor seemed to have been expecting the call. "Oh, that's true," Ma conceded. "Well anyway, he said he had a message, and when I said Doctor wasn't home, he just started telling it to me anyway! Can you imagine?"

"So what was it?"

"The message? Oh, I didn't get the whole thing. All I heard was something about 'tell Hal to stop worrying; I've got a cushy job in the kitchen,' and then Doctor came in. Gracious me! I hope it wasn't a wrong number!"

As Ma was saying this, we heard Dr. Hallam hang up the telephone with a bang. He went off down the hall to the library and didn't come out again until his dinner was nearly ruined, and then hardly ate any of it.

"Strange man," Mother muttered, as she scraped his untouched custard—uncurdled, though I'd stirred it every which-way—into the can. She said it several times. "Strange man!"

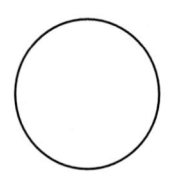

Chapter Three

A few days after the doctor had his telephone call, Ma and I had a fight.

It was my fault. Ma wanted me to quit school and get a job; I knew that. But she couldn't make me quit, and I knew that, too. We really had nothing to fight about. But this day, something about her little prods and hints worked its way under my skin, and I snapped back at her that I'd quit school the day, *the very day*, she quit—

I stopped myself from finishing the sentence, but Mother knew what word I'd been about to say. Any words relating to drinking or drunkenness—any words uncomplimentary to Ma at all, really—were strictly forbidden in our house.

Ma cried first, and then lost her temper right back at me. She called me selfish, and cruel, and ungrateful, and said I couldn't possibly understand all the sacrifices she'd made for me until I was a mother myself. That smarted, but she went farther. She said I wouldn't understand even then, since I clearly had no heart.

I could have saved the situation with a quick apology. Everything Ma had said to this point was routine. She wasn't really looking for a battle. Instead, I coldly answered that a good mother would *want* her child to get an education. I didn't yell. I never yelled when I was angry.

Although I was storming inside and my heart was pounding, I said what I said calmly. To my sobbing, raging, visibly wounded mother, I guess I seemed completely unfeeling.

While Ma reiterated every one of my failures and faults since birth, I got silently ready for bed, and at nine-thirty precisely I lay down as usual and pretended to sleep. Ma carried on for a few more minutes, and then, nonplused, lay down too. We shared a bed (there was only one) and it wasn't big, but that night we lay as far apart from each other in it as we could possibly get.

The next morning, Ma's eyes were red. Mine were, too. I'd hardly closed them all night. But to my relief, Ma seemed calm as she cooked Dr. Hallam's breakfast, and though we didn't talk much, for my part I tried to put as much extra-friendliness into what I did say as I possibly could. When she wished me a happy day as I left for school, I took it to indicate she was willing to put things behind us.

No such luck. When I came home that afternoon, I smelled hooch before I was halfway up the stairs. I opened the door to our place to find Ma spread-eagle on the bed, dead to all shame. The bottle on the floor beside her was luckily a small one, but it was two-thirds empty, and when I walked in, she didn't even stir.

I threw my books down as hard as I could onto the floor.

"What?" Ma murmured, her words slurred. "Who's there?"

I didn't say anything, just picked up the bottle and took it into the bathroom, where I ran the stuff down the sink.

Then I went back and scolded Mother like a child.

Using the same cold voice that got me in trouble the day before, I told her she should be embarrassed by what she'd done. "If you even know the meaning of the word," I added.

"Oh, it's Thea," Ma replied, struggling to see me through an alcoholic haze. "Hello, Thea. Nice to see you."

I'm translating here. Her words were essentially unintelligible. They were cheerful, though, and polite. Nobody was in a better mood or had better manners than my mother when she was drunk.

"Don't pee the bed, you big baby," I snapped back. "I have to sleep in it later."

Ma's only answer to this was a snore.

I sat on the floor and did my homework then, as fast as I could. Mother'd had more to drink than usual, and at one point her breathing became so loud and rough I got up and rolled her onto her side. I knew from experience she breathed better on her side when she was drunk. By the time I finished my homework, she was sleeping normally enough that I figured I could safely leave her, which was good because the doctor had to be fed, and it looked like there was going to be nobody to feed him but me. I knew how to cook quite a few things, but I wouldn't know until I got to the kitchen what groceries I had to work with.

Ma must have started drinking early. As soon as I stepped into the house, it was apparent that only some of the housework had been done. The doctor's bed was made, but the kitchen was untidy, and the breakfast dishes had never been washed. Maybe Ma'd decided that if she could get herself fired, I'd have to quit school.

If that was her plan, I had no intention of letting it work. I did a quick general clearing up, stacked the dirty dishes in the sink, stuffed the breakfast linens into the laundry bag (the laundry hadn't gone out, either), found a clean tablecloth, and dressed the dining table properly. Then I got to work on dinner.

Luckily it was pork chops in the icebox rather than a roast. Chops would take no more than twenty minutes to cook. But the only potatoes on hand were boilers, and the only vegetables in the keeper were celery and carrots. None of those things would cook fast, and all of them would have to be peeled. All I could find to make into soup was a big can of tomatoes in the back of the pantry.

I started on the tomato soup first, making up a recipe as I worked because I didn't have time to look up Ma's. While the soup simmered, I cleaned the vegetables, and then I put everything but the pork chops in pots of water to boil. Though Ma always said it ruined vegetables to boil them, I turned the heat up high because the doctor was due home soon, and he ate early. It seemed like the vegetables took forever to get soft, but when they finally were, I stuck the chops under the broiler and while they cooked I did my best to make plain boiled vegetables appetizing. I browned the carrots in butter and a little brown sugar, mashed the potatoes with cream, and arranged the celery neatly on a dish and poured white sauce over it. I'd done something wrong; and the white sauce was so thick I could've stood the spoon up in it, but it tasted all right. To my surprise, when I was done everything looked pretty good—although in the case of the tomato soup I thought looks might be misleading. The soup's bright color was at least partly the result of me getting confused while I was cooking it and adding red pepper to it twice.

It didn't hit me until I heard Dr. Hallam pulling out his chair in the dining room that besides cooking the dinner, I'd have to serve it, and that in serving it, I'd be giving my mother away. There was no help for it, so I quickly exchanged my apron for a clean one—nothing I could do about the fact that I was wearing school-clothes under it instead of a black dress—took a big breath, and carried the tureen into the dining room.

Dr. Hallam seemed surprised to see me, but not mad or anything.

"Well, well," was all he said, his tone dry. They were the first words he'd ever spoken directly to me.

"Um, Mother's…not feeling very well," I told him as I set the tureen on the table. I could feel my face turning red as the soup. "Dinner's cooked, though. I hope it's all right."

"I'm sure it's fine," the doctor said. "Would you like me to have a look at your mother?"

I honestly thought I'd rather die.

"No, she's okay, really," I answered quickly. "What I meant was, she was kind of sick before, but she's already getting better. You don't have to bother yourself."

"It wouldn't be a bother."

Dr. Hallam caught my eye then, and I saw from his expression that although he understood exactly what kind of "sick" my mother was, he wasn't looking for an opportunity to storm up to the apartment and fire Ma on the spot, even though he'd have had every right to do it. He was genuinely offering medical help.

I also saw that he was sorry for me. I hadn't gotten a lot of sympathy in my life for the way Ma was, and the doctor's had a strange effect on me. It made me want to bawl. I looked away quickly.

When I didn't answer him, Dr. Hallam said, "The soup looks delicious," and helped himself to some.

I went back to the kitchen and stared at the clock for fifteen minutes.

My mother'd always told me fifteen minutes was all it took someone eating alone to finish a bowl of soup, but the doctor was still eating his when I brought in the chops. Turned out it was his second helping.

"I like this," he told me. "Make it anytime." Apparently too much red pepper was just enough for Dr. Hallam.

My face flushed with pride this time, instead of shame, and I brought him the rest of his dinner.

The doctor seemed to enjoy everything, and the creamed celery especially. He ate a lot of creamed celery. But all I had to give him for dessert was leftover pie.

When my mother served leftovers, she always fixed them up in some way, so they didn't seem like leftovers. Leftover roasts got turned into hashes or potpies; leftover fish became fish balls; vegetables were disguised with sauces. Leftover dry desserts, like cakes and pies, got sauces, too, and leftover wet desserts, like creams and puddings, got turned into sauces themselves. But I hadn't done anything with the pie. It was just…pie.

"I'm sorry," I said, as I offered it. "It's from yesterday."

Dr. Hallam surprised me by answering, "Good. That means I won't be tempted to eat it. You're such a fine cook that I've eaten everything on the table except the cloth. I'll be sick if I have another bite."

The doctor sounded different from his usual self when he said this, which made me look at him. And you know what? He was smiling. Actually smiling. He'd called me a "fine cook," which meant he knew that I—not Ma—had made the meal, but he was smiling instead of mad. Naturally, I smiled back.

Dr. Hallam stood then, saying, "Dinner was very nice. Thank you," and went off to the library, where he spent most evenings—doing what, I didn't know. I stayed behind to clear the dining table, then washed all the dishes, including the breakfast ones Ma hadn't done, tidied up the kitchen, put the laundry and dry cleaning by the back door to be picked up, set up the next day's breakfast, and washed the linoleum. By the time I was done it was nine o'clock, so I went up to the apartment and straight to bed. The place was cramped and dingy, but it was home-sweet-home to me, and I was relieved beyond words that, if I'd read the doctor right, Ma and I would be staying in it for at least a little while longer.

Next morning, Ma was the way she usually was on the day after a bender—subdued and ashamed. She got up by herself when the clock chimed five-thirty and ran herself a bath. We had no bathtub in the apartment, and Mother and I took our baths in the same washtub I used for our clothes, diverting the water for it from the sink tap with a length of pipe. I don't think I need to say the washtub didn't fill fast that way. There was no hot water in the apartment, either. If we wanted a warm bath, we had to carry hot water from the house. I'd have helped Ma with that if she'd asked, but she had a cold bath instead. Ma was always sorry when she'd gotten drunk, so I guessed she was taking a penitential cold bath because she wanted me to know she was sorry but couldn't bring herself to say it. But where an apology from Ma—even a little, grudging one—would have made me feel better, seeing Ma shiver only transferred her guilty feelings to me. I didn't say it, but that's how I felt.

After her bath, and for the first time in weeks, Ma got herself down to the doctor's kitchen early enough that I would have been on time to geometry class if she hadn't raided my carfare to buy her bottle so that I had to walk to school.

Over the next couple of weeks, Ma's extra-good behavior gradually faded, and everything went back to normal. I went back to trying not to let the doctor see I was the one starting his breakfasts again, and she went back to hinting five times a day that I should get a job.

"Two years of high school is as good as a diploma for a girl," she said.

Time, my mother, and exposure to cold reality had tarnished

every goal I'd ever set for myself except the goal of completing my high school education. I answered back firmly, "Nothing's as good as a diploma."

*

The day before final exams started, everybody's first period class at Central High was spent making and submitting a list of the subjects we wanted to study the next year. It seemed to be hit-or-miss whether I got what I asked for, though some of my classmates appeared to have better luck. I was only a little late to school that day, and as soon as I sneaked in and sat down, Homer moved from where he was to sit next to me.

Unlike some teachers, Mr. Brody allowed us to talk among ourselves while we picked our classes. "You putting in for trig next year?" Homer asked me.

"I'm *requesting* trigonometry," I replied. "Don't know that I'll get it."

"Of course you will. Why wouldn't you?"

I studied the list of available classes for a minute before answering. Typing might be useful, but if I knew how to type, my mother would nag me harder than ever to drop out of school and get a job. Not worth it, I decided. "I don't *know* why I wouldn't," I said, "but freshman year I asked for general science and got home economics instead, if that tells you anything."

"Okay, but girls need to know how to cook and stuff. Now that's out of the way, you should get what you ask for. Anyway, you got into general science after all, didn't you? I heard you did."

"I got in, but I had to beg," I said—and flushed, because it wasn't a happy memory. "And I had to take home economics, too, so I didn't have room in my schedule for music." I liked music. I liked science better. "And for this year I asked for geometry and biology, but I only got geometry."

"Why didn't you get biology?" Homer demanded, like it might be *my* fault. "There was plenty of room. My biology class wasn't even half full." Homer was school-smart, but he clearly had no idea that the fact that he was the son of a prominent lawyer had any bearing at all on what classes he did or did not get. "Well anyway, put in for trig. I'm taking it, and I'll be bored if you're not in my class so I can beat you."

I asked for trigonometry—not to spare Homer from being bored, but because I'd already planned to.

You'd have thought I'd demanded the moon.

On the last day of school I got the news that, according to the school board, no girl at Central had ever studied trigonometry before, and only a "fast" girl would want to. Mr. Brody (who had taught my algebra class, too) said he'd speak to them for me and vouch for my character, but I'd have to wait until September, when school started again, to know for sure if I was in trigonometry or not.

"It will depend on how many of the boys who signed up for it come back to school next year," he told me. Then he gave me a look that, although his eyes didn't move from mine, somehow managed to take in my shabby clothes, runover shoes, and mended stockings. "Are you sure *you're* coming back?"

"You can count on it," I replied.

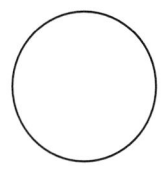

Chapter Four

The summer days were long, and there wasn't enough to do at home to keep me busy. Also, I needed money to give Ma to buy herself some new clothes. I'd grown taller recently, and if Ma didn't get new clothes, she'd have no old ones to give me to remake for myself. Since the neighborhood Dr. Hallam lived in was the last stop on the streetcar line, we had no businesses around aside from a dodgy dry cleaner's, a small grocery, and a florist's shop. I asked for work at all of them, but they were family-run and didn't need outside help. I took a position with one of the nicer markets downtown instead, delivering groceries on a three-wheeled bicycle, although it was a ten-cent trolley ride each way to get to it, which ate up a lot of what I earned. It was hard work, too—especially since I wasn't used to riding a bicycle. Several of the delivery "boys" were full-grown men, and I didn't like the way they talked about pretty movie stars or the other women who worked at the store, but when my bicycle broke down, which it often did (as the newest employee, I got the oldest bicycle), they were always quick and kind about fixing it for me. Instead of a salary, I was paid per completed delivery, which meant every minute my bike was out of order cost me money. That made me grateful for help even from dirty talkers.

By mid-July, I was bringing home about four-fifty a week (and Ma and my boss were both leaning on me hard to make the job permanent) when the owner of the dry cleaner's shop near Dr. Hallam's house got arrested for infringing the Volstead Act. I wasn't entirely surprised. I'd suspected for some time that Ma must be getting snorts from one of the local shops' back doors. The dry-cleaning man was let out of jail immediately (of course), and I was sure he would get straight back to selling booze, so as soon as I saved up enough money to afford notebooks and ink for school, a dress for my mother, and a pair of new shoes for myself, I quit my job and stayed home to keep an eye on Ma.

I'd always been honest about not messing with any of Dr. Hallam's things beyond what I needed to do to keep them clean, but after a week with nothing to read but Ma's Bible, I was bored and desperate enough to dare to slip into his library to see what kind of reading a medical book made. On my way to the library, I gave a tug or two to the slats on a few of the book crates lined up in the hall outside it. There were so many crates I figured at least a few must contain novels. But all the boxes were nailed up tight, and I didn't have a crowbar, so my choice was either medical books or the Bible and, not to sound irreligious or anything, I was tired of the Bible.

For the rest of the summer, I spent a few hours of every day sitting on the library floor, reading.

The first thing I read was all the stuff I could find about male anatomy and…function. You know what I mean…because I was very curious about that, and Ma wouldn't tell me a thing. When that got boring—which it did—I decided to pick out one body organ every Monday and spend the rest of the week reading everything I could find about that organ and all the things that could go wrong with it.

There wasn't summer enough left for me to get through many organs, and despite using the glossary in the back of one of the books a *lot*, I didn't understand all of what I read, but it definitely made the time pass.

When I wasn't reading, I made a little money mowing neighbors' lawns and minding their children, which I used to take Ma out to the pictures twice and for ice cream once as rewards for days she stayed sober. In no time, it was September 1927, and time for me to go back to school. It would be my third year in a row in the *same school*, which was a record for me.

The day before classes started, I went to Central to pick up my schedule, and learned I'd gotten into both the biology and trigonometry classes I wanted, but that P.E. was going to be my first class of the day, taught by the teacher who hated me, so I didn't dare to be late for school anymore. I explained this very carefully to Ma.

"From now on, you're going to have to get up as soon as I call you," I told her. I said it so sternly anybody'd have thought I was *her* mother instead of the other way around. "I can't help you get the doctor's breakfast this year."

Ma made a face like a balky mule, and sure enough, on my first day of school Dr. Hallam had to go to work with nothing in his stomach but a cup of percolator coffee and a piece of toast.

"It's your fault," Mother insisted when I found out about it. "I shouldn't have to do this. It's your turn to shoulder the load."

I was sick with fear that Ma'd manage to get herself fired no matter how good-natured the doctor was, but I didn't dare let her see it. Instead, I sat my mother down calmly and tried to make her watch as I wrote out our expenses and calculated the minimum amount of money I'd need to make to support us. "See?" I said, pushing the paper in front of her. "I'm sixteen. I can't get any job that would pay me this much. If you get fired and I have to go to work instead, you'll have even less money to spend than you do now."

Ma wouldn't look at my figures. She hated math as much as I loved it. But she knew "less money to spend" in our situation meant no money at all to spend on liquor, and I think the doctor might have had a stern talk with her, too, because most days after that, he got his breakfast.

*

Except for P.E., which was the same as always (terrible), I liked school better than ever. I was a junior now, and my class had shrunk to less than half the size it had been when I was a freshman. This was normal, and though it was regrettable in some ways, it was also good in that having so many students drop out meant those of us who were left were all serious about getting an education. We came to class with our homework done and paid attention to the lectures. Naturally, our teachers loved us.

To my surprise, I realized one day I'd somehow started having friends.

For years I'd assumed the reason I didn't have any was because there was something wrong with me. There *were* things wrong with me, in fact. I knew there were. I was skinny, plain, awkward, and prone to blurt out whatever came into my head without thinking. My mother regularly said I was also unfeeling, stubborn, and ungrateful, but if those things were true, my teachers and classmates didn't mention it.

Now it began to look like the real reason I hadn't made friends before was just that I'd never stayed in one school long enough to get a chance to. This was my third year at Central, and now as I walked between classes, boys greeted me in the halls, and girls who were giggling together called me over to share in the joke. It didn't hurt that Homer Escoe was my first and best friend. Big-boned and rangy but nice-looking overall, Homer was popular, friendly, smart (he was on track to be named our class valedictorian), and best of all, didn't seem to notice I was poor. Once he had made it clear he thought I was all right, a lot of other kids—and teachers—gave me a second look. If I'd had an occasional spare dime like my new friends did to spend on a soda at the drugstore soda fountain after school, or been able to count on Ma to get her housework done and dinner started without me rushing home to make her do it, life would have been perfect.

*

A few weeks into the school year, I had to walk home one day. For a change, this wasn't Ma's fault. I'd needed to go all the way across town earlier in the week to look up something for school in the public library, and it cost me two nickels streetcar fare each way.

Only a few blocks from Central, the rain that had been threatening all day began to fall. I'm not talking about ordinary rain, either. I mean wrath-of-God stuff; the kind of Oklahoma downpour that makes animals spontaneously start lining up two-by-two. I didn't own an umbrella or a raincoat. All I could do was remind myself that, as Ma always said, I wasn't so sweet I'd melt like a sugar-baby and trudge on toward home.

I was halfway there and all the way soaked when a car pulled up beside me, and a familiar voice called, "Jump in." It was Dr. Hallam, and as I looked, he reached back to open the car's rear door.

I shouldn't have accepted the invitation. The doctor's car had nice leather seats, and my clothes were sopping. I couldn't resist, though. I dove straight in, wiping the rain out of my eyes with my sleeve.

A man I didn't know was in the front passenger seat.

The doctor said, "John, this is—" and then stopped.

I didn't blame him for not remembering my name. He'd only heard it once, when my mother introduced me when we first moved into the apartment, and we hadn't spoken to each other since the night I'd served him his dinner. "Thea," I reminded him.

"Thea," repeated Dr. Hallam, looking grateful for the prompt. "This is Thea. Thea, this is Dr. Nicholas. I need to drop Dr. Nicholas off at the train station before we go home, Thea. Is that all right, or will your mother worry?"

I said she wouldn't, and also gave Dr. Nicholas what I hoped was a properly friendly yet respectful "How do you do?"

Dr. Nicholas didn't even look back at me before going on with what I guessed must have been the conversation he and Dr. Hallam were having when they stopped to pick me up. Dr. Nicholas did all the talking. I found what he said interesting, but Dr. Hallam didn't look like he was paying much attention. The topic was something called "splenic anemia," and although I didn't entirely understand what Dr. Nicholas said about it, I repeated what seemed like the most important parts several times to myself, so I'd remember them later and be able to look them up in Dr. Hallam's books when he wasn't around.

"They're twins, Ed," Dr. Nicholas said. (I was interested that he called Dr. Hallam "Ed.") "Identical twins. There's no other possible explanation for identical twins presenting with precisely the same condition at the same time."

"Coincidence?" Dr. Hallam suggested.

Dr. Nicholas waved away the word "coincidence" with one hand. "It's clearly hereditary," he said, and then repeated it. "It's clearly hereditary."

It's a hereditary splenic anemia." He picked up some papers from the seat beside him and read from one. "Eight-year-old male twins... repeated bouts of epistaxis, severe enough in one case to warrant nasal packing... Have you tried salt pork for nasal packing, Ed? Works like a charm. ...generalized lethargy...distended abdomen. Et cetera, et cetera. All the usual." Another hand-wave. "Finally referred to us by the local country doctor for bleeding gums, by the way. *Bleeding gums.* Those boys had distended bellies for *years*—two of the most enlarged spleens and livers I have seen in my entire *career*—and they're sent to us because their gums bleed!"

"Interesting," Dr. Hallam said absently.

Dr. Nicholas shook his head. "That's southern Illinois doctors for you. I'm telling you, Ed, civilization in the state ends at Urbana. South of that is barbarian territory. Hillbilly country." Dr. Nicholas thought about this for a minute before adding, "My guess is if you drew a line through the southern border of Champaign County and extended it in both directions to the coasts, you'd find the whole country was that way. The southern and western drawls are diagnostic. The slower the verbal cadence, the slower the brain."

Dr. Hallam caught my eye in the car's rearview mirror and rolled his own.

"Anyway," Dr. Nicholas continued, "once I'd ruled out syph—" He glanced toward the back seat, evidently just remembering I existed, and finished, "That is, the parents and the boys all had negative Wasserman reactions, so I felt confident ruling out both...that... and tuberculosis, but blood tests showed leucopenia. Sure enough, once splenectomies had been performed, both twins immediately improved."

I was glad to hear the little boys were better, and tried to pay attention to what Dr. Nicholas went on to say about exactly how heavy their spleens turned out to be when they were removed (I memorized the number so I could look up what a normal spleen weighed later), and what the pathologist said after studying samples of them under a microscope. The doctor used a lot of words I didn't know, including a long one starting with an "m" I couldn't quite make out, even though he said it several times. I did catch that the twins' spleens were full of *big* cells, though, which I assumed was what made their spleens big.

When we pulled up in front of the train station, Dr. Nicholas hurried to finish what he was saying. "I'm writing this up to submit for publication, Ed. If I leave you a draft, will you send me your comments? I'd be grateful for your input. I'm titling it, 'Familial Splenic Anemia in Identical Twin Boys: A Case Study.' What do you think?"

"I'm happy to read anything you give me," Dr. Hallam answered, taking the papers from Dr. Nicholas. To me he added, "I'll be right back, Thea."

I nodded to let Dr. Hallam know I'd heard him, and said, "Pleased to have met you," to Dr. Nicholas, who didn't bother to answer but went on talking about splenic anemia while Dr. Hallam got his suitcase out of the back of the car for him and gestured to a porter to come and take it to the train. I think Dr. Nicholas left Dr. Hallam to tip the porter, too, which didn't surprise me at all given he was the kind of man to call me and half the country barbarians and hillbillies.

*

A few months into the school year, I guessed Ma had made a new contact when her drinking got suddenly worse. She'd wake up more or less fine in the morning and make and serve Dr. Hallam's breakfast on her own, but by the time I got home from school, she was generally fried to the hat, as they say. If I put her straight to bed and did the housework myself, she was usually able to help cook his dinner and serve it, and if the doctor noticed she was hungover (which, being a doctor, he probably did), he was too nice to yell at her for it. Afterward, Ma'd do the dishes and tidy the kitchen with me, and by the time we got back to the apartment, she'd be totally sober and want to talk. I'd listen for half an hour to let her run down a little, then plead exhaustion on my part to get her into bed. Luckily, once she was lying down, Mother nearly always dropped right off. I needed her to sleep, because the only way I could get all my homework done was to get back up and sneak down to Dr. Hallam's kitchen to do it where I could have a light.

The doctor found me there one night.

From the way I jumped when he opened the kitchen door, he probably thought he'd caught me burgling his house. As I scrambled to get my books and papers together, I apologized for being there.

"That's all right," Dr. Hallam said quickly. "You're welcome to use the table. I just came in for a glass of water." He glanced out the window and seemed surprised to see the apartment was dark. I started for the sink, but he said, "No. No need. I'll get it myself," and waved me back to my chair. "Please continue with whatever you're doing."

The doctor got his water, sipped it, and then asked, "What *are* you doing, by the way?"

When I told him it was my trigonometry homework, he looked interested.

"Really?" He came closer to look. "I didn't go to school in this state. Do Oklahoma high schools require their students to take trigonometry?"

This was so far from the case I almost laughed. "I don't think most Oklahoma students could take trigonometry if they wanted to. Even

Central only offers trigonometry every few years."

Dr. Hallam put down his glass and picked up my book in its place. "Since you don't have to take it to graduate, I'm guessing you must like math," he said, leafing through it.

"A whole lot!"

"And you're good at it?"

"Second, usually," I admitted, trying to sound modest. "Sometimes I'm first."

"Second, or sometimes first," the doctor repeated. "Good for you. What other classes are you taking?"

I told him. "I want to take chemistry next year," I added, "but I'm not sure I'll be let."

"Why is that?"

"I'm a girl."

"You are a girl," Dr. Hallam agreed, starting to smile a little. "What's that got to do with it?"

"Oh, you know… Chemistry's for people who are going to college, and they're mostly boys. If there's room in the class, I might get in."

"I see. So it's assumed that as a girl, you'd rather get married and have children than go to college?"

"Yes."

"And would you?"

"Oh, I'd rather go to college than *anything*," I blurted. The words were out of my mouth before I could stop them. "I can't, though."

"Why not? Have you taken any other science classes?"

"General science in my freshman year. Now I have biology."

"Physics?"

"Not allowed."

"Because…?"

"Girl," I said again.

The doctor gave me back my book. "What will you do if you don't go to college?" he asked, leaning back against the stove and making himself comfortable.

"Get a job." What other answer could there be? "But see, I have this friend… I mean, she's not exactly a friend, but she's someone I know who took biology. She graduated last year, and when I met her on the streetcar over the summer, she told me she's working in a pharmacy now, and she really likes it. Only she said she'd like it even more if she'd had chemistry in school, because if she had, there's a test she could take to get certified, and then she'd get to help compound the drugs and stuff. I'd like a job like that, where I could do chemistry, instead of just working in a shop or an office or someplace."

I felt like I was talking too much.

"Why set your sights so low?" Dr. Hallam asked, not seeming to mind how much I talked. "If you'd like to work in a pharmacy, why not be the pharmacist?"

"Girl," I reminded him for the third time. "And also, money."

"There are female pharmacists. There's one at the hospital where I work. And there are bursaries and scholarships for bright students."

Then he looked at his watch—a wrist model; everything about Dr. Hallam was up-to-date—and said, "But to get a college scholarship, you'll need to do well in high school, and to do well in high school, you need plenty of sleep. Go to bed now."

Still smiling, he finished his water while I stacked up my books and papers. "I'll lock up," he offered, when I was ready to go. "You're welcome to study here anytime—" After a split-second hesitation, he remembered my name. "Thea."

I went up and crept into bed next to Mother as usual, but I had a hard time falling asleep. I didn't take all the hardest classes I could in high school so I could go to college, because I knew I *couldn't* go to college. I took them because I wanted to learn everything I could possibly cram into my brain before I graduated and had to get a job.

It looked to me—it had looked to me for a long time—like people didn't learn much once they left school except for how to do their jobs, which if they were girls like me was likeliest to be housekeeping and baby-raising. Once they were out of school, hardly anybody seemed to try anymore to find out what was *behind* what went on around them; what made stuff *happen*. I already understood things a lot of the adults I knew didn't—mostly math, but not only math—and that scared me. The world was big and complicated, and apparently I was going to have to live in it surrounded by people who didn't understand it even as well as I did. That didn't feel safe.

But what if I *could* go to college? What if Dr. Hallam was right that there was money around for poor girls like me to go to college on, and I could get some of it? Four more years of school would be time enough to learn *so much*. A brief vision of myself as a bob-haired "coed" strolling across a tree-studded college lawn toward a vast, book-stuffed library made my head swim.

Then, as the bracket-clock struck one-thirty, I pictured my mother's face as I told her she'd have to wait four more years for me to take over earning our living. The mental image made me sigh and roll closer to the wall. If I so much as suggested such a thing, Ma'd kill me with guilt. I'd gotten into trigonometry. With any luck, next year I'd be allowed to take chemistry. A job in a pharmacy was nothing to sneeze at, and probably the best I could hope for.

I put my college dreams away in the drawer in my brain marked "Not Allowed," and the next minute, fell asleep.

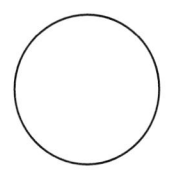

Chapter Five

More than two weeks had passed since the conversation I overheard between Dr. Hallam and Dr. Nicholas on the way to the train station, and something about it still bothered me. Something Dr. Nicholas said sounded wrong to me compared to what I'd read in Dr. Hallam's medical books, though I couldn't put my finger on exactly what. I told myself Dr. Hallam knew all about medicine and *he* hadn't disagreed with Dr. Nicholas, but my brain wouldn't let the matter go. I felt like if I didn't get another look into the doctor's medical books to see what the problem was, my brain might never get another minute's rest.

If there even *was* a problem, that is.

One afternoon when my mother was napping as usual (she hadn't been drinking, but she'd gotten to like her afternoon naps and having me do the housework), I managed to get all my work done fast enough that I still had an hour left over before the time to start dinner. I went to the doctor's library, sat down on the floor, and pulled out the medical book nearest me. One of the organs I'd studied during the summer was the spleen. I opened the book to the "spleen" pages then put it aside and pulled out another book.

When I'd found four books with paragraphs or pages on the spleen and had them opened and lying around me, I started to read.

I hadn't gotten far before Dr. Hallam walked in. I shivered like a rabbit.

The doctor said, "Hello!" fairly calmly, considering I'd probably startled him, too. "May I ask what you're doing?"

Instead of answering this, I gasped, "You're home early!"

"I'm expecting a telephone call. What are you doing?"

I stammered out apologies and confused explanations piled on top of each other while I closed up his books and started putting them—gently—back on the bookshelves.

"I promise I've been very careful," I babbled. "I haven't torn any pages or anything."

For the third time, Dr. Hallam repeated, "But what are you doing?"

He took a breath to say something more, but just then the telephone rang. The doctor's face changed instantly. "Stay there," he said, suddenly stern, and headed down the hall toward the telephone stand almost running.

A few seconds later, I heard him bark, "Speaking. Go ahead," like he had when he'd gotten his other mysterious telephone call months before, and then for a longish time, he didn't say anything, but just listened.

For several minutes after Dr. Hallam said, "Thank you," and hung up the telephone, he didn't come back, and when he finally did come, he seemed upset. I figured he was upset with me for messing with his books until he looked at me. Then I realized he'd more or less forgotten I was even there.

When he remembered, he tried to be friendly. "You're not in any trouble, Thea," he said, walking over to where I was still sitting on the floor. "Were you looking at those books because you had a medical question? If that's it, maybe I can help you. Or did you want to look up something you'd rather not ask your mother?"

My face went red-hot when he said this, because I knew what the "something" he meant was and I *had* looked it up. I said, "Oh no, no," trying to sound casual and unconcerned, and then attempted to tell him the real reason I was in his library as quickly as I could.

I found it hard to put into words. "It was just... I don't know... I was wondering about something Dr. Nicholas said to you that day in your car. What he said seemed kind of different from what I read. Only I can't remember exactly what was different about it, so I was looking in your books to see if I could figure it out."

The doctor seemed confused. "Compared to something you read *where*?"

I gestured. "In your books."

"You were reading my *medical* texts?"

"Well, parts of them. Last summer. And I'm pretty sure one of them said something *like* what Dr. Nicholas said, only…different."

Dr. Hallam pulled out his chair and sat.

"All right," he said slowly, staring at me. "I don't remember precisely what Dr. Nicholas and I were talking about. Remind me."

I wasn't surprised to hear he didn't remember. I'd noticed at the time he wasn't paying attention. "Those twins with the big spleens."

"Oh, right. The supposed 'hereditary splenic anemia.'" The doctor's expression and tone became gentle. "I see. And that's bothering you. Well, children do sometimes get sick and need to undergo operations, I'm sorry to say. I don't think you need to worry about it, though. It's not common."

I realized he thought the idea that children could die was new to me, and that I was afraid for myself. In fact, every graduation at Central included a memorial hymn sung by the school choir to commemorate students who'd died during the school year. I'd heard the record deaths in one year was nineteen (out of a class of ninety) during the Spanish Flu epidemic, but I wasn't at Central myself then, of course. "Oh no, I understand that," I said hastily. "I know kids can die. No, this is something Dr. Nicholas said about the disease the twins have. Only, as I said, I can't remember what it was, so I thought I'd re-read everything I read before about spleen problems to see if I could find it."

The doctor was back to staring at me. He didn't look angry, though. I was glad about that.

"I know I should have asked permission to read your books first," I said, flushing again. "I'm very sorry."

"No, that's all right. It's fine." Dr. Hallam leaned forward in his chair and clasped his hands between his knees. "Let's—go back and start at the beginning. Why and when were you reading those books? I assume from what you're saying you've been reading them for some time, not just after listening to Dr. Nicholas."

I explained about summer, and no school, and quitting my job to help Ma—I didn't say to help her stay sober—and then getting bored and needing something to read. "I should have asked first," I admitted again.

"It's fine," the doctor repeated. "It's fine. I'm happy to share them. But what could you possibly have gotten out of them?" Then he corrected himself. "I take that back. Obviously, you *did* get something out of them. But how? I would have thought they'd be impenetrable to someone your age."

"Well, they kind of were impenetrable," I agreed. I liked the word "impenetrable," and mentally filed it away for future use.

"Especially they were impenetrable at first. But the big one"—I pointed to the book I meant—"has a glossary at the back, and also I got the idea of reading about one organ at a time, which was easier than doing the whole body at once. I liked reading about blood the best. I never thought of blood as an organ before." When the doctor didn't say anything right away, I added, "Also I liked the parts about the liver, I guess because a lot of the liver stuff was about blood, too."

"The liver," Dr. Hallam repeated. "You read about the liver."

"And the heart and spleen. But then school started again."

The doctor leaned back in his chair, shaking his head but—to my relief—also smiling. "You are full of surprises, Miss Thea," he said. "All right. Let's look through my books together and see if we can find what John—Dr. Nicholas—said about the spleen that's obsessing your mind, and I'll help you to understand it."

Together, Dr. Hallam and I pulled all the medical books out again and put them on the desk, and as I found the pages, I re-read everything they said about the spleen with the doctor reading over my shoulder.

"This isn't it," I complained after every book. "I mean, this is what I read before, but it's not the thing Dr. Nicholas was saying in the car."

"No, why would it be?" Dr. Hallam agreed. "As I said, I don't remember our conversation clearly, but there's no reason John would characterize the spleen for me."

"'Enlarged liver and spleen,'" I read aloud. "All the spleen problems cause 'enlarged liver and spleen.' I think what he said had something to do with that." Then I caught sight of the desk clock and cried, "Oh, gosh! I need to help Ma make dinner!"

"Let's just let her handle that tonight," the doctor answered dryly. "Instead of the spleen, should we be looking at what you read concerning the liver instead?"

I thought this over. "No," I decided. "Because Dr. Nicholas was talking about the spleen. He *mentioned* the boys' livers were enlarged, but he *talked* about their spleens. He said— He said the pathologist reported the spleen had…big cells. Is that right? The spleen had big pale cells, and since he said that was in the *pathologist's* report, I guessed it wasn't normal."

Dr. Hallam straightened up a little. "No, it's not normal," he agreed. "I didn't catch that. I wasn't paying proper attention, was I?"

I was trying to think of a polite way to say I thought he hadn't paid attention to Dr. Nicholas because Dr. Nicholas was boring, when the stacks of medical magazines caught my eye.

"Maybe what I'm remembering wasn't in a book," I said. "Maybe it was in one of those magazines."

"You read medical journals *too*?"

"Is that what they're called? Okay, let me look." I sat back down on the floor and started rifling through the stacks. "I didn't get to the ones with the red covers yet." I put that stack aside. "So it wasn't any of them."

Feeling a little shy, I looked up at Dr. Hallam and asked, "Is this you?" I held up two papers that weren't bound into journals but were each a single article. One of the authors of the papers was "Hallam, E. J. III," which kind of matched the name on his medical diploma.

The doctor said it was. "Case studies. And that's Dr. Nicholas," he added, pointing to another author name, which was "Nicholas, J. J."

The topic of the papers was childhood cancers. I thought if Dr. Hallam studied children with cancer, it might account for him being gloomy.

I put the doctor's papers aside and went back to looking. "It might be this mag— I mean, journal," I said, flipping through one. "No. This one maybe."

Dr. Hallam seemed to have forgotten his upsetting telephone call. Squatting down beside me, he started going through stacks of journals, too, scanning the tables of contents. "Nothing about spleens," he muttered, tossing them aside one by one. "Nothing. Nothing. Nothing."

Just as I was about to give up, I found what I was looking for. I couldn't stop myself from letting out a shriek.

"Here!" I cried. "Here it is! It was in this article about Gaucher's Disease!"

"*Gaucher's*," the doctor corrected me, saying the word very French.

Then he suddenly sat all the way down on the floor and stared at me again. "Gaucher's is hereditary," he said slowly. "Good God. They didn't rule out Gaucher's."

He reached over, took the journal from my hand, and started reading, saying "Good God," again after about every paragraph, along with "Gaucher's," almost as often. "I can see why John… I mean, they present the same," he muttered. "'Distended, tender abdomen; easy bruising; weight loss…'"

"Fatigue," I put in. I don't know if he heard me.

"'The appearance of the Malpighian bodies in the path report should have triggered a review,'" Dr. Hallam went on, still talking to himself. "Good God."

The "m" word I'd heard Dr. Nicholas say must have been *Malpighian*. I repeated it to myself a few times so I'd remember it.

As the doctor was reading, Ma came to the door. It was open, but she knocked anyway.

"Dinner, Doctor?" she asked hopefully. Poor Ma! It was well past dinnertime by now. Depending on what she'd cooked, some of the dishes might be getting ruined.

"Thank you. Five minutes," Dr. Hallam answered her without looking up.

Mother looked confused, then retreated back to the kitchen.

The doctor didn't speak again until he'd read the article twice. Then he said thoughtfully, "Do you know what?"

I didn't.

"He's misdiagnosed those boys."

He still didn't seem to be speaking to me. He was staring across the room at nothing. I said, "Yeah?" anyhow, to remind him I was there.

Dr. Hallam turned to look at me then, sat up straighter and even smiled. "Yeah," he repeated, in the same tone I'd used. I wondered if he'd ever said "yeah" before in his life. "Or—I think so. I'm almost sure of it. I need to call John." He looked at his watch and seemed to think for a minute. "All right, I can't do it now, but first thing tomorrow, I need to make a telephone call." He smiled broader. "Your curiosity may have saved a few people—possibly including me—from making fools of themselves." He stood up and put out his hand to help me up too, meanwhile repeating what he'd said earlier. "You are full of surprises, Miss Carter."

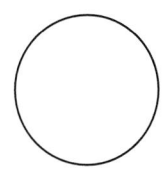

Chapter Six

I was sitting at the bottom of the stairs to our apartment doing homework next day when Dr. Hallam came home. After he put away his car, he surprised me by coming over to talk.

He said first he didn't know yet about the Gaucher's thing. "Maybe tomorrow. In the meantime, I have something for you." He pulled out his wallet. "That is, I have something for your mother that I'm going to give to you. Your mother has been with me for some time now, and it's time she got a raise in pay. I thought that as you are helping her with her work, it might be right to pay it to you."

He held out a two-dollar bill.

Two dollars looked so good to me I almost licked my lips, but I thought it would be more polite to seem reluctant. "Mother's all right with what she gets. She—*we*—get our room and board, too."

"No, this amount is fairer," the doctor said firmly. "And it's fair that it goes to you."

Of course I took it. Two dollars a week would add up in no time to enough for new gym clothes, which would mean one less thing for my P.E. teacher to torment me about. Also, my cotton stockings had at least three mends per leg too many to be respectable.

And—I'll just go ahead and say it—I also wanted money to buy throw-away pads for my monthlies, like other girls had. Mother insisted homemade cloth ones worked just as well and were cheaper, but I hated washing them. With two extra dollars a week, provided I was careful and looked for bargains, I'd be able to afford a lot of nice things.

"Thank you," I said, and slipped the money between the pages of my textbook—one place for sure Ma wouldn't look.

I was so grateful for the doctor's kindness I wanted to do something for him, like give him my life, or my left arm or something. He probably didn't want either of those things, but I thought of something else he might like instead. Dr. Hallam had started walking to the house by now. I jumped up and ran after him.

"Wait!"

He stopped and turned.

"I'll unpack the rest of your books for you, if you want," I said when I reached him, talking fast from nervousness. "I'm guessing you want them on the shelves, but you haven't had time to put them up yet. I could do that. Tell me how you want them arranged—by subject or whatever. It'll only take me a few days."

The doctor hesitated, the same way I'd hesitated to take his money. For some reason, that made me feel good, like I was finally old enough to have something of value to offer.

"Would you?" he asked, sounding grateful. "That would be wonderful! I should have done it myself by now. I've had time, I've just been lazy. I don't need them in any particular order. Shelve them wherever they'll fit. Will five dollars be acceptable? Or is that too little? Ten?"

I laughed and said I didn't want any money for it. "It's just part of the housekeeping."

But the doctor insisted, and since there were a lot of boxes to unpack, and a lot of high shelves I'd have to put them on, I let him talk me into five dollars (he wouldn't go lower). He shook my hand, saying sincerely he thought he was getting the best of the bargain, and we walked the rest of the way to the house together. Then Dr. Hallam went upstairs, and I went to Ma in the kitchen.

I told her I was going to unpack the doctor's books without letting her know I was being paid to do it.

"I saw the two of you talking by the stairs," she said. "Is that when he asked you to do his books?"

I lied and said yes.

Ma smiled. "He likes you."

"Well, he doesn't seem to mind me, anyway."

"He *likes* you, I said," Ma repeated. "You know, if you put yourself out a little, you might be able to make him like you enough to propose marriage. Wouldn't that be nice?"

"*Dr. Hallam?*"

"Oh, I know you're no 'It Girl,'" Ma said, shrugging. "But you're perfectly presentable."

"Ma, he's over thirty! *And* he's rich."

"He's thirty-six," Mother said. I wondered how she knew. "And so what if he's rich? You come from good stock yourself!"

"We aren't exactly in the Social Register, Ma." We weren't even in the telephone directory.

"I didn't say we were socialites," Ma retorted. "But we're as good as anybody and better than many, and as you say, he's rich. Rich men can marry anybody they want."

"Well, what they generally want are rich girls. Just get that idea straight out of your head, Ma. If I start making sheep's eyes at the doctor, he'll fire you just to get rid of me."

Then I headed off to set the dining table, with Mother calling after me, "All I'm saying is to be nice to him, all right?"

*

Next day, Dr. Hallam came straight into the kitchen when he got home. Ma instantly got busy at the stove.

When he greeted us, I got an impression he could hardly hold something back, but all he said—very politely—was, "I need to speak to you, Mrs. Carter, but first I need to speak to Thea, if I may."

Ma threw me an I-told-you-so look as I followed the doctor out.

As soon as we got to the library, Dr. Hallam's smile turned into a huge grin. "*Gaucher's*," he said triumphantly.

"Not the spleen anemia thing?"

"Definitely not splenic anemia. Almost certainly Gaucher's. We'll have a definite diagnosis in a couple of days. Three cheers for those nagging little doubts of yours, Thea!"

I suspect I gawped like a fish. "I was *right*?"

"You were right. Which means John was wrong. He hates that." Another grin. "He'll get over it, though. He'll get over it the moment he remembers how much rarer Gaucher's is than splenic anemia and that publishing a paper on Gaucher's will therefore make a correspondingly greater splash. Well done, Thea! Well done!"

The doctor shook my hand—already shaking all by itself from excitement—and we grinned at each other until I suddenly thought of something that made my face fall. "What about the little twins?" I asked.

Dr. Hallam immediately turned serious, too. "Yes, I know. A diagnosis of Gaucher's is not good."

Everything I'd read said Gaucher's disease was very bad, in fact. "They're only eight years old!"

"Yes. It's a tragedy, Thea. Life is sometimes very tragic. I'm sorry. On the other hand, some patients do live for years with the condition, and I hope you find consolation in knowing you've contributed to our understanding of a very rare disease. Thanks to you, any insights we gain from observing the twins may help guide us at last to effective treatments for Gaucher's."

Dr. Hallam kept repeating that with proper medical care, the twins might live long—long-ish, anyway—and relatively healthy lives, until I calmed down and was able to begin to accept the situation.

Then, still in his kindest voice, he said, "I need to speak to your mother," and gave me his handkerchief.

After I dried my eyes, we walked back to the kitchen, where Dr. Hallam told my mother he'd be leaving tomorrow and be away for a week or so.

"Something fun, I hope?" Mother asked brightly, not noticing I'd been crying. Ma almost never noticed when I was upset or crying, even when she'd been the one to make me cry in the first place. Maybe she just saw me so much I was invisible to her. "Whereabouts are you going?"

Dr. Hallam didn't say where. I guessed he was used to having his business pried into and knew how to deal with it. "A legal matter," he answered briefly. "Don't bother about breakfast tomorrow. I'll eat on the train."

"Ma, leave him alone," I said when he'd gone out.

Though she flushed guiltily, Ma insisted she'd only meant to be friendly.

"Well don't be 'friendly,' because he's not your friend, remember? Anyway, you meant to be nosy."

Ma disregarded this. "Something 'legal,' eh?" she said thoughtfully. "What trains leave early, Thea? The Dallas one? Do you think he's going to Dallas?"

"Not my business," I said firmly.

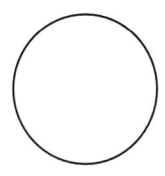

Chapter Seven

With the doctor gone, there was hardly any housework to do, but even so, his books took me longer to unpack and shelve than I expected them to. Dr. Hallam pried the lids off the crates before he left, and there were a *lot* of crates, all full to the top. Some of them contained more things than just books inside—things like pictures and pens and knickknacks, stacks of papers, folders of papers, loose papers, papers tied with string into bundles, old letters, and a wastepaper basket with the waste papers still in it. There was even a pair of shoes. It looked to me like whoever packed up the doctor's old office did it the quickest, most careless way possible.

Dr. Hallam told me I could just put things on the shelves however they fit, but I wanted to do the job right, so I grouped the books by subject, more or less, and put all the articles and journals and bound journals in date order, propping up the unbound ones that wouldn't stand by themselves with various bookends I found in the boxes. When I ran out of bookends, I used the bigger, heavier knickknacks in place of them.

One of the "knickknacks" was a sort of large bullet-like thing—more of a bullet-casing than a bullet, really, only very big, and dented around the open end. It rattled when I shook it, and when I looked inside, I found pictures—snapshots—of doughboys from the Great War. Looking at the pictures made me feel funny. Except for their uniforms, the doughboys were like the boys I went to school with, except I knew some of them—maybe many—were likely dead. In one picture, a good-looking fellow with a bandaged hand was showing off the exact same bullet-thing I'd found the pictures inside, or one just like it. I studied his face for a long time, wondering if he was one who'd made it home.

Eventually I put the pictures back where I'd found them, used the bullet to prop up a row of paper-bound medical journals, and went back to shelving books.

Besides medical and science books, the doctor owned lots of novels—classics and popular ones, too. He even had *Les Misérables* in two volumes. I thought about asking to borrow it, but then noticed it was in French. There were some other books in French, too, and a bunch in German that seemed to be all about medicine, so I put them on the shelf with the medical books. I was somehow not surprised to discover Dr. Hallam knew German and French.

Two whole crates were full of books about history. Though I generally didn't care for history classes at school, which were mainly about the dates of battles and the political views of the current school board, I loved to read books about history. When I peeked into one about the English Civil War—I'll be honest; until that moment, I hadn't known they had one—I was excited to see handwritten notes in the margins. I hoped Dr. Hallam wasn't one of those aggravating people who wouldn't lend their books.

One box was full of paperbacks of Zane Grey cowboy stories, and Sherlock Holmes, and Raffles the jewel-thief. Though I admit I wanted to read them myself, I thought paperbacks might lower the tone of the library as a whole, so I found an inconspicuous spot for them on a bottom shelf in a corner, mostly hidden from view.

When the books were finally all shelved, I put all the loose pens and pencils I'd found into the top desk drawer, the papers into the lower two, and carried the shoes upstairs to the doctor's closet. I wasn't sure they were his (they seemed big), but I didn't know what else to do with them.

When everything was done, I sat on the floor in the middle of the room and admired my work. I felt like I'd earned every penny of my promised five dollars, and I hoped the doctor would think so too.

As Ma and I got ready for bed that night, we heard a car pull into the driveway, and when we peeked out the window, we saw Dr. Hallam paying off a taxi.

As I was about to leave for school next morning, he walked straight into the kitchen.

"How is Dallas this time of year?" Ma asked him, probably imagining she was being subtle and clever.

Doctor Hallam said briefly that he had no idea, then thanked both of us—but looking at me—for all the work we'd done, and gave us each a dollar.

"The library looks absolutely wonderful," he said. "Please feel free to use it anytime you like." Winking—but with his head turned so only I could see it—he added, "Especially the medical texts."

"Goodness," Ma said, as soon as he was out of earshot. "Why would I want to do *that*?" She eyed my dollar. "I don't know why he should tip *you*, Thea. You don't even work for him. Oh, all right, if you're too selfish to *give* it to me, why don't you just lend me that, then? You know I'm good for the money. I need new stockings, and I really think a woman in my position ought to wear silk instead of lisle."

A pair of silk stockings—cotton-topped ones—cost a dollar and a half. I knew where the extra four bits would go.

"I need stockings, too," I said stubbornly.

"Heartless girl!" Ma muttered.

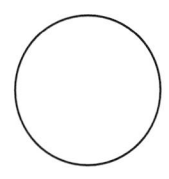

Chapter Eight

Homer had taken to walking me not only to my classes, but to the trolley-stop after school. He carried my books and also did most of the talking, which I didn't mind, since I didn't want to talk for fear I'd give away too much about myself. The Escoes were pretty well off, from what I could tell, with a house the size of Dr. Hallam's and a cook-housekeeper to run it. Nice as Homer was—and he was very nice—I wasn't sure how he'd take it if he knew I lived in somebody's garage apartment and my ma was a cook-housekeeper herself.

"Next year, you'll travel home in style," he told me one day as we left Central. "Dad's got a job lined up for me this summer, and with the money I make, I'm going to turn Mother's old flivver into one keen jalopy."

"A keen what?"

By his expression, I knew Homer was pleased—"tickled," he'd have put it—to have stumped me. He loved knowing all the latest slang. "A keen jalopy," he repeated. "A hotsy-totsy little crate of my own."

"You mean a car?"

"A car's exactly what I mean. No more waiting for the streetcar for *my* friends, no siree! Starting next year, I deliver 'em straight to their doorstep."

"My ma'd kill me if she saw me riding in a car with a boy," I informed him.

Homer grinned down at me. "Yeah, my mother'd kill Meggie if she saw her in a car with a boy, too." Meggie was Homer's younger sister. "What is it with mothers? I'll let you out at the end of the street then. Now how about we stop at the drugstore for a soda, Thea? My treat."

Since Dr. Hallam was paying me part of my mother's salary, I had my own money and didn't need to be treated. And since some of the other girls advised that if you let a boy treat you to ice cream, they started thinking they owned you, I wouldn't let myself be treated. But a soda did sound nice…

"Sure. Why not?" I agreed, trying not to seem nervous. I'd never gotten a soda at a soda fountain before. "I'll get my own, though. You need to save your money to make that— that—"

"Jalopy," Homer supplied. "Thanks, Thea."

The soda fountain was packed with students, and I had such a good time there I ended up being an hour late getting home. Ma apparently spent the extra time drinking, and I served the doctor's dinner that night.

*

I was enjoying my biology class, but when Dr. Hallam looked my biology textbook over, his expression turned pained.

"This is—more than ten years old," he said.

The doctor, I could easily guess, hadn't gone to public schools.

"Yeah, but it's still in good shape, and textbooks don't get replaced until they're worn out. The school board figures as long as the facts they've got in them are still true, it doesn't matter if the just-discovered ones are missing."

"But it does matter," Dr. Hallam objected. "It matters very much."

A couple of weeks later, the postman brought a package from New York with my name on it, and inside were two biology textbooks, freshly printed a few months before.

"I thought you might find those interesting," the doctor said when I went to thank him. "They're college-level texts, but I don't think you'll have any difficulty understanding them. If you do, come talk to me and we'll figure them out together."

I said before I was a blurter. Now I blurted, "Why are you so nice to me? I'm just—nobody. I'm just the help's daughter."

"I hope I'm nice to everyone," Dr. Hallam said, and then corrected himself dryly, "almost everyone," on purpose to make me laugh, I think—which it did. "And you're not 'nobody,' or 'just' anything. You're a young person with a very good brain, and you use it. I like to see that." He regarded me for a minute, then asked, "Would you rather I hadn't gotten you the books? I don't want to make you uncomfortable."

I said quickly, "No, I like them. I like them a lot, and I like that you're nice to me. All I meant was…"

I didn't know how to finish the sentence.

"Enjoy them, then," the doctor said, smiling.

I did enjoy them. I loved them. The only problem with the books was they knew more biology than my biology teacher did, and I found out the hard way my teacher was sensitive about being corrected. To stay out of trouble, on my test papers I wrote whatever I knew the teacher would score as correct, and at home I read the books the doctor had given me to find out what the real answers to the questions were. It meant I had to study biology twice as much as the other students did, but I didn't mind that.

From time to time, I did have to go to Dr. Hallam with questions about what I read in the biology books he gave me, especially things about natural selection and evolution, which were two topics my high school textbook did not discuss or even acknowledge. I also went a few times for help with trigonometry. At first we didn't talk about anything except biology and trigonometry because I knew my guess about the Gaucher's had made a good impression on him, and I figured the more I talked, the bigger the chance I'd ruin it by saying something stupid, but one day I couldn't resist asking him about the "big bullet."

"It's properly called a shell," Dr. Hallam explained, kindly suppressing a laugh. "Although 'bullet' isn't far wrong. A shell is the casing of the kind of 'bullet' artillery pieces fire, with a large explosive charge inside."

"Were you a soldier in the war?" I'd been wanting to ask him that.

"Oh, yes." He made a face. "Yes, there's an old tradition in my family that anytime there's a war going on anywhere, the Hallam men must take part in it."

"Didn't you want to?"

Dr. Hallam fussed with his pen for a minute. "I wasn't entirely opposed, as I recall," he said finally, laying it down. "I suppose I believed it was my duty. I wasn't a soldier in the sense you probably mean, though. I was in the medical corps."

"How'd you get the shell?"

"I didn't," said the doctor, turning to look at it. "A lunatic did, and gave it to me as a gift."

I'd seen a picture in my sociology book of a lunatic confined in a straitjacket because he'd driven himself crazy by abusing himself.

That's what the book said. But I knew there were other things that could drive men insane, and I'd heard war was one of them. "A real lunatic?"

Dr. Hallam hesitated, then asked, "Do you want to hear about it? Then you can decide for yourself whether he was or not."

Naturally, I said I'd love to.

"That shell was one that came down in an American trench one day in the course of a heavy barrage," the doctor began. "It happens to be a German shell, but you may believe me it might as easily have been one of ours. Once a shell exits the mouth of the artillery piece, the average artilleryman feels satisfied he's done his whole duty. Where the shell happens to go after that is God's—or the devil's—concern. In any case, and possibly by mere chance, that particular shell landed right where it was supposed to, in a trench full of soldiers. However, it *did not explode.* That's the important part of this narrative. If the shell had exploded, this would be a different kind of story."

"A sad one, I guess," I put in.

"Very sad," the doctor agreed. "The shell landed, as I said, in a trench full of soldiers, and as you might imagine, the soldiers immediately decamped. Or rather, all the soldiers decamped *save one*; a lunatic corporal we shall call—Corporal Lunatic."

I laughed. Dr. Hallam looked pleased.

"Not only did Corporal Lunatic not run away," he continued, "but he called on his mates to return, shouting something to the effect of, 'Come back, you idiots. If the blessed thing hasn't gone off by now, it's a dud.'"

"What's a 'dud?'"

"A shell that doesn't explode for some reason."

"And was it one?"

The doctor leaned down to take the shell off the bookshelf and handed it to me. "You are holding the proof that it was a dud in your very hands. If the shell had exploded, that part of it would have been reduced to shrapnel, and buried with, or picked from, the bodies of young men. War's a hideous business, Thea. Don't let anyone ever tell you otherwise."

I waited until the doctor's expression lightened before asking, "Did the other soldiers all get back in the trench then?"

"Nobody got back into the trench. No rational man would ever voluntarily reoccupy a trench containing a potentially live shell. That would be madness. No, the other soldiers very sensibly dispersed to find cover in other trenches, while the lunatic corporal waited out the barrage alone, passing the time by disarming and emptying that shell."

"Lordy!" I exclaimed—"lordy" being as near as my mother allowed me to come to a swear. "Wasn't that dangerous?"

"Oh, yes. Insanely so."

"Did he get in trouble?"

"No. He was commended for his coolness under fire."

I shook my head. "Somebody's a lunatic then. I'm not sure it was the corporal." I gave the shell a shake. "I think there might be a picture of him inside here. And some other pictures."

Dr. Hallam sat up, surprised. "Is that where I put them? Let me see."

I poured the snaps out onto the desk. The picture of the smiling—no, grinning—man holding the shell was on top, and the doctor looked at it for a long time.

"Yes. That's him," he said finally. "I forgot he was only Private Lunatic at the time. The promotion came later." He glanced briefly through the other pictures.

"Are any of those men you?" I asked.

"No. I had the camera." The doctor gave me back the snapshots, and I put them back in the shell.

"How long were you in the war?"

"Two years. Well, that, plus the eight months after the armistice I spent waiting for transport home. I don't know if you'd count that as 'in the war,' though, since no one was shooting at me."

We sat for a minute, and then the doctor sighed and said, "Go on. Ask me. Everybody does."

"What?"

"Ask me whether I killed anyone." Every trace of his smile was gone. "Let's get it over with."

I admit it. I had been wondering.

"No, I did not," Dr. Hallam answered, without waiting for me to ask first. "Or at least, I never killed anyone in the field. On the other hand, I was a newly diplomaed doctor treating injuries of a kind nothing had prepared me for, so it's possible—probable, I may even say—that I was unwittingly responsible for more than a few deaths in the wards. I have to live with that."

Before I could say anything more—not that I had any idea what more to say—the doctor picked up his pen again. "Now that we've settled *that*, let's talk about what you're learning in biology."

*

Since the doctor'd said I could, I all but made his library my own. Unlike the public library, where I had to rush in and grab the first books I saw and get home quick before my mother had time to get too drunk to cook, I could pore over Dr. Hallam's books for as long as I wanted, reading pages here and there, picking and choosing, and only checking on Ma occasionally to nudge her through her day. I read the paperbacks first, then asked Dr. Hallam what books I should start on next.

"Oh, the classics, of course," he said. "Wait a couple of years before you start getting into the moderns. You'll want to be able to talk about contemporary fiction at parties, but it won't help you get into college."

"But—I don't think I can go to college," I reminded him—but not forcefully. I didn't want him to take me at my word.

"Do you want to go?"

"Yes."

"Good. Then read the classics."

My mother heard the conversation.

"He shouldn't be saying things like that," she hissed, pulling me into the kitchen.

"What things?"

"You know what things! Things like about how smart you are, and how you ought to go to college. He's setting you up for a fall, Thea!"

There was fear in her eyes—not for my fall, but for herself. I refused to address it.

Instead, I tried to turn her ambitions to my advantage. "Dr. Hallam thinks it's good for people to read so they can talk at parties. I wonder if he'd give parties if he was married?"

I started dinner, letting the idea that Dr. Hallam was fitting me to be his wife work on Ma's brain. I told myself this was perfectly fair of me, since it had been her idea in the first place. It wasn't fair, of course, and if I was going to college, I was only postponing the inevitable. Sooner or later I'd have to level with her.

I tried not to think about it.

*

I didn't need the calendar to tell me the school year was almost over. The days were turning long and hot. I did well on my final exams, coming in first in most of my classes, including biology. I was second in trigonometry, but only by a little. Homer was first, of course.

The school principal stopped me in the hall to ask, "Will you be back next year, Thea?" and when I nodded, he said, "Well, a mother is her son's first teacher."

The sting of being viewed as no more than some unborn boy's mother was eased a few days later when Dr. Hallam met me, carrying a paper in his hand.

"Have a look," he said, showing it to me. "'A Case of Gaucher's Disease in Identical Twin Boys.'" He caught my eye to make sure I knew he was joking before adding, "Another triumph for the team of Nicholas and Hallam, and a strong debut by Carter." Turning to the back page, he pointed out a line that read: "'The authors are indebted to Miss Thea Carter for helpful discussions.'"

"Oh, gosh." I could hardly breathe. "Oh, my gosh."

After telling me I could have more copies—they were called "reprints"—if I wanted them, Dr. Hallam handed the paper to me. I was shaking so hard the pages rustled.

He allowed me to stare at my name for a minute, then began pointing out other things in the paper he thought I'd be interested in, including the part that said the twins were doing better since having their spleens removed. He repeated what he'd said before, that the twins might live for years, adding, "John will be following their case, so they'll get the best treatment available."

I decided if Dr. Nicholas took good care of the boys, I might—partly—forgive him for calling them "barbarians." Only partly, though. He'd said I was a barbarian, too. It still stung.

"Do you know yet if you'll be taking chemistry next year?" the doctor asked then.

I tore my eyes away from "my" paper. "I think I will," I said. "Enough boys signed up so that it'll be offered but not enough to fill it."

"Good. Calculus?"

I shook my head. "Oh, they've never had calculus at Central."

"German? I know you're taking French already, but German is useful for the sciences."

When I explained that German was banned at my school, the doctor sighed. "How about Latin?"

I didn't like this idea much. "All the Catholic kids take Latin, and they hear it every Sunday," I said. "They'd have a head start on me."

"You'll just have to study a little harder then."

Easy for him to say. "I guess I could take Latin."

"Consider it."

Neither of us said anything for a minute. I was trying to figure out a way to get another peek at the place where my name was printed without being obvious when Dr. Hallam asked suddenly, "Would you *like* to learn calculus?"

"Pardon? Oh! I guess so. I mean, *yes*, I definitely would, but I don't know—"

"I could teach you." When I hesitated, the doctor added, "You don't have to, of course."

"No!" I cried. "What I mean is, *yes*, I want to learn calculus, only I don't want to put you to a lot of trouble."

"It wouldn't be any trouble. I'd enjoy it. Let me see what books are available. I still have mine from years ago, but there are probably better ones out by now." He congratulated me again, and suggested I go show the paper to my mother.

Ma's first question when she saw my name was, "Will you get paid?"

"No. Even Dr. Hallam and Dr. Nicholas won't get paid. People don't publish scientific papers to make money. They do it to help people."

"Oh. Well, maybe Doctor will offer you a job, then. Or maybe the other fellow will."

"Dr. Nicholas?"

"Why not? Wouldn't a job in a doctor's office be nice? I'll bet it would pay well, too!"

"Ma, Dr. Nicholas lives in Chicago!"

"Oooh! Marshall Field's!" Mother cried.

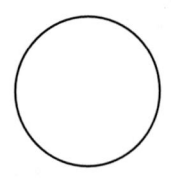

Chapter Nine

A few days later I was in the kitchen, drying the dinner dishes as my mother washed them, when the telephone rang. The doctor was in the library, but when he hadn't come to answer it by the third ring, I answered the call myself with my usual, "Dr. Hallam's residence." I stressed the word *residence* in case it was somebody who needed reminding that even a medical doctor is entitled to an evening off sometimes. A lot of people seemed to think they weren't. Neighbors sometimes didn't even bother to call first before showing up on the doorstep wanting medical advice. The doctor was patient about this, and I never knew him to send a bill to any of them afterward, but I disapproved.

While the operator was still announcing the call was long distance, a man's voice broke in with, "Is Hal there? Can you put him on, please?"

The name "Hal" caught my attention. "May I tell him who's calling?" I asked, and then went to the library to relay the name.

Dr. Hallam was at his desk writing, surrounded by open medical journals. He and Dr. Nicholas were working on another paper together. "Who did you say it was?" the doctor asked distractedly, looking up.

"A Mr. Freeman," I said, for the second time. "I think that's what he said. He asked for 'Hal,' like that other man did, but I think this is somebody different."

Before I finished talking, Dr. Hallam jumped up, threw down his pen and flung back his chair so hard it hit the bookcase behind him. He bolted by me without a word, and when he got to the telephone, snatched up the receiver and shouted, "Hello? Hello?" into it. As I was edging past him to get back to the kitchen, he was whispering, "Good God!" to himself like it was a prayer.

"Is it a woman?" Ma whispered, as I shut the kitchen door behind me.

I shook my head, and she looked reassured.

Long after Mother and I finished doing the dishes, swept the kitchen floor, and set things ready for cooking breakfast the next day, the telephone conversation was still going on. I couldn't make out any words. I stopped Ma from going to set the table for breakfast; she only wanted to do it because she'd be able to see the telephone stand from the dining room. But I admit I sneaked a peek myself when, despite me, she cracked the kitchen door open to look from there. The doctor had carried the telephone with him as far down passage to the library as the cord would reach and was sitting on the floor to talk. His hair, which he always combed straight back, had fallen down on one side, and as I watched, he ran his fingers through it and laughed in a way I'd never heard him laugh before, as free and easy as a boy. As soon as Ma—well, we—had gotten one good look, I pushed my mother out the back door of the house, locked it behind us, and made her come upstairs with me to give him more privacy.

Next day, the doctor applied to get a private telephone line put in the house in place of the party line (as a doctor, he had priority and could have gotten one anytime), and when the installer came, had the telephone itself moved from the telephone stand in the hall to his desk. After that, sometimes in the evening he'd go into the library after dinner and close the door behind him. On those nights, Ma and I did our evening kitchen work to the murmur of unintelligible conversation and more laughter.

*

Dr. Hallam started our first calculus lesson by asking me why I wanted to learn calculus in the first place. I didn't know any better answer to give than just that it was the next math class in the usual sequence.

He shook his head. "No. That's the reason you took all the math classes you've taken up to this point. Calculus is different. You want to learn calculus because calculus is the language of the universe."

Nobody'd mentioned to me before that the universe had a language. I liked the idea.

"You know about Newton's laws of motion, don't you?" the doctor asked.

I hesitated. "Kind of. I mean, I've read them."

"If you've read them, then you probably know there are equations to describe all the ways things move. Now, you could *memorize* all those different equations, or look them up, but that would be tedious, wouldn't it? But when you know calculus, you'll be able to start with first principles and *derive* the equations any time you need to use one."

"Is that easier than looking them up?"

"Oh, yes. Once you've learned calculus, you can do it in your head. And those equations put the physics of the whole universe at your fingertips." He smiled at me. "We all want the universe at our fingertips, don't we?"

"I wouldn't mind." I smiled back.

"Then let's put it there. First, we'll talk about limits."

I was hooked on calculus from the first sentence out of Dr. Hallam's mouth. I could immediately see that what he'd said was true. Calculus was going to be different from any other math I'd ever learned. It looked hard, but also so interesting that the next thing I knew, we'd read through two chapters of my calculus book and it was bedtime.

"Work until you get stuck," Dr. Hallam said, handing the book across the desk to me. "Then we'll talk again."

After that, at least once a week when the dinner dishes were done, I went to the doctor to get unstuck, or just to have him look over my work of the previous few days to see that I'd done everything right. He always left the door open when we were in the library together like that, and during my first few lessons, I'd hear my mother tiptoe down the hall from the kitchen from time to time to listen—I guess to make sure we were really doing math problems and not something else. But calculus was always the only thing going on between the doctor and me, and whether Ma was happy or disappointed about that, I wasn't entirely sure.

During the summer of 1928, Ma's drinking got worse again, or maybe I was just recognizing the signs of it better. I discovered to my despair it wasn't enough to keep cash out of Ma's hands, as I'd been trying to do. Dr. Hallam's business at the laundry and the grocery and the drug store were hers to give, and it didn't take the shopkeepers long to figure out how to get it. Even when I was off school during the summer, I couldn't always be on the spot to take deliveries to the house myself, and it took the boys from the grocer's or dry cleaner's less than five seconds to slip a pint bottle into an order.

"Are you trying to die, Ma?" I demanded when I found one— empty—in her underwear drawer. "This stuff's poison."

She pointed to the label. "It's not! It's Old Forester."

"It's Old Forester like you're a good Baptist," I retorted. "That's just a used bottle that's been refilled. Anyway, real whiskey's poison, too."

"That can't be so! Whiskey's medicine! Doctors can prescribe it, and even Baptists are allowed to have it when it's prescribed by a doctor."

"Baptists are allowed to have opium when it's prescribed by a doctor, too, but if they take too much, it kills them like heathen." Then, for at least the fiftieth time, I urged Mother to talk to Dr. Hallam, though without saying explicitly what she should talk to him *about*. Ma knew perfectly well already what I was suggesting the conversation should be about, but it offended her if I said the word aloud. "Maybe he could give you something that would help you stop."

"Stop what? I don't need to stop anything," Ma replied stiffly.

Be careful what you wish for, they say. In mid-August, Ma did stop drinking for a while. It wasn't because of anything I said, though, but because of something she did.

I was half awake one night, too hot to sleep. Mother got up to go to the toilet. She did that most nights, so I didn't think anything about it until a minute later, when I heard glass break in the bathroom. I guessed right away what it was. I jumped up and sure enough, when I opened the bathroom door, Ma was standing staring into the sink at the pieces of a shattered bottle.

I was genuinely concerned that if Mother tried to clean up the glass, she'd cut herself. She'd already made enough "trips to the toilet" without my being aware of it to be shaky on her feet. But I was also angry, and my voice was icy as I told her to get back to bed. "If you think you can walk that far," I muttered, making sure she heard the sneer I was wearing on my face.

Infuriated—although possibly less by my tone than by the sight of good booze going down the drain—Mother whirled around and smacked me across the face. She hit hard—probably harder than she meant to. In a fury of my own, I went back to bed myself and left her to deal with the mess she'd made.

In the morning, Dr. Hallam saw the bruise on my cheek and made sure I knew he'd seen it in the quiet way he had of just looking and then lifting his eyebrows, but beyond asking politely in a general way if I wanted him to speak to my mother, he didn't say anything about it. Mother didn't say anything about it either, but for a couple of weeks afterward she was unusually agreeable to anything I said, and, as I mentioned, stayed perfectly sober.

All my life, the times when Ma wasn't drinking had been like holidays for both of us. Not buying liquor left Ma with money in her pocket to spend, and for the first few weeks of every spell of sobriety, her sense of virtue buoyed her spirits. This time was even more a holiday than most, since I had money of my own I didn't mind spending to reward Ma for every sober day. But where in the past I'd always hoped (even prayed, though I wasn't otherwise the praying kind) that the change would be permanent—that Mother would never take another drink in her life—I knew by now that a holiday, by definition, is brief.

While her sober spell lasted, I let her help me pick out a new skirt and blouse for myself, the first brand-new things I'd worn in years, and I paid for a housedress and two pairs of lisle stockings for her. I hoped not getting her the silk hose she wanted would motivate her to stay sober longer, to save her drinking money to buy them herself. When I gave her the choice of a new hat or a vaudeville matinee, Mother chose the matinee. While the big city theaters were closed in late summer, their touring companies came to places like Oklahoma City, and the show we saw was such a good one that Ma and I seriously considered seeing it again the next day. Instead, we dressed in our best and gave ourselves a night out downtown at a real picture palace with red plush seats and gold leaf everywhere. We saw *Ben Hur* because Mother adored Ramon Novarro.

Afterward, we shared a strawberry phosphate at an ice cream parlor.

"This is as good as being rich, isn't it, Thea?" Mother sighed, looking around. "I mean it. If I had a million dollars, I don't think I'd want anything more than a nice night at the pictures and a strawberry phosphate."

"And Ramon Novarro," I put in wickedly.

Ma thought—or pretended to think—I was being serious. "Whyever would you even suggest such an indecent thing?" she said huffily. "Why, I must be more than twice his age!"

"Well, Dr. Hallam's more than twice mine," I countered.

"That's different. It's good for a girl to marry an older man. A man's not ready to settle down until he's older, for one thing, and for another, young men don't generally make enough money to take proper care of a wife."

This reminded me of a question I'd wanted to ask for years. "How much older was Dad than you?"

Mother frowned and pushed the phosphate glass away. "Three years," she said. "That's how I know what I'm talking about. I got married thinking your dad and I would live nice, like some other people I knew did. I thought on his salary we could have a house, and a carriage, and servants... parties." Ma stared vacantly for a minute—into the past, I think.

"You did have a house. And you had parties, too, didn't you? I think I remember one. You had on a yellow dress with a lace fall in front." I pictured her in my mind, an angel in my baby eyes, laughing as she circled the table after dinner guests had gone home, finishing off what was left in all the glasses.

Ma shrugged. "Oh, that old thing. I wore it for years. Yes, we had a few parties. Not many. Instead, we had babies and a hired girl, and scratch, scratch, scratch every month to pay the bills. Do you remember when you and I used to go to Dallas, Thea? Your dad and I had to make that same trip in a wagon. We went there to shop, because there wasn't any decent shopping in that pokey little town we lived in. We should have lived in Dallas. I wanted to, but your dad wouldn't hear of it." She sighed and said, as she often did, "I was born for better things."

I was tired of hearing it. "What's better than this?" I argued. "Didn't we just wear new clothes to the picture palace and drink a strawberry phosphate? You said a minute ago you were as well off as if you had a million dollars."

Ma's expression turned bitter. "Well, if I said that—and I don't by any means remember that I *did*—I was joking." She stood. "Let's go now, before we miss the last car home."

A few days later, Mother burned a nice beef roast for no good reason, and I knew she'd started back down the same old road.

I couldn't say I was learning to deal (at all) with my mother's ugly choices in life, but I was learning to deal with kitchen disasters. After I put Ma to bed, I ran—literally—to the closest grocery, and had a chicken bought, cleaned, cut up, and in the pot fricasseeing in less than an hour.

*

The weather cooled, the cicadas quieted down, and the school year—my senior year—started. Homer met me on Central High's front steps on the first day, deeply tanned, his sandy hair bleached nearly blond by the sun, and looking a little taller than he had the last time I'd seen him.

"How was the job?" I asked. "Did you save enough money to build your jalopy car?"

"Just 'jalopy,'" Homer corrected me, grinning. "Say 'car,' or say 'jalopy.' Don't say both. Yeah, I got enough. You're not going to know the flivver when you see her next. When I get done with her, she's going to look just like a Plymouth Eight, only sporty." Dr. Hallam drove a Plymouth Eight. There was nothing sporty about it. "The job was pretty keen, too. In fact, it's got me seriously thinking about studying law, like my dad, instead of being an engineer."

I laughed, and rested my hand on Homer's arm for no good reason. It was the first time I'd touched him like that, and judging by his face, he liked it. "I can see you as a lawyer," I told him, not adding that secretly I'd prefer to see him as an engineer. "What classes did you get?"

Homer'd gotten every class he wanted, of course. I was happy, and surprised, to be able to tell him I had, too.

"We'll have chemistry right before lunch," Homer said, comparing his schedule and mine. "That's convenient." I guessed by describing it as "convenient," he meant he wanted us to have lunch together. "Wait—Latin? You're taking *Latin*? Did you convert or something?"

I assured him I hadn't. "Just thought it might be useful sometime. I got the young P.E. teacher this year, too, instead of the old grouchy one. And guess what? I'm learning calculus!"

Homer looked at me, and then down at my schedule again.

"Not in school," I laughed. "At home."

"Cripes," Homer said dubiously. "I don't know, Thea. From what I've heard, calculus is too hard to just learn out of a book."

"No, I mean someone's— I mean I've got a— a—" I didn't quite know how to explain about Dr. Hallam—even to myself. "A tutor," I finally said.

"A *tutor*?" Homer seemed unaware of exactly how poor I was, but he knew I couldn't afford a tutor.

"Not one I have to pay," I explained quickly. "He's a— friend of my mother's. Sort of a friend. When I told him I wanted to learn calculus, he said he'd help me and got me a book."

Homer seemed unconvinced. "Are you sure he actually *knows* calculus?"

"Of course he does," I said indignantly. "For one thing, he's a doctor—"

"A *medical* doctor?"

"—and for another, I'm a quarter of the way through the book, so if he didn't know what he was talking about, I'd have figured that out by now!"

"Okay, okay. I believe you."

Homer and I stared silently at each other for a minute, ignoring greetings from passing friends.

"What's wrong?" I finally asked.

"Nothing." Scooping my books out of my arms, Homer turned and started up the stairs.

"Piffle," I said, following him. "Something's wrong. Why don't you just tell me?"

"It's nothing," Homer repeated.

I reached to take my books back. "I need those," I said coldly. "My first class starts in five minutes."

"No, I'll carry them," Homer said quickly. "I want to." He forced a fake smile that, to my relief, quickly turned into a real one. "I'm sorry. I didn't mean to sound sore or anything. I was just surprised, that's all."

"Surprised that I can learn calculus? You and all the rest of the men in this world."

"Not all of us. Not me. I like it that you're not a Dumb Dora. It's the thing I like most about you." (I'd already surmised it wasn't my looks.) "It's just— Well, for a minute it just felt kind of funny to think of you knowing more than I do. That's all. I'm not mad about it."

Tucked into my notebook was a reprint of the paper on Gaucher's Disease with my name on it. I'd brought it specifically to show Homer. Now I thought I'd better not.

"It's just calculus," I demurred. "It's just one little thing. I don't have the least idea how to make a jalopy."

"You're a peach, Thea." Homer cautiously touched my arm the way I'd touched his—unnecessarily. "Hey, you know what? I'll bet my dad knows somebody who could tutor me in calculus. I'll ask."

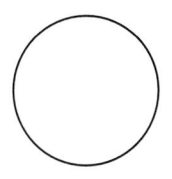

Chapter Ten

A few weeks into the new school year, Dr. Hallam said to me, "It's time for us to think seriously about getting you into a college. Have you thought about where you want to go?"

I hadn't. I was afraid to. "I'm— not sure I can go anywhere."

"Because…?"

"Well, money."

"Yes, you'll need some kind of bursary," the doctor agreed. "Getting scholarship money to pay your way in college will require extra effort on your part, but I'm sure you can do it. That is, if you want to."

Ever since Dr. Hallam had first suggested college might be a possibility, I'd been going back and forth in my mind wondering whether I should or I shouldn't, I could or I couldn't; but I'd never questioned for a minute—not even a second—whether I *wanted* to go.

"I want to," I said. "But are you sure I can? Sure for *certain*, I mean. Because I don't want to get my hopes up higher than my chances."

Dr. Hallam smiled. It seemed to me he was smiling more often lately. "There are no certainties in life," he said, "but your probability of success is high. Is that enough?"

High.

Yes, high was enough. I drew a long breath and said, "Tell me what I need to do."

The doctor said if I was willing to go to a state college, I probably didn't have to do anything more than continue to do well in high school. "But if you want to go someplace better—" He paused, letting the remark hang in the air while he waited.

The word "better" made me mentally squirm. I didn't want to be like my mother and imagine I was somehow "born" for better. "I'll go anywhere they'll take me," I said.

The doctor pulled a pen and paper out of his drawer. "Well, we'll certainly send in an application to a state college. That's prudent. Would you prefer Norman, or the A&M in Stillwater?"

"Stillwater, I guess."

"All right," Dr. Hallam said, and wrote this down. "But if you have no objection to going out of Oklahoma, you should go to the best place you can qualify for. Your performance on the College Board exam will determine where that is."

Dr. Hallam talked for a while about the College Board exam. He'd taken the old version, he said. "That one was a series of essays designed to find out what prospective students didn't know as much as what they did. Students used to doing well on exams found them quite demoralizing."

"I'm demoralized just hearing about them. I don't have to do that, do I?"

"No, you'll take the new test. It assesses scholastic 'aptitude,' allegedly. It's three hours long, instead of three days."

I liked the sound of that. "How many essays?"

"None. It's all short answer. I believe each section—there are six or seven sections, as I recall—comprises around three hundred questions.

No, now don't panic," Dr. Hallam added quickly, seeing from my expression that I was. "You're not *supposed* to be able to answer all the questions. That's the point. There are strategies to maximize your performance on timed tests, and we'll talk about them."

"All right," I said doubtfully. "What about my grades and things?"

"Those are considered. Since yours are excellent, they certainly won't count against you no matter where you apply, but universities give more weight to the College Boards than high school grades because high schools vary so much."

"All right. Makes sense. What else do I need to do?"

"Well, it would be useful to get your mastery of calculus assessed and certified, so you don't have to retake it in college. You can leave that to me, if you would. Letters in support of your application can be useful. Are there any teachers you've had who you think would be willing to write a letter for you? What about your chemistry teacher? Are you and he on a friendly enough basis for you to feel comfortable asking?"

"Our relationship is more like he's my teacher and I'm the stick he keeps to beat the backs of the boys in class he doesn't think try hard enough. He's always asking, 'Are you going to let yourself be beaten by a *girl*?'"

Dr. Hallam considered this for a minute. "Well, keep him in mind, anyway. What about your math teachers?"

"Mr. Brody said the same thing to the boys about me being a girl, but on the other hand, he was always really nice about me being late to class."

The doctor advised me to keep up the relationship if I could.

The next evening, as I served him his dinner, he asked me out of nowhere if I liked music. "Specifically, classical music."

I confessed I had no way of knowing if I liked it or not, never having heard any that I knew of. "I read a few years ago there was an orchestra in town, but I've never been to one of their concerts or anything. I think what our school orchestra plays is classical. I wouldn't say I like it, but that might just be because they're terrible players."

Dr. Hallam nodded. "Let's acquaint you with it, then. Before you pick what to do with your life, you should know the world better."

Next day he came home from work late with a gramophone and a big stack of records, mostly classical, and the day after that, a radio was delivered to the house while I was at school. Ma showed me the radio with trepidation. Anything electric made Ma nervous. We'd lived in a few places wired so badly that anything electric was apt to shoot sparks.

"Will it start to go all by itself?" she asked me, whispering like she was worried a loud noise might be enough to trigger a broadcast. Since it hadn't even been plugged in yet, I was able to tell her with perfect confidence it wouldn't.

After dinner, while Ma did the cleanup and dishes alone (I wasn't entirely sad to leave the job to her) I helped Dr. Hallam pound a long metal spike into the ground, twist a length of thick wire around it, and stick the other end of the wire through the library window. After that, he climbed onto the roof of the house with a coil of thinner wire over his shoulder and tied the wire to the chimney. The loose end of the thin wire went in through the library window, too. After twisting the two wires around pins on the back of the radio, Dr. Hallam turned the set on.

The radio immediately started humming, and the tuning dial glowed faintly. Ma, who'd come in to watch, hurried back to the kitchen, looking anxious. When the glow brightened, Dr. Hallam said it meant the tubes in the radio were warmed up, and began turning the dial to find a station.

I was so excited just to watch I didn't immediately notice when the radio actually began to play. The initial noise was only static, which was a new sound to me that soon became familiar. I didn't recognize the first tune that came out of the speaker, but I knew I'd never forget the thrill it gave me to hear it. The only programs we could find on the dial right then were snatches of music too far away to make out clearly and the local farm report, but that first night (and for some time after), even hearing the farm report gave me a thrill.

"The Chicago Symphony broadcasts its concerts every Sunday night of the season, and the season is about to start," the doctor told me. "Would you like to listen to them with me?"

I said I most definitely would. "I'd enjoy listening to anything on a radio. Even just talking."

"You'll have plenty of opportunities to hear talking," Dr. Hallam said dryly. "There's an election coming up. Whether the talking will be enjoyable is another matter."

Later, as we came out of the library, Dr. Hallam and I got a quick glimpse of Ma's backside as she ducked into the kitchen.

I explained quickly, "I don't think she meant to be snooping. She was just curious. We've only heard a radio once or twice outside shops downtown."

The doctor looked thoughtful, and the next day he came home with a smaller radio for the kitchen. "You must be lonely sometimes, Mrs. Carter," he said as he set it up. "I hope this will help you to pass the time."

Ma spent hours every day after that listening to what she referred to as "her" radio—church services on Sunday mornings while we ate breakfast and weekdays to whatever music she could find. Some days she listened more than she worked, in fact, but she also complained less about me—and the whole world—"neglecting" her, which made doing some extra housework myself worth it to me.

Every Sunday of that winter and spring, I sat on the floor in front of the radio and, whenever static didn't get the better of the Chicago Symphony, paid close attention to the first "serious" music I'd ever heard. After the first concert, the doctor worked at his desk while I listened, but on the season's opening night he sat on a chair next to me and described what the people who were lucky enough to be at Symphony Hall were seeing.

"This applause is for the concertmaster," he explained. "He's the best violinist, and he comes out first and leads the musicians in tuning up their instruments. That's the sound you're hearing now."

"Our orchestra does that," I said. "Only when they do it, it sounds like cats being skinned."

"Considering that violin strings used to be made of catgut, that's an apt simile, Thea. Now everybody's waiting for the conductor to come out. The conductor's name is Stock, by the way." The doctor said "Stock" German-style: "Schtock." "He always waits a few minutes before he takes the stage to let tension build."

The roar of applause when the conductor finally did walk out was so loud it made me jump and say, "Lordy!"

"No, he just thinks he is," Dr. Hallam smiled, adding casually, "I've spoken with him a few times."

"Mr. Stock? Really? You've talked right to him?"

"*Maestro* Stock," the doctor corrected me. "You can make a friend of any musician by addressing him as 'maestro,' but if you don't call a conductor that, he might run you through with his baton. Some members of my family are patrons of the orchestra, so Maestro Stock is obliged to stop by their box occasionally and speak nicely to them."

His family had a *box*? "What are patrons?"

"Donors. People who give the orchestra money. A few of my relatives are genuine music lovers, but that's beside the point. People in their position are expected to support the arts even if the only thing they get out of a symphony is a nap."

I wondered—not for the first time—if a man whose relatives were things like "patrons" of orchestras had any idea how big a scholarship a girl with nothing would have to get to be able to graduate from college. Or for that matter, if he understood what it would feel like to go to college and be poorer than everybody else there.

I didn't ask either of these questions. Instead, I said, "I didn't know you were from Chicago. You don't sound like you are."

Dr. Hallam gave me a strange look. Or rather, he gave the air around me, or maybe the wall behind me, a strange look. He didn't seem to see *me* at all.

"Years of speaking lessons made me the man I am today," he said in an odd, cold voice.

Then he quickly went back to being himself. "Oh, good! Here's the Brahms. Listen, and we'll talk about it afterward."

"What if I don't like it?" I asked uneasily, as what seemed to me like an overwhelming number of notes poured out of the radio all at once.

"That'll give us just that much more to talk about afterward," Dr. Hallam replied.

On evenings other than Sundays, the doctor encouraged me to play the records he'd bought. Most of them were songs from operas, and I had to listen to a *lot* of opera songs before I found one I liked. But once I liked one, I got to like others, too—eventually to the point of having strong feelings about which singers were worthy to perform my favorites. Dr. Hallam said I was annoyingly opinionated on the subject, but I think secretly he liked it.

Between the music and books and calculus lessons, I felt like I was two Theas, living two lives. One Thea believed she was going to college. She memorized Latin vocabulary, read the classics, discussed music, began sentences with, "If I may," and never lapsed into Southern Oklahoma dialect. The other Thea's dreams only took her as far as a high school diploma. That one ironed and cooked and cleaned and scanned the classified section of the newspaper to see what kind of jobs a girl high school graduate could get.

"Nineteen a week," Mother said, pointing out a clerk job I would need to learn typing to qualify for. "We could live on nineteen."

We.

"We could if you kept working for the doctor," I said. "Otherwise, we'd have to pay rent out of that nineteen."

"I bet an apartment like this one wouldn't set us back more than five dollars a week."

"Maybe. But we couldn't live in one like this. If we couldn't use the doctor's kitchen, we'd need to get an apartment with one." I didn't say so, but I'd also made a secret vow to myself that if I couldn't go to college, I at least wanted to live in a place big enough for me to have a room of my own.

Being thwarted made Ma cross. "Well, what do other girls do when they're just starting out?" she grumbled. "Gracious me, they must get by somehow on nineteen a week!"

"They have roommates, like Janie did," I said. Then I watched with very little sympathy as my mother mentally struggled with the idea that no gravy trains stopped at our station. She coped with this realization the same way she coped with any bad news and was in no shape to make dinner that night.

*

Soon after this, Dr. Hallam came to my mother with two pieces of news. The first was that movers would shortly be arriving with his furniture. This was a surprise, since neither Ma nor I knew he had any. After more than two years in Oklahoma City, it appeared the doctor had finally decided to go ahead and settle in. The second thing he told her was that a friend of his was coming to stay for a few weeks. "Mr. Diedrich is used to living simply," the doctor said. "I anticipate he'll be an easy guest."

Ma loved the job of ordering the movers around to get the doctor's things into the house and arranged. I was at school, so I didn't see it, but I'm guessing the movers probably didn't love the experience quite as much. Ma ordered bread and cold cuts and soda pop in to feed them at lunchtime and saved me back a bottle of Nehi Cola. I'd never had bottled pop before. I liked it a lot.

While I drank it, Mother and I wandered through the house looking at and commenting without shame on Dr. Hallam's things. We guessed the doctor must have lived in an apartment before because he by no means owned enough furniture to fill a big house, but two bedrooms were now fully fitted out, and the bed he'd been sleeping on before had been moved into a third bedroom, along with enough random pieces for it to serve as a sleeping room in a pinch. The dining table and chairs Dr. Hallam had bought in Oklahoma had been moved down to the basement and replaced with a much nicer set that included both a large sideboard and a corner cabinet for china.

"Mahogany," my mother said dreamily, running her hand across the shining surface of the table. "If you take my advice, Thea, you'll never let the help serve a single meal on this before you've checked for yourself to see a proper liner went on under the tablecloth. One hot dish could absolutely ruin a finish like this."

Since chances were good that *I* would be "the help" who set the table, I took note of the advice.

The dining room was beautiful, but the living room went all the way to elegant. The fringed rug on the floor was like something out of the *Arabian Nights*, the long sofa was red leather, and the chairs were upholstered and deep. Unlike the parlor sets in the Sears, Roebuck catalog I previously regarded as the ultimate in chic, nothing in Dr. Hallam's living room matched anything else, yet it all looked absolutely right together.

Besides the furniture, the movers left boxes of linens in the upstairs hall and barrels of dishes beside the china cabinet in the dining room still to be unpacked, but overall the place looked wonderful and didn't echo anymore.

Two days later, Dr. Hallam came into the kitchen where Ma and I were cooking with a letter in his hand.

"As you know," he began uncomfortably, speaking mainly to my mother, "my friend Mr. Diedrich will be arriving in two days. Now it develops that another friend will arrive in town a few days after that."

"Another friend?" I echoed.

I didn't mean anything by saying that, but the doctor made me blush by replying—though with a smile—"Believe me, I'm as surprised as you are to find I actually *have* two friends. This friend is Dr. Nicholas—Thea has met him—and I feel obliged to invite him to dinner. Dr. Nicholas is traveling with another mutual acquaintance who happens to be married and is accompanied by his wife. Mrs.

Carter, could you manage a dinner party for five on such short notice? Or, since putting a lone woman at a table with four men seems heartless, could you manage if I were to go so far as to invite a second woman? With Mr. Diedrich, that would make us a party of six."

Mother immediately began assuring Dr. Hallam that she—meaning we—could easily handle a dinner for six.

I wasn't quite so sure. "How fancy a dinner do you mean?" I interrupted my mother to ask.

"Nothing fancy at all," the doctor said quickly. "If Dr. Nicholas wants fancy, he can stay in Chicago and eat at the Palmer House. I'm aware, though, that even a simple dinner requires a great deal of planning and work." He looked at me as he said this, knowing—we both knew—that the work he was talking about would likely fall at least half on me. "There's always the alternative of a restaurant," he added.

Neither Ma nor I liked the idea of obliging the doctor to entertain his own friends in a restaurant. Ma quickly resumed her reassurances that we could handle things while I decided putting on a dinner party sounded kind of fun. Not fun like the dinner parties in movies where people in evening dress threw food at each other, but fun enough to be worth a little extra work.

"Shouldn't you get ladies for Mr. Diedrich and you, too?" I asked. "I think there's supposed to be even numbers of each at the table."

"On this occasion, we will waive the point," the doctor said—to Ma's obvious relief.

Later, when Mother went to serve the doctor his dessert, she stayed in the dining room while he ate it to discuss what the menu and flowers for the dinner should be, and afterward bustled around the kitchen checking the panty and cleaning supplies. As soon as the doctor finished dinner, she went to the dining room to put away the last of the china that hadn't been unpacked yet and count the wineglasses.

"Doctor says he won't be serving wine, but I don't believe it for a minute," she told me, bringing the glasses in for me to wash and polish. "He has to say that because of his position, but I'm sure he knows a dry dinner will *never* do."

"I think he does mean it, Ma."

Mother laughed gaily and patted my shoulder. "Well, shine up the glasses anyway," she said, trying to wink knowingly (she could never get the hang of a wink). "Because I know you're wrong. And what do you think? We're going to have to borrow table silver!"

"Hm?"

"Those few place settings the doctor's been using are all he owns. What do you think of *that*?"

"I don't think anything of it."

"It means you'll get to pick your own silver pattern! Not that old family silver isn't nice to inherit and all, but the new patterns are so pretty!"

I was tired of hearing her fantasies, especially since she never listened to mine. "Ma," I said firmly, "it doesn't matter to me what silver Dr. Hallam does or doesn't have because I am *not* going to marry him! All right? Get another dream. That one is never coming true."

The doctor gave Ma permission to use his account at the best department store in town to buy a few things the house still needed. She came home with those—and a new black dress and pair of silk stockings for herself.

"Ma…" I sighed.

"He told me to get what I needed!" Mother said, looking guilty.

It wasn't hooch, so I let it go.

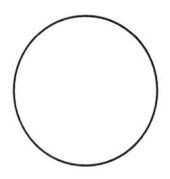

Chapter Eleven

When Dr. Hallam came home from work a few days later, he brought his friend with him. Ma saw them coming from the window, and after one look, rushed over to smooth my hair and pull my blouse down at the back. "Now, you *smile* when you're introduced!" she whispered sharply, which made me guess Dr. Hallam's friend must be good-looking.

He was, and not only that, but he also appeared to be a few years younger than the doctor. From Ma's flutter as she was introduced I knew she was already sizing him up as a potential son-in-law.

"Dennis, Miss Thea Carter," the doctor said when he got to me.

I recognized Mr. Diedrich's curly hair and dark eyes as soon as I saw him, and unfortunately, I said so. "Why, you're the lunatic!" I blurted without thinking—then immediately wished I could die. (Ma looked like she wished I could, too.)

The "Lunatic Corporal" didn't take it amiss, though. In fact, his shout of laughter almost ruptured my eardrums. "I guess Hal's been telling stories," he answered me, and winked. "Let's us talk later, Miss Carter. *I've* got a few stories, too." Being from Kansas, he had a homey accent and a country boy's easy way.

As soon as the two men left the kitchen, Ma started speculating about Mr. Diedrich. "Is he another doctor, do you think?"

"I doubt it. I think Dr. Hallam would have introduced him as '*Dr. Diedrich*' if he was."

"Oh, of course. Do you suppose he's married?"

I laughed, and didn't answer.

"Do you think he is?" Mother pressed.

"Ma, that is purely his business." Then I asked, "What're you looking at?" even though I could see perfectly well what she was looking at—my bust—and was annoyed about it.

"I wonder if you're ever going to fill out," Ma sighed. "Why don't you cook that special soup the doctor likes, and when I serve it, I'll be sure to mention you were the one who made it? Men like to know a young lady can cook."

I refused to make the soup, but that didn't stop Ma from getting in a word about my domestic abilities anyway. "Oh, Thea did it. Thea's a good little housekeeper," she said later when Mr. Diedrich thanked her for arranging his room. In case he wanted a wife who could talk at dinner parties, she added, "She reads a lot, too."

After dinner, Mr. Diedrich made the doctor give him a tour of the house. "Where the hell's your piano, Hal?" I heard him ask as they passed the kitchen door. (Mr. Diedrich swore kind of a lot.)

I didn't hear what the doctor said, but I did hear Mr. Diedrich's answer. "So, were you *punishing* yourself? Hell's afire, boy! Just get a damn piano, will you? I want to hear you play."

By his own request, our guest became "Mr. Dennis" to me on the second day of his visit, and after asking me politely if I'd mind it (because my older sister was married, which properly made me "Miss Carter"), he called me Miss Thea. He called Mother "Miz Grace" without even asking, probably because he guessed she'd love it, which she did. Ma had grown up near the Arkansas border where "Miz Firstname" was an even more respectful title than "Miz Lastname," since a woman's last name was more her father's or her husband's than her own.

Mr. Dennis was very different from Dr. Hallam. Not just in that Mr. Dennis had grown up poor on a farm and the doctor was a city-boy with money, or because Mr. Dennis showed all the interest in Dr. Hallam's house and neighborhood the doctor didn't—"There's an attic?" I heard the doctor ask him incredulously—or because the doctor was blond and Mr. Dennis was dark. The two were about the same height and if you looked, had about the same build. But even standing next to each other, Dr. Hallam's dignified way of holding himself made him seem taller than Mr. Dennis, while Mr. Dennis's loud laugh and physical energy made him seem bigger than the doctor. A room with Mr. Dennis in it was full of thrusting elbows and knees and jokes and laughing, and whirlwinds of motion. If Dr. Hallam was in the room too, it also had one quiet place from which the doctor sat observing what was going on, usually with a little smile on his face. Despite their differences, and despite the fact that, as Mr. Dennis told me, the two hadn't seen each other in more than three years, they were the best friends imaginable.

*

The dinner party was set for Saturday. I let my calculus slide for the week and used the extra time to polish every dish and glass in the china cabinet and starch and iron the best table linens until they were stiff and glossy enough to almost stand up by themselves. Ma spent most of Thursday and Friday getting the rest of the house ready, and while Dr. Hallam was at work and I was at school, Mr. Dennis made himself available to help her. Ma'd just about decided Mr. Dennis wouldn't do for a husband for me after all because he said he was "between jobs" and was vague about what kind of job he'd had when he was working, but he made her laugh and he willingly washed windows and floors, which put her in such a good mood that even though I figured all the fancy groceries she'd ordered for the party had probably gotten her at least a pint, she didn't drink at all that I could tell.

She and the doctor settled on a rib-roast for a main course and a bowl of yellow roses for the table (Ma loved yellow roses), and the doctor brought home a chest of table silver to use that he'd borrowed from Miss Foster, his nurse. Ma was disgusted—and showed it—that the silver was only plated, and Dr. Hallam came to me privately to ask me to tell her not to mention it at the dinner because Miss Foster was the extra woman he'd invited to come.

On Saturday morning, I made a triple recipe of tomato soup, the one part of the dinner that could be cooked well in advance.

My mother's nose was a little out of joint about the soup. It wasn't her recipe, and it wasn't her choice. She felt the doctor should serve consommé.

"If it has to be tomato," she sniffed, "at least it should have sherry in it. Tomato soup is always better with sherry. If Doctor would pick some up when he gets the wine, we could add it to the soup when we reheat it."

"There's not going to be any wine, Ma." I'd told her this already.

"Of course there will be. I already put the wineglasses on the table."

"We're using them for water."

"What about cocktails before?"

"Nope."

"Well, what if somebody asks for one? A good host should always have something on hand in case somebody asks." She leaned toward me conspiratorially. "Thea, what if we just took care of that little detail ourselves? You and me. All on our own. We might save Doctor a lot of embarrassment that way!"

"Alcohol's illegal, Ma."

"Everybody drinks it!"

I raised an eyebrow at her, and she wilted.

"How's the dough coming along?" I asked then. My mother's yeast rolls were delicious.

Ma lifted the clean dishtowel she'd laid over the dough-bowl to peek. "Rising nicely. I wonder if you would keep an eye on it for me? I'll be back in time to punch it down. I've got a long day ahead of me and I think I'd like a little nap." It was only mid-morning, too early for anybody to need a nap, no matter how long their day was going to be, but she appeared to still be embarrassed about pushing me to bring alcohol into the doctor's house, so I assumed she just wanted to hide out for a while.

"Go ahead," I agreed. "I'm almost done with the soup. I'll put it on the top shelf of the icebox, okay? There's room."

"Whatever you think."

When the soup was finished and the dough was still half an hour or so from being doubled, Dr. Hallam and Mr. Dennis called to me from the library to ask me to sew a button on Mr. Dennis's jacket, which I did, and then stayed to listen to them make jokes at each other's expense.

In the middle of our laughing, I asked, "What about those stories you were going to tell me, Mr. Dennis? What did Dr. Hallam used to get up to during the war? Did he get in a lot of trouble?"

"Never got into trouble," Mr. Dennis said, shaking his head like he was delivering bad news. "Pure as a choir boy. The dullest man in the army. Now, *after* the war... I think I might have heard the words 'court martial' said once or twice in reference to you, didn't I, Hal?"

The doctor glanced at his watch and said abruptly, "Lunchtime."

"No, I want to hear!" I cried. "*Court martial*? Lordy, what did he do?"

"I'll tell you when you're older," Mr. Dennis said, winking. "Want to see some pictures?"

Naturally I did, so Mr. Dennis pulled a little tin box out of his jacket pocket.

I asked if it was a cigarette case.

"It was until Hal made me give up smoking," Mr. Dennis sighed. "Years ago. Said it was a filthy habit. I'm keeping pictures in it until he tells me pictures are a filthy habit, too. Look at this: The scion of the House of Hallam in khaki."

The photograph he handed me was of Dr. Hallam in his army uniform, hatless, and looking deadly, deadly serious. It appeared to have been cut from a larger studio portrait.

"How old were you?" I asked the doctor. If I hadn't already known better, I'd have guessed no more than eighteen.

"Oh, still in knee-pants," Mr. Dennis answered for him, while Dr. Hallam said, more believably, "Twenty-six, I think."

Besides the studio picture, the cigarette case had some snapshots in it, including a wartime one of the doctor with a white apron on over his uniform and a cigarette between his lips.

"You're a fine one to talk about filthy habits!" I laughed.

I only meant to tease him, but I guess it was the wrong thing to say. Dr. Hallam looked as shocked as if I'd shown him my knickers.

"Smoking," Mr. Dennis said quickly, turning the snap for the doctor to see. "Smoking wasn't filthy until Hal quit doing it. Here's one of my kid sister. It's from years ago, though. She's all grown up now."

Dr. Hallam repeated, "lunchtime!" and Mr. Dennis put the pictures away.

We went to the kitchen, where the men said they'd be fine with sandwiches. After I got out the bread and things, Mr. Dennis joined right in and made sandwiches with me. The three of us ate together, which was all right, since it was Ma and not me who was technically "the help," and we sat at the kitchen table because the dining table was already set for the dinner. My mother wasn't around, and I admit I never thought of her even once, although of course it was lunchtime—past lunchtime—for her, too.

It wasn't until I was cleaning up after lunch and the men had gone back to the library that I happened to notice the dough-bowl still sitting exactly where it had been an hour before.

When I lifted the towel, I knew instantly my mother hadn't come back to the house to punch the dough down while I was in the library. It hadn't been punched down at all. It had fallen; and after falling, it had risen partway again and fallen a second time. In other words, it was ruined. Ma had evidently forgotten all about it. A quick look at the clock told me that, with all the other cooking she had to do for the party, there wouldn't be time for her to make another batch of yeast rolls. We'd have to make-do from the bakery. I headed for our apartment to give Ma this news and a good-sized piece of my mind.

She was asleep when I got there, but she was way beyond "napping." Ma was all the way to dead drunk, and snoring so loud I was surprised I hadn't heard her from the house.

I literally cried with fury. Everyone had been looking forward so much to the dinner party and now she'd wrecked it. Tears ran down my face as I shook my mother harder than I'd ever shaken her before, and yelled, "Get up, you stupid bastard, I hate you." "Bastard" wasn't the right word for Ma, and it wasn't the word I wanted, but at that moment I couldn't remember any worse ones. One part of me wanted to smack my mother across the face the way she sometimes smacked me, but I managed to stop myself from going that far.

When I couldn't rouse her right away, I got scared. Bum alcohol could kill a person. What if Ma'd gotten some? She wasn't careful. She'd take anything she could get. A hip flask lay on the floor next to the bed. I grabbed it and headed for the house.

I burst into the library without even knocking first, silently holding up the bottle for the doctor to see.

I couldn't speak, but I didn't need to. Dr. Hallam jumped out of his chair and grabbed his medical bag, and when the two of us got to the back door, Mr. Dennis was right behind.

Up at the apartment, the doctor went straight to the bed. He checked my mother all over, listening to her heart, and pulling open one of her eyes. At one point he asked me for the flask, and when I gave it to him, he sniffed it, said, "It's all right," and put it aside.

Straightening up, he added, "I don't think she's in any danger, but let's get her into the bathroom, and see if we can get some of that stuff out of her stomach."

He motioned to Mr. Dennis, but I went to help him instead. I thought my mother'd be more comfortable not being handled by two men. Dr. Hallam took off his jacket and rolled up his sleeves, and then showed me how to put my shoulder under Ma's arm to lift her. Together we got her onto her feet, with the doctor urging her along much more gently than she deserved, and calling her Grace. Ma was sort of awake by now, but I think not enough to be sure who he was.

When we got to the bathroom, the doctor stopped dead in the doorway, looking confused. "Where's the bathtub?" he asked, staring at the holes in the walls where water pipes should have been.

"We use that. The washtub," I explained, pointing out the washtub propped against the wall while I shriveled inside with humiliation. I pointed with my chin, since I was holding onto Ma with both hands.

The doctor didn't say anything more. Together he and I got Mother to the toilet, where the doctor made her vomit a couple of times with gulps of water in between. Ma was too drunk to cooperate much, and no wonder. She'd polished off a whole hip flask, and there wasn't much of it left in her stomach. After the second vomit, Dr. Hallam and I got her back to the bed—Mr. Dennis opened it for us—where I washed Ma's face with a wet towel before rolling her onto her side as usual and covering her up.

"What now?" Mr. Dennis asked softly.

"Now we let her sleep it off," Dr. Hallam answered, repacking his medical bag. "I'll check on her every few hours. She'll probably be fine by tomorrow. Well, relatively fine."

"I should stay."

I expressed this as a statement, flat and cold, and not as a loving offer.

The two men exchanged looks. "You may stay if you like," Dr. Hallam answered, speaking carefully.

"Well, I *don't* like," I cried angrily. "If you want the truth, I don't care to be anywhere near her! Why does she do this?" I looked up at Dr. Hallam and started to cry. "Why does she *always do this*? Every time I'm happy, she wrecks it! It's like she hates me!" This was an overstatement, but while I was saying it, it didn't feel like one.

Mr. Dennis took my arm. "You come be with us," he said. "Your Ma won't know if you're here or not." I didn't take any persuading.

When we got back to the kitchen, I sat down in my mother's usual chair with the hateful, petty thought that if she didn't like it, she could stay sober enough to sit in it herself.

Mr. Dennis asked for the second time, "What do we do now, Hal?"

Dr. Hallam didn't answer until he'd poured a glass of water, chipped some ice to put in it, and set it in front of me. "Drink that," he ordered, and then added to Mr. Dennis, "I'd better go make some telephone calls."

"There's no way to save the party, I guess," said Mr. Dennis. "Damn! I was really hoping something good would come out of you talking to John Nicholas. I mean, the fellow's a"—he looked at me and didn't finish saying what he thought John Nicholas was—"but he's very sharp, and he knows all the right people."

The doctor smiled—a grim smile, not a happy one.

I set down the waterglass, which I'd drained. "What 'good?'"

Mr. Dennis took a breath to say something—some soothing nothing, I think—and Dr. Hallam turned toward the library, probably to go call the dinner guests and say the party was off. I jumped up and caught hold of the doctor's jacket to stop him, repeating, "What 'good?'"

The doctor hesitated. "John would like to get me back to Chicago, that's all. He suggested his friend—our other guest—might be someone who could help me."

"Do you want to go back?"

"Well, I…wouldn't mind it. If the circumstances were right."

"Then that does it," I cried, wiping my eyes on my sleeve. "I am *not* letting Ma ruin this dinner party like she ruins everything else! Don't call anybody. I'll cook the dinner myself."

I walked over to the stove and began putting on my apron to show I meant what I said.

Dr. Hallam was totally against the idea at first. He gave lots of reasons it wouldn't work, all of which I had answers for except the one about how, even if he wanted to let me—which he said he didn't—I wouldn't have hands enough to cook a dinner and serve it at the same time. "Your mother couldn't have done it either," he said. "She was counting on you being in the kitchen."

Mr. Dennis came to my rescue.

"I'll help," he said. "I don't know anything about serving, but I can help in the kitchen."

"Denny, you can't boil an egg," the doctor contradicted him flatly.

"All right, I can't boil an egg," Mr. Dennis conceded. "I admit it. I have never successfully boiled an egg. But I've worked in a kitchen before, and I know how to follow directions. I bet I could boil an egg if Miss Thea told me how."

"From the dining room? You're a guest, remember?"

"Honestly Hal," Mr. Dennis said earnestly, "that's the best part of Thea's plan. I absolutely cannot work in your kitchen and sit at your damn dining table at the same time. And that's an answer to a prayer."

"Denny…"

Mr. Dennis put up a hand. "Hal, I love you dearly," he said. "You are more than a brother to me. But I do not like your friends—some of your friends—and I do not like dinner parties. No, this is perfect. Miss Thea and I will get as much of the cooking done early as we can, and when the guests come, I'll carry on in the kitchen while she serves at the table. I'll make sure nobody sees me, and you can say my arrival was delayed, or I had to leave early, or whatever the hell else you want to say to explain where I am. Just let me cook. Okay?"

"We can do this," I put in. "I'm sure we can do this."

Dr. Hallam still looked doubtful.

Mr. Dennis smiled suddenly and reached to give the doctor a little push toward the kitchen door. "Out of the way, old man. Go shine your shoes or something. Miss Thea and I have work to do."

The next few hours were crazy. First Mr. Dennis and I laid out everything we thought we'd need for cooking while the doctor drove to the nearest baker's to try to get dinner rolls.

"Out," he said, when he came back. "Where's another bakery I could try, Thea?"

"Forget it," I said. "It's too late in the day, and baker's bread is no good anyway. I'll make biscuits."

Dr. Hallam's eyes widened. "You can't serve biscuits! Biscuits are—"

Mr. Dennis and I—two Southerners, at least in regard to biscuits—stared at him, daring him to continue.

"Delicious," Mr. Dennis finished the doctor's sentence for him. "Biscuits are delicious. Don't be a snob, slicker."

"Biscuits will be fine," the doctor said dutifully. "How are you at serving, Thea?"

I got Mr. Dennis started peeling vegetables, which he turned out to be lightning fast at (he really had worked in a kitchen), then left him to it while Dr. Hallam and I went into the dining room. Once there, the doctor put a serving bowl and a ladle into my hands and walked me around the dining table, critiquing my performance as I pantomimed serving food from the left.

"Ladies first, of course," he said, "starting with the lady on my right. Then the men in order counterclockwise. John first"—he pointed to what was going to be Dr. Nicholas's place—then Dr. Edgar"—our other guest—"and me last. Dave Edgar's a trencherman, so pass everything twice, and a third time if he seems interested. Pass the dishes first, and then make a second circuit with the sauces. If you try to carry both at once, you're likely to spill."

Then he had me put the bowl and ladle down and watched me pretend to clear dishes away from the right. I hoped he wasn't wrong when he said, "You'll do fine."

When I got back to the kitchen, still by no means entirely clear on the fine points of serving, the vegetables were all ready to cook, but time was getting short. I simplified Ma's planned Duchesse potatoes into plain mashed browned under the broiler (which is all Duchesse potatoes are anyway, except for being piped into fancy shapes) and crossed out two or three steps from each recipe for all the other dishes. Since Ma wasn't going to be making the souffle she'd promised, I ordered Dr. Hallam—an educated, fully qualified, and highly respected actual medical doctor—like he was my personal errand boy to go out and buy ice cream.

The roast could take care of itself until it was time to make gravy, so after I slid it into the oven, I went up to the apartment to have my bath. Ma was still sleeping when I got there, but breathing more normally now.

My bath was cold—no time to bring up any hot water—but this time I liked it that way. When I was dry, I put on Ma's new black dress and her nicest apron. I was tall enough now that the length of the dress was all right on me, and once I tied on the apron nobody could have told it was baggy across the bosom. Ma's newest pair of hose were silk all the way to the tops and probably cost two dollars, but I didn't feel any shame about taking them without any intention of giving them back to her later. They were the first silk anything I'd ever worn, and I was angry at Ma all over again for making the occasion such a bad one.

Once I was dressed, I put my hair up in a bun like Ma wore hers, regretting for the one millionth time that she refused to let me have it bobbed, and then I wet the cake of mascara I'd secretly bought and used the tiny brush that came with it to dab some on my lashes. When I remembered Ma'd sworn she'd blister my hide if she caught me making up my face before I turned eighteen, I dabbed on a second coat of mascara and tinted my lips with Ma's own lipstick.

Then I went back to the house, where Mr. Dennis told me I looked wonderful.

It was nearly time for the guests to arrive. I slipped into the dining room and got the doctor's champagne saucers. I'd spent a lot of time polishing them, so I decided I might as well put them to use. The icebox door had been opened so many times the ice cream was soft, but I put a scoop into each saucer, poured a little melted raspberry jam over it, added another scoop of soft ice cream and another pour of jam, and then set all the glasses straight onto the ice block to get as cold as possible before time for dessert. The jam wasn't homemade and might not even have been a good brand (I didn't try any), but it made a pretty contrast with the white ice cream, and as I poured it, I repeated to myself what the doctor'd said to me, that if the guests wanted fancy, they could eat in Chicago. The celery stalks had been sitting in ice water for an hour and still hadn't curled the way they were supposed to, but I put them in the celery glasses anyway and set the glasses on the dining table next to the salted almonds. Then I stuck my head back into the kitchen to tell Mr. Dennis to start heating the soup and went to help the guests with their wraps.

I liked Dr. Hallam's nurse Miss Foster right away. I was just the housekeeper, so nobody got introduced to me, but as I showed her where the toilet was—which I called the "cloakroom" because the doctor had said I should—she told me quietly I could call her Francie and that she'd heard all about me. From her smile, I guessed Dr. Hallam had only told her the good parts, and I probably blushed. The other woman guest was Mrs. Edgar, whose fat husband Dr. Edgar looked me up and down—twice—right in front of her. I was disgusted, but tried not to let on.

Just like he had the first time we'd met, Dr. Nicholas totally ignored my existence.

Everybody stood around in the living room for a few minutes, talking about this and that and probably wishing Dr. Hallam had broken the law so we could serve cocktails, while I went and checked on the soup. When I came back and gave the doctor a nod, he said, "Let's get started, shall we?" and gave his arm to Mrs. Edgar. Dr. Edgar redeemed himself with me for his ogling (a little) by noticing that Dr. Nicholas was totally ignoring Francine, too, and offering her his own arm, and then everybody went into the dining room.

I was too nervous to notice what was going on at the table during the soup and appetizer courses, but once the roast had been served, I began to enjoy listening in on the conversation. The three men at the table were all doctors and pretty much only talked about medical things, but that was fine with me. I loved medical conversations. As a nurse, Francine probably could have contributed a few things to what the men said, but she kindly gave all her attention to Mrs. Edgar instead, who only talked about her children. I understood why Mr. Dennis hadn't wanted to be at the dinner. Not being either a medical person or a mother would have made him a real outsider.

While I was making my second round with the roast (which involved a long stop at Dr. Edgar's place while he calculated exactly how much of what was on the platter he could serve himself and still leave what decency required him to in case Dr. Hallam wanted seconds), Dr. Nicholas brought up his idea for the new paper he wanted Dr. Hallam to write with him. It would be on—guess what?—Gaucher's Disease, providing the new patient he'd recently had referred to him turned out to have Gaucher's.

"Naturally, I'm going to make perfectly sure of that first," Dr. Nicholas said, as though making perfectly sure of his diagnoses was a policy he'd never, ever violated in his life.

"Naturally," Dr. Edgar said, gesturing to me to bring him more biscuits.

"You know, Ed is a brilliant diagnostician," Dr. Nicholas added. (Dr. Hallam caught my eye and smiled wryly.) "And by the way... is it true that pediatric oncology at Cook County is going to be expanded?"

Since Dr. Hallam just *happened* to be an expert on pediatric oncology (and interested in a job in Chicago), the talk after that was nothing but pediatric oncology in Chicago, with even Nurse Foster and Mrs. Edgar having things to say on the subject. Being a mother made Mrs. Edgar a sort of expert on the "pediatric" part at least, and Nurse Foster was an expert on Dr. Hallam, whom she praised to the skies. Her silverware was only plated, but the reference she gave the doctor was sterling.

Dr. Edgar finally interrupted the selling of Dr. Hallam by demanding to know if there were any more of "those delicious dinner rolls," and then saying, when I showed him there weren't (because he'd eaten them all), "Well, how about dessert, then?" How that man could still be hungry after the way he'd already stuffed himself was beyond me.

After dessert, I served coffee in the living room. The coffee tray was so heavy Mr. Dennis insisted on carrying it all the way to the living room door for me before handing it over and then sneaking away fast before he could be seen. I managed not to drop it, or to spill any coffee when passing the cups, and after the guests had drunk their coffee, they were finally ready to call it a night and ask for their coats. Francine got me aside to tell me my biscuits were the lightest she'd ever had, and Mrs. Edgar asked me—well, ordered me, really—to send her my recipe for tomato soup.

"Dr. Hallam will tell you where," she said, and breezed off without even looking at me.

I had no intention of sharing my soup recipe except maybe with a nice lady like Francine, but I was flattered to know she'd liked it.

Best of all, Dr. Edgar and Dr. Hallam parted with hearty handshakes and promises to "be in touch." My feet hurt, my arms ached, and my dress—Ma's dress—was clammy where a river of sweat had run down my back, but none of that mattered to me because the party had clearly been a big success.

When I staggered back to the kitchen, Mr. Dennis was gnawing roast straight off a rib like a cannibal. He'd saved me back helpings of everything, and some ice cream for the doctor. We all ate, and then we all did the dishes together, laughing and talking like brothers and sister. At least, I think that's what we were like. My brother and sister were too old for me to ever have washed dishes with them, so I couldn't be sure. By the time the dishes were clean and put away, it was after midnight. Dr. Hallam said the rest of the work could wait for morning and we should all go to bed.

"Would you like the spare room for tonight, Thea?" he asked me, his expression very kindly but also embarrassed.

When I said no, he insisted on walking me up the stairs to the apartment and coming in with me to check on my mother. I think she was awake, but she pretended not to be. Dr. Hallam looked her over briefly and said she was fine. As soon as he went back down, I stripped off my dress—Ma's dress, that is—threw it on the floor, crawled in next to Ma, and slept like a log in my slip and step-ins.

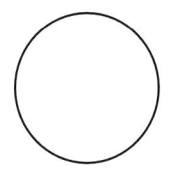

Chapter Twelve

I was aware when my mother got up the next day, but it was my turn to pretend to be asleep. I didn't get down to the house until after nine, where I found the kitchen much cleaner, but my mother nowhere around. When I stepped out into the hall to look for her, I heard the doctor talking to somebody in the library, and when I sneaked closer, I realized he was talking to Ma.

They were together there for quite a while. As far as I could tell, Ma didn't cry or try to justify herself, like she often did. I couldn't hear what the doctor said to her, but whatever it was, when she came back to the kitchen, she apologized to me for the first time in her life, or mine.

Also for the first time, I didn't say everything was fine or pretend like nothing had happened. Ma didn't seem to expect me to. I listened to her apology, then made myself toast and coffee and ate while she quietly shined up the pieces of Francine's despised silverplated tableware and packed them neatly back into their case. After that, the two of us did another quick clean of the kitchen together before going back up to the apartment, because Sunday was supposed to be Ma's day off. I spent the afternoon doing our regular laundry, including dunking Ma's dress I'd borrowed in white gasoline to clean it and hanging it behind the garage to drip dry where nobody cared if the grass got killed by the drips or not. Mother slept most of the day.

When I came home from school on Tuesday, Ma met me at our apartment door, stone sober and amazed. Workmen were in our bathroom, she said, installing the bathtub and water heater Dr. Hallam hadn't realized until dinner-party day that Ma and I didn't already have.

"They came right after breakfast. Doctor told me to expect them. He apologized to me and said he was sorry for not having it done sooner. He assumed when he bought the house this apartment was ready to live in."

I'm happy to say that my mother looked ashamed as she told me all this. The truth was I felt she deserved shame. She was the terrible employee of a very nice boss who should have fired her on the spot when she almost ruined his dinner party. The only reason he hadn't, it seemed clear to me, was because he wanted me to get my chance at an education and a good life, which was really my mother's job to see to, not his. I hoped if she felt shame enough, Ma would reform.

I hoped—but I wasn't counting on it.

Our bathroom was finished on Wednesday, and on the Monday after it, Mr. Dennis went back to Chicago.

It was bad that he had to go. It was even worse that on Sunday, the day before he went, the doctor and he had some sort of quarrel.

I'd been thinking I felt tension building between them for almost the whole last week Mr. Dennis was with us. I was very sensitive to building tension because tension built with Ma, too. It built from her being happy and at peace with the world to her needing to be very drunk to cope with it at all. But I didn't know how bad the situation was between the doctor and Mr. Dennis until the two of them took a walk together after breakfast and both of them came home sad-faced, and in Mr. Dennis's case, I think also angry. His nature was generally so cheerful I hadn't known before he could *get* angry. They spent a few hours apart after that, with Mr. Dennis outside pacing the yard and the doctor in the library, and then Mr. Dennis went in.

On our day off, Ma and I still ate our meals in the doctor's kitchen, since we didn't have one of our own. This day, we decided between ourselves it would be more tactful of us to go into town for lunch and leave the men alone in the house. We ate at a cheap Chinese restaurant, a Chinese business being one of the few things open on a Sunday in Baptist country.

"I hope Doctor and Mr. Dennis patch things up double-quick," Ma said, pushing sprouted beans into a pile at the edge of her plate. "I don't mind a little rice now and then, but the rest of whatever you call this is too foreign for my taste."

Much later, when Ma and I slipped into the kitchen for dinner, we could hear the two men in the library hotly debating something with the door closed.

"What do you think about just having some ice cream instead of cooking?" I whispered to Ma, after opening the icebox and finding a pint there. "It'll be fun to have all the ice cream we want for a change, won't it?"

Ma stopped straining to make out what the doctor and Mr. Dennis were saying to each other and indicated with signs that a big dish of ice cream was the exact kind of dinner she liked best. I sent her upstairs with the ice cream carton and two spoons and said I'd meet her there as soon as I'd set up for breakfast.

"I won't be a minute," I promised.

I did set up the breakfast things, but as soon as I'd done that, I took off my shoes and tiptoed down the hall in my stockinged feet to listen at the library door. I had an idiotic idea I'd listen for a few minutes to find out what the doctor and Mr. Dennis were quarreling about, then walk in and, with a few well-chosen words, broker peace between them.

But even with my ear flat against the door, I couldn't make out enough of what either man said to understand the problem, much less solve it. Dr. Hallam always spoke quietly, and on this occasion his voice was no more than a low murmur. Mr. Dennis spoke louder and he talked more, but the only remark I made out clearly was, "Dammit, come on, Hal! There's some risk, sure, but I'd be willing to take it."

I couldn't distinguish any of the individual words in the doctor's subsequent answer, but it sounded to me like they added up to "no."

A long silence after this made me afraid the two men had given up on settling their differences and would soon come out, so I tiptoed away from the library door much more quickly than I'd tiptoed to it, put my shoes back on in the kitchen, and hurried up to the apartment.

The lights in Dr. Hallam's house stayed on late that night. Next morning, I watched from the window as the doctor and Mr. Dennis walked out to get into the doctor's car and drive to the train station, both looking like they'd shrunk two inches and lost ten pounds since the day before.

"That Mr. Diedrich might at least have been polite enough to give me a little something for the extra trouble," Ma said, watching with me as the doctor's car rolled down the drive. "He didn't even say goodbye." She hadn't noticed either man's obvious grief, only that she hadn't got her expected tip.

I might have reminded her it was she, not Mr. Dennis, who had been "extra trouble" during his visit but didn't bother. Frank talk hurt

Ma's feelings, and when her feelings were hurt, she expected me to comfort her. I wasn't in the mood.

"I don't think Mr. Dennis has a lot of money, Ma," was all I said.

*

The period of humility and sobriety that followed Ma's dinner-party-day binge was shorter than usual, and then she was right back to drinking. I talked with the doctor about it. I was generally comfortable enough to talk with him about almost anything now—although not quite enough to specifically mention either my mother or drinking.

I was required to take Public Speaking at school to graduate, and I was turning out to be absolutely horrible at it. Dr. Hallam, in an obvious effort to shake himself out of the black mood he'd been in since Mr. Dennis left, offered to help me.

"You'd probably make a better speech if you talked about something that genuinely interested you, instead of any of these topics." He indicated the list of suggestions in my textbook. "What's something you love and would like to share?"

Instead of answering him, I found myself blurting, "Why do people do stuff they know is wrong?"

"Good, but you need to reword that a little," the doctor said, pointing to the instructions in my textbook. "How about, 'some reasons that…', or 'it is the case that…' The premise for this type of speech is supposed to be phrased as a statement, rather than a question."

"I didn't mean for a stupid speech," I said moodily, shrinking down in my chair. "I mean for real. Why do people keep doing things they know are wrong?"

One of the things I liked best about Dr. Hallam was that no matter what question I asked him, he always carefully considered it. Putting down his pen and folding his hands, he said, "Why does anybody do anything? It's usually because they imagine there's some benefit to themselves in it."

"Well, but what if there isn't? What if what they're doing is bad for them?"

"Bad for them in what way? Bad for them because it erodes their moral fiber or because it's physically self-destructive?"

"Both."

"Both. All right." The doctor nodded. "Well, I'm not qualified to discuss moral questions. That's not my line. But I've dealt with a lot of people who have done things that are very bad for them physically, so I believe I may tell you with some authority that these people have nearly always been aware what they were doing was bad for them, and many times they've hated themselves for doing it. They do what they do because they can't stop themselves. The compulsion that drives them is too strong."

My temper—I had one—blazed up. "They can stop," I said bitterly. "If other people can stop doing bad things, then they can stop too."

Dr. Hallam stared down at his desk and sighed.

After a minute he said, "I had a patient once who weighed over three hundred pounds. His breath was short. His joints ached. His heart was failing. He was almost literally digging his grave with his teeth. When I asked him why he ate so much, he told me, 'I eat because I'm hungry, Doc. You have no idea how hungry I am.'"

I looked away. "He was just greedy."

"Well, that's the thing, Thea. You don't know that. I don't know it, either. Neither of us knows how hungry that man was, or whether, if we had the same appetite, we'd eat just as much as he did." Dr. Hallam picked up his pen again. "Here's a topic for you: 'Ten reasons I believe teachers of Public Speaking should be handsomely paid.' An A-plus grade is guaranteed."

As soon as he'd made me laugh, the doctor turned serious again. "I truly think she's doing the best she can."

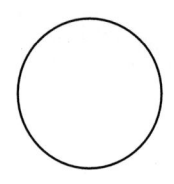

Chapter Thirteen

Like it or not (and to be honest, I kind of *did* like it), Homer officially claimed me as "his girl." He squired me around Central, carrying my books, and treated me to ice cream as often as he could persuade me to come with him to the drug store after school, which was seldom because I had to get home to look after Ma. She hadn't gone on an actual binge since the day she'd nearly ruined the doctor's dinner party, but she was rarely entirely sober anymore. She started keeping her bottle stashed in her corset where I couldn't decently get to it and take it away, which meant all I could do most of the time was to keep an eye out to see she didn't hurt herself or anybody else.

I didn't supervise Ma's Sunday afternoons, though. Sunday afternoons were all mine. Homer took me out driving in his jalopy on Sundays, and I refused to miss our rides even for my mother's sake. One or two other Central High couples usually came with us, and the female halves of the pairs clubbed together to provide a picnic lunch. I paid for my share out of the three-fifty a week I was now getting for keeping Dr. Hallam's house, and marveled at how many sandwiches a high school boy could consume at a sitting.

Our drives usually took us four or five miles out into the country, where we stopped and had our picnic, then took a stroll that always—somehow—resulted in the various couples becoming widely separated from one another. After an hour or so apart, we'd all meet at the car again and go home.

What the other couples got up to during their time alone I never knew for sure, but it was probably the same as what Homer and I did, which was to lie down in the grass—Homer always considerately spreading his jacket out for me first—and exchange a few fumbles and kisses. This activity was enjoyable to me, but also somewhat fraught. The line between being a "sport," who would permit a liberty or two, and being "fast," and letting a boy go too far, was a fine one, and we girls were the ones who had to walk it. The expectation was that boys would try anything; it was up to us to restrain them. I was luckier than the other girls. Thanks to the reading I'd done in Dr. Hallam's books, I could anticipate how the fumbles, especially, were likely to affect Homer, which gave me a decided advantage in knowing when the time had come to shut them down. In the case of Homer, a reliable technique for cooling his ardor was to bring up the subject of calculus. Despite the efforts of the college boy who'd been hired to tutor him, learning calculus was giving Homer fits. He wouldn't let me help him.

Lying beside me one Sunday in late autumn, his left arm under my head for a pillow and his right hand resting on my ribs just below the place I knew he really wanted to put it, Homer murmured, "Still thinking about going to college, Thea?"

"Of course. Why wouldn't I be?"

"Just wondered."

"Well, don't wonder. I'm going."

"Yeah. Me too." His right hand moved subtly higher. "What school?"

"Dunno yet. Why?"

Homer propped himself up on his left elbow and looked down at me. Since he'd kept his arm under my head, this posture put his face within inches of mine. I expected he would kiss me (we were getting pretty good at kissing), but instead he begged suddenly, "Come to A&M with me!"

The intensity with which he asked made me uneasy. "With you and several thousand other people, you mean," I answered, trying to laugh. "I'm considering it. It's on my list of places to apply."

"Don't just consider it. Come. I want you to." Looking at me earnestly, Homer said, "I...like you, Thea. A lot." Cautiously, he put his hand on my breast. Being a "sport," I allowed him one squeeze before I moved out from under it.

"I like you, too." My voice wasn't quite steady. "Let me take the College Board exams first. Then I'll decide."

"You don't have to take College Boards to go to A&M. They know Central's a good school."

"I know, but I *do* have to take them. Not for college, exactly. I have to take them for myself. I have to know where I stand."

"Who cares where you stand on the College Boards? *I* know you're smart. Come to A&M with me, Thea. Please? We'll go to college together, and afterward, we'll...get married. Maybe. If you want to, I mean."

I sat up abruptly.

I'd done it. I'd scored the marriage proposal my mother'd wanted for me since— since I was born, I guessed. A decent boy with good prospects, from a good family—"good stock," if you wanted to put it that way—could be mine if I wanted him.

It was Homer's turn to feel uneasy. "Don't you want to?" he asked, sounding plaintive.

I drew a long breath. "Think about what you're saying," I urged. "Think about whether you're sure *you* want to. You're talking about something that wouldn't happen until years and years from now. You could easily change your mind along the way."

Homer tugged me gently down again, and into his arms. "It wouldn't be years and years," he murmured into my hair. "We can get married as soon as I turn twenty-one. We could get married sooner, in fact, only I promised my dad I'd wait until I was voting age."

I snuggled against him. Kissing was nice, and I didn't mind having Homer touch me a little, either. But what I really liked was being held. I closed my eyes for a minute and basked in the sensation of being loved—all right, *liked a lot*—and protected.

"You don't *need* to go to college," Homer repeated meanwhile. "I know how smart you are."

"Let me take the College Boards first," I murmured. "Then I'll decide."

"You'd like it in Stillwater. It's a nice campus, and other kids from Central besides me will be going there. That's good, right?"

"I'll think about it," I promised again.

*

When I came to the library for my calculus lesson a few days later, Dr. Hallam greeted me and asked how school had been going lately—in French.

"What?" I asked, startled. I studied hard in French class, though, and once I'd thought for a minute, I was able to answer in French.

He laughed—which I liked to hear. He hadn't laughed much since

Mr. Dennis had gone. "Grammatically speaking, that's not too bad. You didn't hesitate over your tenses. But who's been your teacher? The Kaiser? I haven't heard an accent like that since the war."

I explained about Monsieur Baumann. "He's very nice, though."

"No doubt he is, but—! Look, I don't want to scare you, but you'll probably have to demonstrate that you're competent in two foreign languages to graduate from a first-rate university. You'll take placement exams at entrance, and if you can qualify in at least one language then, it'll save you a world of time and trouble later. The placement exams aren't too difficult, but that accent will never pass. If you'll allow me to, I'll see about getting you a tutor."

"I don't think too many French people live in Oklahoma," I told him doubtfully.

The doctor said he already had someone in mind.

Picking up my calculus book from his desk, he opened it and smiled. "Look!" he said, showing to me. "Nearly done! Which is good, because I've arranged for you to take a proficiency exam at the college down in Norman next month. It's the one they use to assess their own incoming freshmen, but high school students are allowed to take it, and assuming you score well—which you will—it'll be accepted as proof of competence by most universities. That way, you won't be asked to take calculus again."

"Next month!"

"Early next month."

I stared at him.

"You'll do fine," he assured me again. "Oh, good—we're up to Newton's method. I like that."

"How's Mr. Dennis?" I asked—all right, blurted. "Is he all right?"

Dr. Hallam turned a page or two before answering, quietly, "He's fine, of course. Why wouldn't he be?"

"Because…" I knew I shouldn't say it, but I did anyway. "Because you're not."

The doctor started to say something—then stopped himself. "Mr. Diedrich is fine," he repeated instead. "Let's talk about Newton's method."

*

My French tutor was a woman—tall, thin, and despite her name (she was married), genuinely "Fwanch," as she pronounced it. She rang at the front door of the house like she was there for a social call instead of to work, and when I let her in, she stopped in the middle of the doctor's living room to give it a thorough look-over before saying, "*Bon*. Let us proceed," and immediately sitting down in the nicest chair. I'd intended to have my lessons in the kitchen, where I was most comfortable, but decided against it. I got the sense that if Mme. Bailey had disapproved of Dr. Hallam's furniture, she'd have turned right around and gone straight back out the front door, so I guessed the kitchen wouldn't be good enough for her. Judging by her clothes, I didn't think Madame had any better right to be snobby than Ma and I did—but on second thought, I recalled that Ma actually was kind of snobby, so I sat down on the couch and waited nervously.

"Eh, you are Dr. Hallam's small project, then?" Mme. Bailey began, giving me a hard and somehow distinctively French look up and down. Handing me one of the papers she'd brought along and was now fanning herself with, she said, "Begin by speaking this, if you please."

The text on the paper was in French, and I read it aloud while Mme.

Bailey corrected my pronunciation on all the words I said wrong, which was almost every one of them including "oui" and "non." After that, we "conversed" for a while, by which I mean Madame grilled me (in French) about myself and my life. I didn't know the French words for "none of your business," so I had to take it.

At the end of one hour *précisément*, Mme. Bailey jumped out of her chair mid-sentence—my sentence—and hurried out the front door, calling back to me over her shoulder that she'd return again on "the Thursday." She left too suddenly for me to do the polite thing and see her out, or to give Ma time to sneak all the way back to the kitchen from where she'd been standing with her ear to the living room door.

When I got to the kitchen myself I asked her, in my best imitation of Dr. Hallam's dry way, "So did you find out what you wanted to know?"

I knew Ma well enough to recognize that her first impulse was to play innocent. She pulled out her recipe book and began leafing through it like a cook-housekeeper who has nothing on her mind but making dinner. But Ma understood me, too—well enough to know if she didn't ask direct questions, I'd keep my business to myself.

"Oh, you know…" she said with feigned semi-indifference. "We had a perfect *stranger* in the house, so I thought I should check to make sure everything was all right. She's a French lady, I guess. Is that so?"

"Yes."

"Is she the French teacher you have at school?"

I'd told Ma about Monsieur Baumann a few times, but of course she didn't remember. "No. This one's supposed to help me with my accent. Dr. Hallam says I sound like a Boche."

"A what?"

"A German."

"Gracious me! How can you sound like a German if you're speaking French? Well anyway, I think it's good for you to learn something nice instead of just studying arithmetic all the time. It's very cultured to be able to speak French."

To stop her from saying, as I suspected she was about to, that the doctor probably wanted me to learn French so we could have a French honeymoon, I explained quickly, "I want to be able to converse in at least one modern language before I get to college."

Ma lowered her cookbook and stared at me. "College?" You'd have thought I'd never said the word "college" before in her life.

"Yes," I answered her firmly. "I actually have to know *two* foreign languages to graduate, but one of my languages will be Latin, and I don't have to speak that one, just read it."

I watched from the corner of my eye as Ma's face flushed deep red.

"College!" she muttered under her breath, and went back to flipping through her cookbook pages, this time so hard she tore one. "What a lot of nonsense!"

"It's not nonsense. Plenty of girls go to college now, and afterward they get good jobs and make lots of money. What's wrong with that?"

"What's right with it? That's what I want to know! Name me one thing that's right with it, Miss Smarty! Who's going to marry girls who've gone to school so long the bloom is all off the rose and they're dried-up old maids? Who? Doctor?"

I sometimes asked myself that very question. Not about Dr. Hallam. About Homer.

I didn't say this. Homer was at the top of a long—and lengthening—list of things my mother was not allowed to know about.

"I don't want to marry the doctor anyway, Ma. And he doesn't want to marry me."

"Doesn't he? Well, why is he paying for all those books and lessons and things for you, then? Why would any man pay for all that for *anybody* unless he expected to get something back for himself?"

This was another question I sometimes asked myself.

"Unless," Ma went on, her face darkening, "he *is* getting something for himself out of it. Is he? Is that it?" She leaned across the table to grab my arm.

"Don't be ridiculous," I said coldly, pulling away.

Ma's eyes were blazing. "Don't lie to me, Thea! Is that what's going on? Right under my nose?" She came around the table to grab me again, this time so hard it hurt. "*Is it?*" she demanded. Then she called me a word I won't repeat. The breath that blew it into my face was boozy.

"Get hold of yourself," I ordered, wrenching away from her grasp. "When you call me that, you're slandering me, and it says in the Bible that slandering someone is demonic."

"James, chapter three," Ma recited automatically. She was sober enough for this to make her reconsider. "All right, promise me then," she said, attempting to speak more calmly. "Promise me what I said wasn't true."

I went to the pantry and slammed it open. "What you said was dead wrong," I retorted, beginning to bring out what we needed for dinner, "and you ought to be ashamed of yourself for even thinking it. Look: I don't know if I *can* go to college, Ma, but I'm going to try, and the sooner you accept that, the better. Now let's start cooking. That's our job, remember?"

Ma didn't move. "What if you can't go? What then?"

It was wrong of me to keep Ma's false hopes alive. But wrong as it was, I answered, "Well, if I can't go to college, at least I'll have a high school diploma," as if Dr. Hallam hadn't already told me I'd get into any Oklahoma college I applied to.

While I silently peeled potatoes, Ma talked happily on and on about how much money high school graduates could make.

*

The Sunday after my second French tutoring session, Homer arrived earlier than usual to wait in his jalopy for me at the end of Dr. Hallam's street. As a part of his campaign to get me to enroll at Oklahoma A&M, he'd convinced me to drive out to Stillwater with him to have a look at the place. Ma didn't start the heavy drinking of the day until after eleven or so, and she sat in the kitchen while I made and packed sandwiches and apples and fruit jars of peach-leaf tea into a shoebox.

When she asked what I was doing, I was honest with her. Fairly honest.

"Some kids from school are going out to Stillwater," I said. "I thought I might as well go along. I've never been there."

"Some kids" was just Homer, who was taking me driving alone for the first time, and I gambled on my mother not knowing there was a college in Stillwater.

"Oh!" Mother looked momentarily torn. She was on the verge of asking to come along to Stillwater, but owing to Prohibition, she could only safely drink at home.

Hooch won—as usual. "Well, I guess that's all right," she said. "I've heard it's very pretty out that way."

"That's what I've heard, too. Look: I'm leaving you a sandwich, see? It's already made, so when you want lunch, all you have to do is remember to eat it." Ma'd lost weight lately—enough for the doctor to have noticed and spoken to her about it. In his usual way, he was kind, but forthright, and in *her* usual way, Mother ignored his advice. "And there's cold tea in the ice box. It's got a lot of sugar in it"—Homer liked his tea very sweet—"but I doubt you'll mind that."

"No, I won't mind. I like sweet things." Ma stared out the window. "I guess it'll be hot tea season soon, won't it? The leaves are starting to fall."

It was early November, but autumn came late in Oklahoma.

"Would you like ice cream?" I asked. "There's some left from last night."

"No, no. I'm fine. No ice cream. As a matter of fact, I think what I'd really like is a little nap."

I knew about her "naps." "Why don't you listen to the radio instead of napping? See if you can find that Dallas station again."

"I might just do that."

I knew she wouldn't. "Okay. Well, remember about the sandwich."

"I'll remember." Mother gave me her cheek to kiss. "Have a good time in— Where is it you're going? Stillwater. That's right. Have a good time with your friends in Stillwater, and tell me all about it when you get back."

*

Homer's hello kiss was more passionate than his previous ones. Evidently he felt his bold admission that he liked me "a lot" had moved our relationship up a notch. I thought it had too and responded in kind.

"I've got something to tell you," Homer said as I settled back onto my side of the seat. The plethora of levers and pedals the flivver required to have continually manipulated to keep it going—nothing was automatic in a 1923 Ford—congested the space between the driver's and passenger's places and prevented us from cuddling on the road. "But I'd rather wait until we're out of the city."

I was afraid he was planning to declare his love, or possibly even propose again, more definitely this time. "That's fine. I can wait," I said, with more sincerity than he knew. "In fact, don't tell me at all if you'd rather not."

"No, I want to. But it's a little hard to say, so let's get on the road first."

"Fine. Whatever you want."

When we were past the edge of town, Homer was ready to talk.

"I've, uh, I've stopped calculus," he admitted. "Don't be mad."

Mad? The only thing I felt was relief. "Are you going to try again next year at college?" When Homer flushed, I added quickly, "It's all right. Whatever you decide is fine with me."

Sighing, Homer explained, "I don't know if I *can't* get it, or if I just don't apply myself enough to get it. My dad thinks that's it—that I don't apply myself. The thing is, he never took calculus himself, so how would he know? Anyway, whichever it is, I've…quit. Quit trying to learn it. For good."

"That's fine," I repeated quickly. "If you don't think you'll ever need calculus, why bother with it?" To my surprise, as I spoke, I found myself half-wishing—only half—that Homer *had* proposed to me again. A good marriage could be a safe haven for a woman, and I craved safety.

"That's what I thought," Homer said, sounding relieved. "I was just afraid you'd take me for a quitter. You're doing real well at calculus, aren't you?"

If Dr. Hallam was right, I was doing really, *really* well at calculus. "Yes, but I need it if I want to study chemistry."

"Is that what you're going to be? A chemistry teacher?"

Homer wasn't the only person to assume I'd be a teacher. "No, a chemist," I corrected him. "An actual chemist. Like, in a lab."

"Huh. Okay."

"And you're going to be a lawyer, I guess."

Homer gave me a rueful smile. "Yeah, assuming I can pass the bar exam." Homer's failure to grasp calculus had evidently shaken his confidence. "Dad says if I keep my grades up, I can clerk in his office summers, and he'll take me on in his practice once I graduate."

More safety. More security. And I could share it, if Homer proposed marriage to me and I accepted. "You're a very lucky man, Homer," I said.

Seizing my hand, Homer put it to his lips and kissed it soundly. "I know I am. Hey, you want to try driving? Come on. I'll pull into this field, and you can give it a whirl."

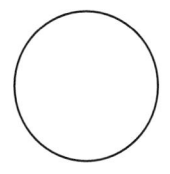

Chapter Fourteen

"That was easy," I told Dr. Hallam, as I climbed back into his car for the drive home. "I *think* it was easy, anyway. Maybe I missed something."

"No, I'm sure you're right," the doctor said quickly. "It was easy for you. I'm confident the test was perfectly straightforward. It wouldn't benefit the university in any way to lay traps for its calculus students."

"Okay. I feel better. It was easy."

As he turned onto the road from Norman toward Oklahoma City, Dr. Hallam asked, "What would you think about picking up something from a restaurant on our way home?"

"Because you figure Ma won't have started dinner yet, even though she should have? You're probably right. She won't have. I'm sorry she's the way she is. She doesn't earn half what you pay her. Honestly, if I were you, I'd fire her."

I was looking out the window, but I could hear the smile in the doctor's voice as he answered, "Oh, I knew what I was getting when I hired her, and I hired her anyway, so I have only myself to blame."

"You *knew*?" I turned to look at him.

"I had a pretty good idea. In my line of work, I see people like your mother all the time. I'm familiar with the type."

Hesitantly, I asked, "So, do they ever...get better?"

Dr. Hallam sighed. "Rarely, in my experience. I'm sorry. I don't think you should give up all hope. I have known a few cases of complete recovery from dipsomania and even worse addictions where a patient was highly motivated to recover. I'm afraid I haven't seen any means to motivate your mother, though."

"Me either." I picked at the edge of my jacket. "She's motivated by money, but only to get as much as she can to spend on booze, so that's no help. She's always said she wanted to see me married to some nice boy, but she isn't motivated to quit drinking to help me get one. In fact, now that I've got a nice boy kind of interested in me, I can't even tell her about him. You've seen how she acts around men she thinks might marry me. She'd scare him away!"

"The right 'nice boy' won't scare easily, Thea. I know that's a bromide, but I believe it's a true one."

"Why am *I* not worth stopping for?" I went on, hardly even hearing what the doctor said. "Just me. Why don't *I* motivate her? I love Ma, and I try to be good, but no matter what I do I'm still not worth it to her to stop drinking for."

"Thea, you're her *child*. How could having a mother who can't—won't—control her own behavior be the fault of a child?"

"But I'm *not* a child. Not anymore. I should be old enough to know how to be worth it to Ma to not drink for, but I'm not. What am I doing wrong?"

"Well, what am I?" Dr. Hallam asked.

"What?"

"My parents haven't spoken to me for years."

Shocked, I sat up and gaped. "Why not?"

I guessed from his expression the doctor was already regretting what he'd just said. "Oh, let's say—" He hesitated. "Let's just say my parents and I are by nature incompatible."

"Your parents don't talk to you for being *incompatible*? Their own *son*?"

"Forget that," he said impatiently, waving his hand. "It's not important. The point I *meant* to be making is that your mother is a fully-formed, independent entity, and if she's a flawed one—and she is—no amount of goodness and worth on your part will ever fix her. Motivation comes from within, not without. The happy ending you both deserve is for your mother to fix *herself*. Your mother has a disease, Thea. You didn't cause it, and you can't cure it. That's all I meant to say. My own parents are an irrelevant side issue."

"I don't know how you could be incompatible with any nice person," I said, fully aware the remark was disrespectful of his parents.

Dr. Hallam smiled. "Thank you. Now, what about my idea of stopping to get something for dinner? What does your mother like?"

I was just about to say, "Anything but Chinese," when the doctor added, "Or rather, what do *you* like? You're the one who had to take a calculus exam. You should get to pick."

If Ma were sober when we got home, I'd feel bad about showing up with food she didn't like, but the chance she'd be sober was close to zero. "Do you like Chinese?" I asked.

"Love it."

"Chinese, then," I said. "I love it, too."

*

The yearly Central High Christmas Dance was always well-attended despite the fact that most kinds of Baptists, not to mention the Methodists, discouraged dancing, and Hard-shell Baptists absolutely prohibited it. Ma was far from Hard-shell, but when Homer invited me to the Christmas Dance, I warned him there was very little chance my mother would let me go.

I was wrong.

"Will there be dancing?" the Baptist in her felt obliged to ask.

"Ma, it's a *dance*."

"Oh." Ma thought this over. "I guess you can go if you want to. I used to love to dance myself. You'll need a better dress, though." She looked me up and down as though surprised and disappointed to discover her remade old "best" dress wasn't suitable for a party.

"I can make one. It doesn't have to be anything real fancy." The current fashion in dresses was a sleeved tube for daywear and a sleeveless one for evening. I could have sewn one with my eyes closed.

"What about dancing shoes?"

I hadn't thought about shoes. "Yeah, I guess I'll need those, too." I hoped my budget would stretch that far.

I managed to find an artificial silk I could afford and brought home samples. Ma and Dr. Hallam both recommended china blue.

"Would you like me to speak to Fran?" Dr. Hallam asked, when he heard I planned to sew the dress by hand. "I believe she has a sewing machine."

"Fran" was the doctor's nickname for Nurse Francine Foster, the lady from the dinner party, who not only let me use her machine, but sewed most of my costume herself, teaching me tricks along the way that stretched my scant four yards of fabric far enough to add little gores around the hem that turned my silk tube into a real party dress.

"Bless my mother for teaching me to sew," she said through a mouthful of pins as we were doing the final fitting. "Now, who's the lucky fella?"

I stopped twirling in front of the mirror (the gores rippled like water) long enough to say his name was Homer. Francie immediately asked if I meant the Escoe's boy.

"Yeah, that's him. Homer Escoe. Do you know him?"

"I know the family," Francie said. "I can't pretend I move in those kinds of circles myself. Well, you're as pretty as a picture in that blue, so see to it Homer treats you right."

Then she offered to lend me a pair of nice pumps that only needed a smallish wad of cotton in each toe to fit me fine.

The day before the dance, Dr. Hallam suggested to Ma she should see me and Homer off from "downstairs," by which he meant his own living room. "You'll naturally want to meet the boy," he said.

I hadn't mentioned that I'd have an escort, and Ma hadn't anticipated it. "There's a boy?" she asked, startled.

"I told you about him, Ma," I said—okay, lied—impatiently. "Homer. From chemistry class." As far as I knew, I'd never mentioned Homer to Ma in the context of my chemistry class or any other context, but luckily, she was aware enough of how little attention she paid to anything to do with my school or school friends to buy the fib.

"Oh, that's right. Homer," Mother repeated. "Well, I suppose you're right. I should meet him. Thank you, Doctor."

The night of the dance was the first really cold night that winter. Homer had to pick me up with his Sunday suit hidden under a plaid jacket. He brought me carnations and baby's breath on a tinseled elastic band to wear on my wrist, and politely helped me to put on my mother's coat while she peppered him with arch questions. Ma was cold sober and dressed in her best, trying hard to look like she belonged in a house like the doctor's.

Once we'd added our coats to a pile of other coats on a table just inside the Central High Boy's Gymnasium door, Homer finally had a chance to look me over properly.

"Gosh!" he said then, and whistled, obviously liking what he saw. "That's a spiffy little number you've got on there, Thea!"

I twirled for him. He liked the wave-effect, too. "Hotsy-totsy?" I suggested, to tease him.

"Absolutely hotsy-totsy!" he enthusiastically agreed. "The cat's meow! The absolute berries! If you cut off some of that hair, you'd look like Norma Talmadge!"

This last remark almost spoiled the compliments for me. The fact that I was just about the only female at Central High with un-bobbed hair was a personal sore point.

The rest of the evening went great. I danced mostly with Homer, but times when various chaperones dragged him off to make him oblige a wallflower or two—seeing that wallflowers danced and nobody spiked the punch were the chaperones' main jobs—I attracted a steady stream of partners from the stag-line, boys who'd known me for three years and never shown the least flicker of interest until they saw me in a dancing dress and silk stockings. At eleven o'clock sharp, all the lights were turned on, and anybody who didn't get out the door quick enough was made to stand in a circle in the middle of the gym and join in singing, "Auld Lang Syne." Only a few of us knew all the words, and apparently not everybody in the circle was sure of the tune, either.

The song over, Homer and I retrieved our coats from the pile and the jalopy from a nearby field where Homer'd parked it.

In a dark spot two blocks from the doctor's house, we parked for a while—of course. Even nice boys like Homer expected a little something in return for their flowers and compliments. Homer boldly suggested we climb into the back seat, but didn't venture even a tiny protest when I turned him down. I think he was as unwilling as I was to risk having things go too far. But we kissed and cuddled as well as we could in the front seat before driving the rest of the way home, with Homer allowing me to operate the jalopy's throttle on the way for the practice. The throttle was a lever positioned behind the steering wheel, and I had to lean on Homer's shoulder, my cheek close to his, to reach it, but neither of us minded that.

At the doctor's door, as Homer kissed my cheek—chastely, in case neighbors were watching—he murmured, "Made up your mind to come to A&M with me yet, sweetheart?"

Homer'd called me "doll" before. He'd even addressed me, lightheartedly, as his "tomato." But "sweetheart" was serious.

My heart begged me to answer, "Yes!" but my brain still wasn't sure. The two of them compromised on, "Almost."

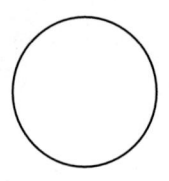

Chapter Fifteen

My calculus test score arrived two days before Christmas, and was even better than I'd hoped it would be. Dr. Hallam was so pleased with it he called it an early Christmas present, but after all he'd done for me, I knew I owed him a bigger, better one.

In the three years Ma and I had worked for him, the doctor had never celebrated Christmas in any way except by spending more time doing hospital work so the other doctors could be home with their families. This year I saw to it that when he came home late Christmas Day, a real Christmas dinner was waiting for him—turkey; stuffing; all the usual trimmings; and pie, too. I knew I'd hit on just the right gift when the doctor took one look at everything laid out on the dining table and immediately excused himself to go upstairs. He said he needed to wash his hands, but he'd already been upstairs and already washed his hands. I guessed what he really wanted was time to pull himself together.

When he came back, he was smiling. Immediately going to the china cabinet, he started getting out plates and bowls and so forth and putting them on the table, insisting that Ma and I eat with him. I'd guessed he would probably want us to, but hadn't liked to presume.

A dinner by candlelight in a lovely dining room was the kind of thing Ma liked, and her spirits soared high as the moon. As we ate, she told lots of stories about what Christmases were like back in the '80s and '90s when she was young. I'd heard all the stories before, but she told them well, so that the funny ones made us laugh, and the touching ones—well, touched us. Ma could be very charming when she wanted. Over pie and coffee, we got Dr. Hallam to talk about the Christmases he'd spent in France during the Great War, and if I'd never heard about the war anyplace else, he might have made me think it was all games and fun. He didn't mention any of his childhood Christmases. I didn't mention mine, either.

Back at school in January, 1929, Homer had a late Christmas present for me—a silver lavaliere necklace with a half-pearl set. I liked it—lavalieres were all the rage at school—but Ma was beyond thrilled. She said a gift of jewelry from a boy meant he had serious intentions.

"Mark my words: It'll be a ring next!" she told me happily.

I gave Homer a pen. Boys are hard to buy for. A pen wasn't an imaginative gift, but I made sure it was a nice one. Giving nice gifts was an important brick in the façade I had to keep up of being at least lower middle-class. I spent all the money I'd been saving to get my hair bobbed on it, plus my whole Christmas bonus from Dr. Hallam, but I didn't begrudge a penny because Homer really liked the pen and used it every day.

In February, the doctor mentioned again that I should try to get a letter from at least one of my teachers in support of my applications to college.

"There's still plenty of time, of course," he said, "but you'll probably want to get as many things out of the way as you can before graduation."

"I'll try my old math teacher," I promised.

The next Monday I stopped Mr. Brody as he passed me in a school corridor.

From the way he immediately guessed, "You want a letter, right? Come see me after school on Wednesday," I thought he might have a letter written and waiting when I got there.

Instead, when I got to his room, Mr. Brody seemed the opposite of glad to see me. He waved me impatiently to a chair in the front row, and demanded as I sat down, "You want a letter from me, am I right? In support of a college application?" Before I could nod, he said firmly, "Well, you won't get one."

I was too shocked to say anything back, but when he asked if I wanted to know why, some notion of politeness made me say, "Yes, sir."

"I never give letters to girls," Mr. Brody announced, picking up a pencil and drumming the eraser end on the desk. "Girls should never go to college. College wasn't made for girls. College"—Mr. Brody waved the pencil around—"has one overriding purpose. And do you know what that purpose is? It is to *make men*. Do you understand me? It exists to make *boys* into *men*."

"But I—"

"You're about to tell me you're just as smart as a boy, aren't you?" I hadn't been, but Mr. Brody didn't let me answer. "If you are intelligent"—he said it like he doubted I was—"then no doubt someday you'll be an adornment to the world of women. But colleges exist, as I said, to *make men*. Learned men, specifically; as business makes able ones, and the military, men who are..." He had to think for a minute what kind of men the military made. I think it might have been on the tip of his tongue to say "obedient" (he'd told us once in class he'd been a sergeant in the army), but instead he came out with,

"Military service makes men *strong*. But as soon as girls get into those places, what happens? The men become weak as women, while the girls themselves become mannish!"

Mr. Brody glared at me for a minute. "For the first time in the history of our country," he went on, "universities are turning young men away! And do you know the reason for that, Miss Carter?"

I thought I did, but didn't say so. I thought it was because, despite the efforts of the Mr. Brody's of the world, increasing numbers of girls were qualifying for college, and going.

I was right.

"They are turning young men away to put girls in their places!" Mr. Brody raged. "In my day, as in the days of the founders of this nation, any boy who qualified was guaranteed a place at a university. And now they must give way to girls! The very girls who should become those young men's wives and the mothers of their sons"—no mention of their daughters, of course—"are crowding them out of the universities of this land! What next? Will they then take the young men's *livelihoods*?"

When it became clear to him I wasn't going to answer this, he continued, "Now, you may not care about the future of our race. Maybe your parents don't even care—though I'm guessing they do, since yours, at least, haven't let you cut off all your hair. Her hair is a woman's crown of glory, and it's a sign of how degraded the current generation of girls is that they don't recognize that. But you may count on it that *I* will never contribute, be it with a letter or anything else, to the current diabolic scheme to corrupt the natural order of the universe!"

I might have been more impressed with this speech if it hadn't been obvious Mr. Brody'd given it more than a few times before.

"Why didn't you just tell me 'no' on Monday?" I asked, my voice shaking. "'No' is all you needed to say."

Mr. Brody threw down his pencil. "Miss Carter, I am a teacher. It is my responsibility to teach young people their places in the world!"

It was clear from Mr. Brody's face he thought *my* place was somewhere near the bottom of the heap.

I think he wanted me to argue. I think he wanted me to give him more chances to lecture me about my "crown of glory," and "my place in the world," and so on. Instead, I stood up, hands shaking, knees knocking, and thanked him for his time.

As soon as I was sure I was out of Mr. Brody's sight, I broke down and cried. I cried all the way home on the streetcar, and all the way through the housework, and part of the way through making the dinner Ma fortunately felt good enough to help cook, for a change. Ma saw me, of course, but I wouldn't tell her what I was crying about, and once I'd reassured her it was nothing to do with Homer, she stopped asking. Dr. Hallam would have noticed, but I avoided him; and fortunately, he didn't remind me again about getting a letter for a week. A week was long enough for me to be able to say calmly when he did mention it that Mr. Brody had refused to give me one. The doctor looked surprised, but said it was fine, that letters weren't necessary. He didn't bring up the subject again.

*

Toward the end of February, Ma and I both came down with colds. Mine got better in a week; Ma's got worse and worse. Although Dr. Hallam offered every day, Ma refused to let him come see her until her breathing finally got to sounding so bad it scared both of us. After listening to her chest, the doctor said she had pneumonia and needed to spend a few days in the hospital. He took her there himself in his car and stayed to see her settled in comfortably, since it wasn't visiting hours so I couldn't do that for her myself. The next morning, he hired a "daily" from an agency to do the housework and cooking so I could spend as much time as possible with Ma.

"As much as possible" wasn't a lot. The hospital only allowed visits for one hour in the mornings and two in the afternoons (three on Sunday). But maybe that wasn't a bad thing. Lots of time alone—sober time—made my mother think. Not only had she been sick enough to almost die, but it occurred to her that if the daily housekeeper did a good job, the doctor might fire her and take on the daily in her place. By now, Ma was absolutely determined to marry me off to Homer, and her being unemployed and homeless wouldn't help that scheme along one bit. When Dr. Hallam came to her bedside to have another one of his serious talks with her, Ma listened better than she had before. He didn't mince any words. He told her flat out if she kept drinking the way she was doing, he wouldn't give her good odds of living to dance at my wedding.

"She's promised to reform," Dr. Hallam told me. "Maybe she means it this time."

"She does. She always means it." I tried not to sound bitter, but I couldn't altogether help myself.

After three days in the hospital and another week at home in bed, Ma started getting back on her feet, a little more each day. It was a month before she was her old self again, and she didn't have a drop the whole time. I wondered how long she'd stay dry.

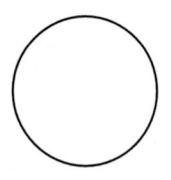

Chapter Sixteen

Dr. Hallam stuck his head into the kitchen. "Is your mother around?" he asked. He had a paper—a letter, it looked like—in his hand.

"She's upstairs. Should I call her?"

He came all the way in. "As a matter of fact, I'd rather talk to you," he said. He held up the letter. "This is from Dave Edgar. You remember him."

I nodded.

"He wants me to come to Chicago to give a Grand Rounds talk."

"Is that…good?" I asked hesitantly. "I mean, *really* good?" I understood that being asked to give a talk was an achievement by itself, but since the invitation was from Dr. Edgar, I was hoping it meant something more; something to do with a job.

If it was, the doctor didn't want me to know. Instead he said, "I'm not getting my hopes up about that"—which I thought was a lie. I thought his hopes *were* up—"but he's proposed 'Recent Advances in Pediatric Oncology' as my topic." Guessing that I might not understand what this implied, the doctor added, "It's a broad subject, and consequently should attract a large audience."

"An audience interested in pediatric oncology," I suggested.

"Exactly."

"Which is being expanded at Cook County Hospital in Chicago."

Dr. Hallam smiled. "Not much gets by you, does it, Thea? Well, be that as it may, please tell your mother for me I'll be gone most of next week."

I said I would, and the doctor started to go—then turned back. "Why don't you and she make a little holiday of it?" he suggested. "I believe you have a sister—is that right? Maybe you'd like to take this opportunity to visit her."

I got a funny feeling in my stomach when the doctor said that. I hadn't seen Jane since I was seven. I hardly remembered her. Yet somehow, whenever I thought of my sister, it was with love. On the other hand, the way Ma said Janie's name made it sound like a swear.

"No, thanks," I said, my voice sounding sadder than I'd intended. "I'm not sure where she lives, even."

"I'm sorry."

"S'okay."

For a minute, it was on the tip of my tongue to ask the doctor whether he'd visit Mr. Dennis when he was in Chicago, but I stopped myself. Dr. Hallam was having a happy moment, invited to give a big talk in his specialty. I didn't want to spoil it.

"If you're going to see Dr. Edgar, I'll give you my soup recipe to take," I said instead. "His wife wanted it." I wasn't sure how much influence a bowl of tomato soup could have toward making Dr. Edgar offer Dr. Hallam a job, but it was all I had to offer.

On Monday morning, as he was leaving for the train station, the doctor gave me advice. "Keep your mother busy, if you can," he said. "Give her a good time. Make her feel that staying sober is worth the effort. It won't hurt you to take a break from studying." He shook my hand before climbing into the taxi, palming me five dollars to keep Ma busy and happy on.

"You don't need to—" I started to protest.

But the taxi door was already closed, and the next minute he was gone.

*

On Thursday, as usual, Mme. Bailey came to give me a French lesson.

I hadn't by any means gotten to really like Mme. Bailey, but aside from being cold, snooty, judgmental, and sure to douse any nascent bud of self-confidence she detected in me with a sluice of French imperfect subjunctives, I thought she was all right. The only objectively negative quality she had was one that—to my shame—I didn't mind. Madame liked to gossip. She spent at least half of every lesson filling me in on the secrets of everybody she knew, which was a *lot* of people. Apparently, half the population of Oklahoma City was trying to learn French. Mme. Bailey did most of her gossiping in French instead of English, which allowed her to pretend, and me to pretend to believe, that what she said was educational instead of hateful. I didn't ordinarily hear much gossip. Dr. Hallam was the most oblivious man I'd ever known (Mr. Dennis was better acquainted with our neighbors five minutes after he arrived than the doctor was after living next door to them for three years), and my mother was too proud to gossip with anyone but a *real lady*, and in her line of work, she didn't meet many of those.

I was unusually excited and happy that Thursday afternoon and inclined to be chatty myself. Just before Madame arrived, Dr. Hallam called to give me a message about a patient to pass on to Francine. He'd telephoned her first, but he'd given her the week off, and she wasn't at home. After I'd written the message down and read it back to him, he added, "Will you also tell her they're treating me very well here, and that she may make of that what she wants? I don't want to say more than that, but I feel I should keep Fran informed."

I almost blurted, "Informed about what?" but managed to stop myself.

"All well with your mother?" he inquired.

I knew what he was asking, of course. "Sober as a judge," I assured him.

Dr. Hallam thanked me for taking the message and I hung up the telephone just the front doorbell rang.

Madame Bailey was taking one last drag on her cigarette when I opened the door. After stubbing it out carefully on the doorframe so she could relight and finish it later, she breezed in, looking around the room as critically as she always did.

After greeting me, she settled herself in her usual chair and adjusted her skirt. Although she wasn't young, she wore it very short. "The doctor's office is closed and he has gone away, I am told," she said. "Will he return, do you think? Or has he run away like the last time?"

She said all this—approximately this—in French. I wasn't entirely sure I'd understood her correctly, since I didn't get what she meant by it.

"*Pardonne-moi?*" I stammered. "*Le médecin est,* um, *simplement allé à* Chicago. To give a talk," I added in English. "He'll be back on Saturday, if you need to speak to him."

Madame was so intent on what she had to tell me she didn't even bother to correct my bad French. Instead, she made a noise with pursed lips that sounded like it might be spelled "pfui," maybe.

"Why would I need to speak to such a man?" she sneered, speaking English this time. "Chicago? Oh, he will not stay long there. He's not welcome. Not after before." I could tell from her expression she was bursting with news on the topic.

"Whoever told you he wasn't welcome in Chicago?" I asked. My face got hot. "He was *invited* there."

Madame waved her nicotine-stained fingers contemptuously. "Sure-sure." Fanning herself as usual with her papers, she switched to French again and continued, "Well, he'll probably come back on Saturday, as you say. It's too soon for it to be safe for him to stay in Chicago. That will be too bad for him—to have to come back, I mean—because I am certain he must be lonely here. There are so few of his kind in this place." She gave me a sideways look that said she was not only available to answer questions, but absolutely begged me to ask them.

His kind?

"Doctors, you mean?" I inquired stiffly.

Mme. Bailey made the "pfui" sound again. "Bah! Don't pretend to be a little girl. You know what I'm talking about. I mean—!"

I wasn't a little girl, but I genuinely did not know the word with which Madame ended this sentence.

"A— flower," she ventured, speaking English again when she saw my confusion. "Not like just a *fleur*, but a certain *kind* of *fleur*. A—" Madame wracked her brain. "*Une marguerite. Mais en anglaise.* What is it?"

I knew the name of the flower she meant. I also knew what the term implied. I had read all about it—under its proper name—in Dr. Hallam's medical books. My face went even redder. "I'm sure you are mistaken," I said coldly.

"Daisy!" Madame burst out triumphantly. "That's it! *Oui*! *Une* daisy! A Nancy boy, eh? How sorry the doctor must be that we don't have 'clubs' like that here, where he and his little friends danced. Although such dancing didn't end well for them last time, did it? Unless perhaps they were able to keep dancing in jail?"

Though I suddenly knew I wanted no part of this conversation, I couldn't stop myself from saying, "I don't believe for a moment Dr. Hallam has ever been to jail."

"Oh, not him. No," Mme. Bailey conceded, with what looked like regret. "But his friends, they went. Some went even to prison! *Enfin*, what kind of man has friends like that? *That* kind of man. A man *like* them."

I was on the verge of asking her why she was telling me all this when the answer came to me. It was because I'd visibly enjoyed the other gossip she shared. Gossip about Dr. Hallam was no different to Madame than gossip about anyone else.

But it was different to me. Though I was shaken by what she'd just told me, I'd have been ashamed to stay another five minutes in a room with someone who spoke ill of the doctor. Defiantly, I stood. "I think it's time for our lesson to be over," I said firmly. "In fact, I don't think I need any more lessons from you. Thank you for your help, and goodbye."

I don't know what Dr. Hallam had been paying her, but evidently it was enough to cause Mme. Bailey to instantly regret having offended me. "No, no," she said quickly. "You have a long way to go still! And you are a very good student. Very good. I will speak to the doctor. You'll see he will want you to continue."

"I don't think so," I said, starting toward the door. "And don't bother to speak with him. I'll speak to him myself."

Relentlessly, I herded Madame out as she continued repeating alternately in English and French that I was a very dear and good student. Having shut the door behind her, I watched through the sidelight as she stopped on the porch to retrieve the half-smoked cigarette from her purse and light it before walking away, and then I walked away, too, in the opposite direction.

Fifteen minutes remained of our lesson hour, and I spent them—and longer—standing by the doctor's empty fireplace, staring at his chair. It wasn't the nicest chair in the room, the one Madame Bailey always sat on. Dr. Hallam was the kind to leave the nicest chair for others. He was also the kind to forget how to smile when his friends were in trouble, and he was the kind to involve himself—and probably his money—in their "legal matters." He was the kind to rejoice to get a call not from "Mr. Freeman," as I'd misheard it at the time, but from a friend with the news he was now a "free man" who could come to visit.

He was all those things, but surely he couldn't also be—

As I continued to stand and think, a million little things I'd seen and heard over the past two and a half years came back to me that seemed to confirm Mme. Bailey's insinuations as to how a prominent doctor from a well-off Chicago family (who no longer spoke to him) had ended up in the relative backwater of Oklahoma City. Not least of these million things were the doctor's obvious joy in Mr. Dennis's company and Mr. Dennis's in his. Somehow, though, Madame's revelations hadn't had the effect she obviously intended, of making me think less of the doctor.

At least, they hadn't yet.

According to the doctor's own books, homosexual behavior was deviant, which made the doctor himself deviant if he engaged in it. If

I wasn't repulsed by that now, I undoubtedly would be when the shock of what I'd just learned wore off.

"Thea?" Ma called. She opened the living room door and stuck her head in. "Is the French lady gone? I thought she must be. It's almost four. How would it be if we went to see *In Old Arizona* again tonight? I know we just saw it, but that Warner Baxter is so good-looking! Now, don't pretend you haven't noticed!" She wagged her finger playfully at me.

"I noticed," I said numbly.

"So how about it? I'll cook up something quick for dinner, and then off we go!"

I had homework to do, but sitting in the dark for two hours, with no obligation to talk to anybody and plenty of time to think, was what I needed.

"Sure," I said wanly. "Off we go."

*

Dr. Hallam came home two days later.

When he walked into the kitchen, I was almost surprised to find I wasn't repelled in the least by the doctor's smile, his handshake, his friendly greeting, or by the way he asked Ma and me, with apparently genuine interest, if we were both well. I also wasn't in any way revolted by the way he listened politely to Ma's excited recounting of the plots of the moving pictures we'd seen, and the shopping we'd done in his absence. I wasn't sure whether this was because I didn't believe what Mme. Bailey had told me (and which my own experience suggested might be true), or that I didn't care about it one way or the other.

"I don't know what to make of it, Doctor," Ma was saying when I pulled my attention back to the conversation. "Thea's gone and quit her French lessons! Just like that!"

Dr. Hallam raised his eyebrows at me.

"I'm still taking French," I pointed out, avoiding his look. "I have French class every day at school."

Even with my head turned away, I could sense that the doctor wanted to ask questions.

He didn't, though. "I'm sure Thea's right that it was time to quit," he said instead. Looking around the kitchen, he added, "It's nice to be back."

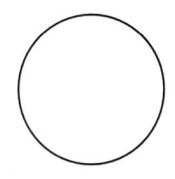

Chapter Seventeen

My heaven-ordained role (if Ma was right) of safeguarding both my virtue and Homer's was getting harder to play. I found myself thinking a hundred times every day there was nobody in the world like Homer. His smile, his intelligence, his silly jokes, even his pride in his jalopy were adorable, and his admiration for me gave me a confidence I never had before. I liked his company more than anybody else's in the world, and when he took me in his arms, I all but melted. There was no denying it. I was falling in love with the lunk.

Along with love, I discovered, came desire.

Dr. Hallam's medical books hadn't prepared me for desire. They didn't even use the word. The word the books used for some of what I was feeling was "arousal," which the books described in clinical terms as one of the points on a line that culminated—again, in the books' words—in coitus. In fact, female arousal was a skippable point, according to the books.

Desire, it seemed to me, wasn't skippable, and it was on a line of its own that started with regard, progressed through warm regard, hand-holding, cuddling and kissing (my favorite bits), and then…some other things Homer and I sometimes got up to. Ultimately, the line reached love. Until now, the "other things" had still been a long way from coitus for me, although possibly not for Homer.

But now I'd reached "love"—at least the near edge of it—and coitus didn't seem so far off anymore. Going forward, I'd need to be extra careful.

Jalopy rides out into the country had been discontinued for the winter, and even when we resumed them in spring, until mid-May the ground was still too apt to be muddy to make lying down on it appealing. There was always the jalopy's backseat, though, and one Sunday when the second couple who was supposed to go out motoring with us cancelled, I found myself in it with Homer's hand down the front of my blouse. It took a lot more effort than it once had to make myself remove it.

"Honey, we don't want a baby," I whispered. "Not yet, anyhow."

"Bet we'd make a cute one," he murmured.

"Bet you're right. But not yet."

Homer nuzzled my neck. "There're things we could do to stop that. My God, you are so beautiful! So beautiful…" His voice trailed off.

I was not beautiful. "There are things *you* could do, you mean." I blocked his hand again. "In the state of Oklahoma, the only thing *I* can do is say 'no.'"

Homer drew back a little and looked at me. "You mean like…?"

"Yep. You're eighteen now. You can buy them at any drug store."

"I guess so. Yeah."

Clearly, he didn't like the idea. He went back to nuzzling.

"We could get married," he suggested tentatively, mid-nuzzle.

"We can't be married in college." What I meant by that—what most colleges meant by it—was that two college students couldn't be married to each other. A married student could enroll, provided their partner didn't. From what I could tell, this was because school administrators feared that speculation by the unmarried students as to what the married students got up to might give the unmarried ones "ideas." "And even if we could," I added, "we still couldn't have a baby."

I was killing the mood—Homer's *and* mine. I wasn't sure I regretted this.

Homer sat up and sighed. "I'm pretty sure my mom and dad would help us."

"They couldn't help me go to college."

I knew what was coming and braced myself for it.

"You don't *have* to go to college," Homer said for the thousandth time. "I mean, you can if you want, but you don't *need* to. I'll always take care of you."

"My dad died when I was five, Homer."

He saw my point. "Well, okay, but Mom and Dad…"

Homer gave up on this line of argument without finishing it. I'd never met his mother and father, but I'd told him before that, unlike him, I wasn't totally confident if I did meet them they'd both think I was the absolute cat's whiskers and instantly adore me. "So—what if I got a lot of life insurance?" he asked thoughtfully.

I laughingly turned down the offer, but allowed Homer—and myself—to enjoy a few more kisses.

When they got too heated, I cooled Homer down again by asking, "You heard who's going to be salutatorian, didn't you?"

The valedictorian and salutatorian for our class year—1929—had been announced. Homer, as expected, had been named valedictorian. A girl I hardly knew was going to be the salutatorian. A lot of people had been surprised by this news, including me.

"Yeah, I heard." Homer sat up higher. "I heard and I'm disgusted. It should have been you, Thea. You're twice as smart as Lydia."

I sat up too and laid my head on Homer's shoulder, where he couldn't see the tears in my eyes. "I don't know about twice as smart, but my grades were better than hers. It's all right, though. I'd have given a terrible speech anyway."

"That's not the point." Homer pulled me closer. "The speech isn't the point. The salutatorian is supposed to be the second smartest student at Central, and that's you. Anyway, your speech would have been fine."

"Mr. Mack told me it's because you and I are both good at science and math and Lydia's good at English. Some of the teachers didn't think the graduation speakers should both be good at the same subjects." I didn't add my private opinion that Lydia had been chosen over me because she was feminine and ladylike (also pretty), which made her a better example than I was of the kind of female graduate Central High School wanted to be known for producing. Lydia was even already engaged to be married—confirmation, if the likes of Mr. Brody wanted it, that she embraced her "place in the world."

"I took harder classes than she did, too," I added.

Having said this, I waited hopefully for it to occur to Homer that if you included calculus, which I had a score to prove the University of Oklahoma felt I'd learned to college standards, I'd taken harder classes than *he* had, too. If Homer had nobly insisted upon going before the committee and demanding to be allowed to step aside as valedictorian in my favor, I would have refused to let him make the gesture, of course—but I would have liked it.

He didn't, though. Homer, who had recently been experimenting—lightly—with using profanity, answered this remark with a sample of his latest research instead, then raised my face to his with one finger and resumed kissing me.

I kissed him back. If I wasn't salutatorian of my class, at least I was loved, and being loved was as good as an academic honor. In fact, it might even be better.

"Enough, enough," I breathed, five minutes later. "Come on. We've got to get home." I pushed Homer away and slid to the opposite end of the jalopy's back seat.

"Okay, okay," Homer groaned. "I know. How about two more smoochies, and then we go?" He leaned toward me and firmly planted one "smoochie" on my mouth. "I like that you're a nice girl and all, Thea, but damn! You sure do get my motor running!"

I arrived home that day virtue still intact, but as I said, keeping it that way was getting harder.

Surprisingly—surprising to me, at least—my own difficulties had the effect of making me increasingly sympathetic to Dr. Hallam's situation. According to his books, the doctor's kind of "deviance" made him feel the same desire for Mr. Dennis that I felt for Homer. If that was the case, it seemed perfectly natural to me for the doctor to want to continue moving with Mr. Dennis along the same line Homer and I were on all the way to its ultimate point. And if they wanted to, why shouldn't they? They were both of full age and obviously like-minded on the subject. From what I could tell, though, nobody else agreed with this conclusion, so I kept it to myself

*

In late May, Dr. Hallam met me in the passage outside the kitchen. "Your practice booklet," he announced, holding up an envelope for me to see. "At least, I think it is. This came in the mail just now, and of course I didn't open it, but I'm fairly certain of what it is."

Only a few of the college-bound seniors at Central were scheduled to take the College Board's new scholastic aptitude exam before graduation rather than after, but I was one of them. This meant traveling to Dallas, since the exam wouldn't be given in Oklahoma City until late June, but getting it over with as soon as possible was worth the trouble of a train ride to me.

The doctor was right about the envelope's contents. The official "Practice Booklet" was both my entry ticket to the hall where the test was going to be given and the College Board's means of familiarizing me with the format of "multiple-choice" questions, which were very new and, according to Dr. Hallam, controversial.

"Don't rush," he counseled, looking over the booklet with me. "Wait until you're calm to start working on it. When you feel you're ready, you can use the library. Let me know when you want to begin, and I'll see you're not disturbed. Now take a few deep breaths," he added, smiling. "You're shaking."

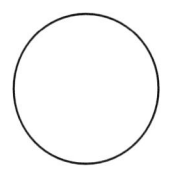

Chapter Eighteen

I'd planned to take the train to Dallas alone on the Friday before the exam and stay overnight at the YWCA—the only place besides a private home where I could legally stay by myself until I was eighteen—before taking the exam Saturday morning, but Ma wouldn't let me. She couldn't claim the Y wasn't perfectly safe, but she insisted a lone girl on a train was sure to be the target of mashers.

To my surprise, Dr. Hallam agreed with her. "A hotel would be safer. If you ladies will permit it, I would be honored to escort you."

Naturally, Ma wasn't going to turn down a trip to Dallas.

In Ma's mind, an "escort" was someone who paid for everything, so she allowed the doctor to arrange for the train tickets and hotel, me in a room with Ma, and Dr. Hallam on a totally different floor because my mother was worried about "appearances." She planned to go shopping while I took the exam. "Dallas has such wonderful shopping!" she chirped happily.

Five minutes before the train to Dallas was due to arrive, I marched Ma into the station Ladies' Waiting Room to have a little talk with her. It was the kind of talk mothers usually give their daughters rather than the other way around, but things with us were always kind of backward.

"Ma, before we go, I want to remind you of something. Okay? The doctor isn't your father, or your husband, or even your friend. He is your *employer*, who also happens to be doing us a big favor. That means when you're out shopping, it would be totally wrong and unmannerly for you to ask him to buy you anything."

"As if I would do such a thing!" Ma cried, looking guilty. "What do you take me for?"

I ignored the question. "No hinting, either," I added.

"I never!"

"Good. I'm glad you never, because it would be very rude if you did." In case words like "wrong and unmannerly" weren't strong enough to restrain her, I added, "You're the one who taught me what women who accept presents from men are likely to get called even when the situation is perfectly innocent, so be careful."

Ma turned away, grumbling.

I'd packed a box-supper for us to eat on the train ride, depriving Ma of the chance to have dinner in the dining car, as she'd wanted, and at the hotel—a really nice hotel—I was too tired to do anything but go straight to bed, so she didn't get to have a late coffee in the hotel dining room either. That put her in a bad mood. I think it was with some notion of making up for those disappointments that, a couple hours later, Ma slipped out of our room alone. I didn't hear her go.

When I woke up and saw her empty bed, my first impulse was to dress and go after her. It wasn't midnight yet, and although I'd never stayed in a hotel before (aside from a few flophouses going by the name of hotel), I guessed somebody at the desk downstairs would have seen Ma go by. A desk clerk might even have been the one to direct her to the nearest convenient source of what she was looking for, which was surely a few stiff ones.

On second thought, I lay back down instead, furious that I'd allowed myself to imagine because she'd been sober for a few months, Ma would stay sober forever. In the morning, I was due to take an exam that meant a lot to me, which was the exact kind of thing that always triggered one of her binges. How did I not know that by now?

Pillows are the kinds of friends who can keep secrets, so I buried my face in mine and cried and said all the bad words I knew into it. Then I lay still and waited for my other good friend, sleep, to pay me a visit.

Around one in the morning Ma came back, but she was steady enough on her feet to be able to sneak in quietly, so I pretended not to hear her.

By seven-thirty next morning, when she and Dr. Hallam walked me to the auditorium where the test was being given, Ma seemed perfectly fine, but the doctor wasn't fooled.

"Even in the best cases, there are often lapses along the way," he murmured to me reassuringly when Ma wasn't paying attention. "I'll keep an eye on her."

Then he wished me luck, my mother kissed me, and after giving my practice booklet to the proctor at the door, I entered the auditorium.

"Do not break the seals on your test booklets until I tell you to!" another proctor was shouting as I found an empty desk. "Once you are seated, do not get up for any reason! Raise your hand if you need assistance, and someone will come to you!"

I took the two pencils I was given, laid them side by side on the desk in front of me, and folded my trembling hands.

*

I came out of the exam four hours later feeling different about myself. I was much less afraid I'd only appeared to be smart enough to go to college because my high school was a small enough pond to make even a minnow seem like a big fish. Though I couldn't expect to get my scores for weeks yet, I thought mine might be as high as six-fifty, and a score of six hundred was considered a good predictor of success at any Oklahoma state university. The doctor kept encouraging me to dream bigger than that, but a degree from a state school was a big enough dream for me.

Dr. Hallam found me in the crowd coming out and took my arm. "How did it go?" he asked, leading me to where Ma was waiting in a taxi.

I had enough time to say, "Not too bad, I think," before climbing in, and then Ma took over the conversation. She'd bought herself a new hat, and she talked about the hat she'd bought, and all the hats she hadn't bought, and all the hat shops she'd been in, and all the hat shops she'd passed by, all the way to the train station and onto the train, where I rested my head against the seat-back and immediately fell asleep.

When I woke up, the doctor treated us all to dinner in the dining car, where the conversation at first was about hats again, and then about anything else that came into Ma's head. I knew what she was doing. She was avoiding the topic of College Board exams like her life depended on not acknowledging that the morning had brought me one step closer to my dream of going to college. I let her have her way, and so did Dr. Hallam. We both knew by now there was no point in trying to make her understand.

*

The new Thea, the one who had potentially scored at least a six hundred on a standardized national academic aptitude test, was bolder than the old, untested Thea had been.

The day after the exam was a Sunday. Dr. Hallam usually worked on Sunday. Unlike the Baptist doctors, he was willing to. But this Sunday he was off, and although I usually tried not to bother the doctor on his days off, after breakfast I went to the library door and tapped on it. Ma was in the kitchen listening—half-listening—to "The Baptist Hour," and probably assumed I was going upstairs to study.

The doctor looked up from his reading and invited me in. "We haven't had a chance to talk yet. Come tell me how the exam went."

I told him I thought it had gone well overall. "I'm not sure about some of the analogies. Would you say a carrot was related to a beet as a turnip is to a potato, or as a lettuce is to a cabbage?"

Dr. Hallam thought this over. "Turnip and potato, I guess," he said.

"Good. That's what I put. Am I disturbing you, by the way? I kind of wanted to ask you something, but it can wait."

Dr. Hallam put his book down. "I am completely at leisure," he said. "What do you want to know?"

"I want to know—" I hesitated. "I don't exactly know how to put this, but I want to know why you're so nice to me. You're always helping me, and it's not like I deserve it or anything."

"Of course you deserve it!" the doctor exclaimed, laughing. "If I've helped you a few times, it's because you needed help, and I was in a position to give it to you, that's all. What other reason would there be?"

As soon as he asked the question, the smile left his face.

"None," I said quickly. "There's no other reason. Ma thinks there might be another one, but I know she's one hundred percent wrong."

I didn't specify what Ma thought the reason was because we both already knew. "But since it's not *that*, what is it? I'm not your kin. I'm not in any way your responsibility. Why do you bother with me?"

Dr. Hallam leaned back in his chair and linked his hands behind his head. "I don't quite know what to say to that," he said, smiling again. "None of this was planned. Not at all. I just…"

He mused for a while.

"You know what image came to my mind the first time I saw you?" he said finally. "You were sitting outside my office, waiting while I interviewed your mother. I looked at you and I saw a little green sprout coming up through a crack in the pavement. Being a city fellow, that's been a common sight all my life: A little plant—a weed, usually—trampled underfoot and surrounded by concrete, but absolutely determined to grow. And in your case, not just to grow, either. Any living thing tries to survive. That's nature. I could tell just by looking at you that you intended to *flourish*. I guess I wanted to help you with that."

"By not firing Ma," I suggested.

Dr. Hallam shrugged and smiled at the ceiling. "Don't give me more credit than I deserve. Keeping her on hasn't been any sacrifice for me, since you see to it her work gets done. I knew from our interview that your mother's work history was somewhat—erratic. I thought you'd probably benefit from staying in one place for a while, especially when I learned you were in high school and wanted to graduate. And after that, one thing led to another."

"But now you're helping me go to college. How did you get all the way from not firing Ma to *that*?"

"How? Well, when I first spotted you in the pavement, I assumed you were a dandelion. Dandelions are nice little flowers, and very hardy, but they're common." He unlinked his hands and sat up straight again. "Then one day—or rather, one night—I discovered you were something more than a dandelion. You were second in a trigonometry class you'd had to persevere against significant odds to get yourself into, and you made it plain to me you intended to keep on persevering until you'd extracted the best education out of your school it could give you. In other words, you were as tough as a dandelion, but an altogether rarer flower."

"That night was the first time in my whole life I ever even thought of going to college," I said.

"I could see that. To be honest, I thought at the time I might have made a mistake by saying what I did, and I told myself not to press the point further. I was aware there were many obstacles in your path."

"When did you change your mind? About pressing the point, I mean."

"You can't guess?"

I flushed. "That Gaucher's thing?"

"Absolutely 'that Gaucher's thing.' Everything about 'that Gaucher's thing' amazed me, and still does. A high school student, with no aid but a highly technically oriented glossary, read, remembered, and ultimately accurately applied information gleaned from a source never intended for a layperson's use. Imagine yourself in my position. Wouldn't you have been amazed?"

It would have been immodest for me to answer the question, so I didn't.

"I'm not sure what kind of flower you are, Thea, but it's unquestionably a choice one." Dr. Hallam smiled again. "What's your favorite?"

"Flower, you mean? Maybe…begonias? I guess?"

"We'll say you're a begonia, then. And in my opinion, a good university is the garden that will bring you into full bloom. I'm looking forward to seeing that happen."

"You're too nice. You're so nice I wish I had some way to pay you back for all your niceness."

The doctor shook his head. "I'm not as nice as you think, in the first place; and in the second, there's no debt to pay. I'm enjoying this. Believe me, there's no satisfaction in the world so great as seeing one's efforts profitably bestowed."

While I was still blushing over this, he added, "I'm going back to Chicago next week, incidentally. I leave Wednesday morning, and I'll probably not be back until late on Friday."

I was getting to be as nosy as my mother, I guess, because I asked, "For—something important?"

As I think I said before, Dr. Hallam knew how to keep his private business private. His only answer to my question was a smile.

*

In late May, Homer had a birthday, and the cost of a funny card to pass among our school friends to sign for him, a serious, somewhat mushy one to give him privately, and my gift of three real Irish linen handkerchiefs (monogrammed) cleaned me out. I had enough money in my purse for a new pair of shoes I desperately needed, but nothing extra for buying (or making) a graduation dress. My only option besides my regular school clothes was my Christmas dance dress, but it was sleeveless. Girl graduates weren't allowed to wear sleeveless dresses to the graduation ceremony on the grounds it was disrespectful to display bare arms in front of the assorted pastors, priests, and ministers—always at least three—who'd be present to address and bless the graduating class. A white dress was usual but not required, but sleeves were mandatory.

I asked my mother for help. "Can you lend me a dollar and a half, Ma? I'm sorry to ask, but I really need to buy something. I'll pay you back in two weeks."

Ma knew by now about the three-fifty I got every week from Dr. Hallam.

"Why not next week?" she asked suspiciously. "I'm not made of money, you know."

"There's something else I need to buy next week."

I'd earmarked my next week's pay for a corsage for Mother. It was traditional for graduates at Central to present their mothers with a corsage before the graduation ceremony as a token of love or thanks or something, but I didn't want to tell Ma about it and spoil the surprise.

"Well, what's the dollar and a half for, then? Gracious, Thea! You spend money like it's water!"

I explained I needed one-fifty to buy a yard of artificial blue silk. "The same stuff I made my Christmas dress out of, remember? I want to add sleeves to it so I can wear it to graduate in."

It took a minute for this to sink in, but when it did, Ma was so horrified she all but fell off her chair. "You can't do that! Girls wear white at graduation!"

"Blue's fine," I said, trying to sound indifferent about what dress I wore. I wasn't. I wanted white. "What would I do with a white dress afterward anyhow? And a dress you can only wear once isn't practical."

I expected this argument to convince my mother, who prided herself on being practical (though she wasn't), and who'd told me many times—approvingly—that back in *her* day, even a girl's wedding dress was expected to serve as her Sunday best for at least a year.

Instead, Ma went on insisting, with increasing agitation, that white was the only *possible* color I could graduate in.

When I wouldn't give in—I couldn't; I didn't have money for a dress, and that was that—she finally got desperate enough to tell me the real reason she was upset. "You have a beau, don't you?" she hinted.

"Yeah. Homer."

"So…?"

"So what? If you want to say something, Ma, just say it, would you?"

Ma dropped her voice to a whisper. "Can't you see it for yourself? Everybody knows you have a beau. What do you think they'll say when you show up for graduation in a dress that *isn't white*?"

Oh, lordy. So that was it. I thought of Mme. Bailey. If she was there to see it, she'd probably have the story all over town before the school orchestra finished squalling the recessional.

Well, let her.

"Ma, I don't give a damn what people think," I said tiredly. "Especially I don't give a damn what people with dirty minds think."

Ma was too upset about my dress to even notice the swears. "Well, you *should* care!" she cried. "And even if you don't, I do!"

I happened to be ironing, and I went on ironing without bothering to answer this.

After a long pause, Ma asked, "How much would a dress cost? I mean if you made it. How much would the goods cost?"

"What does that matter? I told you. I'm going to wear my blue."

"Three dollars? Would three dollars do it?"

"I'm not asking the doctor for three dollars, if that's what you think!"

"Would three dollars be enough?" she repeated.

"Ma, I've got two-fifty in my purse, and I'm going to buy shoes with it. I need shoes a whole lot more than I need a dress I'll never wear again."

After another long pause, Ma said, "I've got three dollars."

Mother was offering me *money*? I considered pinching myself to see if I was dreaming.

"Keep it," I said. "I'm wearing the blue."

"No, I want you to have white. Answer me, Thea. Do you think three dollars would buy the goods for a dress?"

I did a little figuring, taking into account that I'd rather wear blue silk—even artificial silk—than white wash-goods. "No. Not for nice fabric. Four, four-and-a-half, maybe."

After a short, almost physical struggle with herself, Ma said, "All right. I've got that much. Finish ironing those pillowslips and we'll go shopping. You need a white dress."

I asked Francine for the use of her sewing machine again, and as she had at Christmas, Francie not only said "yes" but ending up sewing most of my dress herself. Sewing was a job to me and not one I particularly liked. Francie loved it.

Ma's four-fifty wasn't enough to buy any of the beaded trims or fringes that were currently popular, so Francie and I chose a simple style. At my final fitting, I was surprised to find the dress's bodice embellished with lace.

"Pretty, isn't it?" Francie asked proudly. "That was Alice's suggestion. I never wear frilly dresses myself, but that looks good on you."

Alice was Francine's librarian roommate. "It's perfect," I agreed, admiring myself in the mirror. "But I can't just *take* it. Lace is expensive. Tell me what I owe you, and I'll pay you back as soon as I can."

Francie laughed. "Oh, applesauce! I never charge for things I pull out of my remnant bag. That's just a leftover from a wedding gown I made for another girl. If it'll make you feel better about it, we'll call it a graduation present—from Alice and me."

That day, as usual, there was a biggish stack of mail in Dr. Hallam's box for me to bring in. I swear I was just looking for my College Board scores and not snooping when one particular letter caught my eye. It was postmarked "Chicago," and instead of a complete return address, all that was written on the back flap were the initials "D.D." I had a pretty good idea who it came from.

But it wasn't my business, so I put the doctor's mail on his desk as I always did and went back to the kitchen.

*

Dr. Hallam came home from Chicago late Saturday, not late Friday. I hoped he'd spent the extra time making up his quarrel with Mr. Dennis, but managed to stop myself from asking.

"Did you have a good time?" I asked instead.

"Fairly interesting." The doctor smiled at me. "*Quite* interesting, I should have said. And you?"

The words "quite interesting" and the smile together suggested to me he'd gotten, or expected, a job offer.

But what was good and "interesting" for Dr. Hallam was sad for me, and the smile I returned for his wasn't entirely sincere. "Me? Oh, I'm fine," I replied.

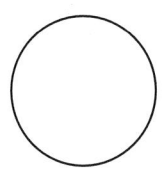

Chapter Nineteen

My final grades were going to be all "As"—except, of course, for my grade in Public Speaking.

I'd improved at giving speeches. Even my teacher, Mr. Mack, said I had. But an "A" in the class was out of my reach. I'd gotten more "Cs" early on than my more recent run of "Bs" could make up for. An "A" on my last speech of the year—doubtful—plus a little charity on Mr. Mack's part, could only raise my final grade as high as a straight "B," although luckily a grade of "D," the lowest mark I could get if I gave any speech at all, could only take me down to a "B minus."

There's something freeing about knowing a situation is hopeless. After a solid year of giving desperately earnest speeches on desperately earnest topics, the final one I wrote and repeatedly practice-delivered as usual to the four walls of the garage apartment was titled, "Seven Reasons High School Public Speaking Teachers Should Be Handsomely Remunerated." Dr. Hallam's suggestion, made back at the beginning of the year and not meant to be taken seriously, had been "Ten Reasons," but seven was all I could come up with.

I hated giving speeches as much as ever, and I had no idea at all how this, my final one, was likely to be received, but two days before the last school day of the school year, something like the fatalism (or whatever it was) that kept Marie Antoinette upright in the tumbril carried me to the front of the classroom, where I cleared my throat, took a sip of water, and began.

Reasons Seven and Six went by without much reaction from my classmates. They were waiting for me to turn earnest, I guess. At Reason Five, I heard titters and looked up from my notes in time to see Mr. Mack (the man who'd reminded me fifty times per speech all semester to "Look up from your notes occasionally, Miss Carter!") hitch himself forward in his chair and smile broadly.

Reason Four garnered outright laughs.

I was almost afraid to say Reason Three, which consisted solely of the name "Bob Woodruff," with no further exposition. Bob was our class—no, the whole school's—clown, bright enough that if he'd ever stopped joking around and applied himself he might have given even Homer some academic competition—only he never did. The despair of his teachers, Bob was very popular with his fellow students (it didn't hurt that he was good-looking and athletic), and I was afraid my little joke about him would cause me to lose my audience's sympathy. Mr. Mack had warned our class repeatedly that no speaker could afford to lose his audience's sympathy.

Bob, however, laughed harder at Reason Number Three than anybody else did, except possibly Mr. Mack.

Another thing Mr. Mack had told the class was that once people started laughing, it put them in a mood to go on laughing. This was proved, I felt, by the fact that Reasons Two and One (One being that Public Speaking teachers deserved to be rewarded for putting up patiently with bad speakers like me), were much better received than they had any right to be. For the first time in my life, I had the thrill of receiving applause that was genuinely enthusiastic instead of merely polite, and I returned to my seat confident I'd won myself a solid "B" in Public Speaking.

*

The last day of school was a long-established, though unsanctioned, day off for Central High's senior class. We came to school as usual and then "sneaked" away just before the first bell rang. I say "sneaked," but everybody knew we were going to go. Every year, a few parents (and some jealous underclassmen) complained about the custom, and a few teachers swore they'd give any student who wasn't in attendance a failing grade, but the complaints were ignored, and the threats were empty. The school administration was probably glad to get rid of us. The graduation ceremony was still two days off, but in our minds we seniors were already free, and we acted that way.

Homer and I managed to pack five more seniors besides ourselves into the jalopy, beating our previous record by two, and the Ford's stated capacity by three. The girls sat on the boy's laps, and nobody minded the crush. We drove around town until afternoon, shout-singing the Central High alma mater out the jalopy's windows and stopping for ice creams and phosphates as we pleased. I let Homer pay for mine, since I was bankrupt.

As he dropped me off at home—Dr. Hallam's—Homer whispered, "See you tomorrow night, Doll!" adding, as he had at every parting for a month, "You're coming to A&M, right?"

For the first time, I answered him, "Yes."

I hadn't formally accepted A&M's offer, which included enough scholarship money to get me through if I worked summers, because Dr. Hallam said there was no hurry and I should wait to see what answers I got from the University of Illinois and the University of

Chicago before I chose, but secretly, my mind was already made up. As I saw things, there was no possibility at all of me getting into Chicago. The fact that the doctor'd gone there told me all I needed to know about what standard they expected in a student, and the tuition and cost of living there were high. Although I felt there was a slight chance Illinois might admit me, bursaries and scholarships at all colleges were naturally reserved for their best prospects, and I was only me.

The college at Stillwater was a good school, it was only a bus (or jalopy) ride away from Oklahoma City, and the cost of living there was low enough that if worse came to worst and Ma couldn't stay employed herself, I was *almost* sure that with a part-time job during the school year to supplement my summer work, I could manage to keep her housed and fed.

Homer, of course, was the final advantage A&M had over any other university. There was no saying he'd stick with me until we graduated from college. He swore he would and seemed to mean it, but I knew things could happen. Loving Homer was easy for me. Trusting him was harder, but I was confident—pretty confident—I could do it.

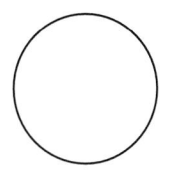

Chapter Twenty

"Oh, Thea," Ma murmured, looking down at her corsage as I pinned it to the front of her best dress. "Oh, Thea. Honey."

"There you go," I said. "You're the mother of a high school graduate. I hope that makes you very proud." My voice was thick, and I had tears in my eyes. I didn't remember my mother ever calling me by an endearment before.

"Of course I'm proud," Ma said. "I wish being a girl graduate made you proud, too, but I know it doesn't."

"Whatever gave you that idea? Of course I'm proud!"

"If you were proud, you wouldn't still think you had to go to college. A proud girl wouldn't think she had to prove she was as smart as a boy."

"Ma, we've been through this. That's not why I'm going."

Mother changed the subject. "So my littlest is all grown up," she said, putting on a sad expression that may or may not have been genuine. "I had you so late in life I never thought I'd live to see this day. I'm not sure I ever wanted to."

"Well, whyever not? Ma, you're not even sixty! You've got years ahead of you yet." I tried to laugh. "Anyway, I'm not going far.

Stillwater's just up the road. We'll see each other all the time." We'd have to see each other a lot, I thought grimly, if Ma was going to live all those "years ahead" I'd just promised. The more neglected she felt, the more Ma drank.

I was about to say more about how near Stillwater was when Ma suddenly exclaimed, "Oh, gracious me! I almost forgot! There's something in the icebox for you!"

The "something" was a bouquet of red rosebuds. Bouquets of rosebuds for girl graduates to carry were another Central High tradition. The ones I'd seen when I went to order Ma's corsage cost four dollars, but families who could afford to have their girls graduate from high school were generally of at least middle-class means. Eight dollars was Ma's whole weekly salary, not counting room and board, and she'd put every dime she had saved toward my graduation dress. I wondered how she'd managed to get flowers for me, too.

The mystery was solved a minute later when Dr. Hallam walked into the kitchen.

"Come look at Thea!" Ma cried when she saw him. "Isn't she just a picture?" When she added, "I paid for her dress," I knew who the money for my bouquet had come from.

The doctor looked us both over, nodding and smiling like he cared what we or anybody else wore, which I was pretty sure he didn't. But to be polite—he was always polite—the doctor dutifully repeated, "Very nice; very nice. You are both remarkably lovely," several times.

On an impulse, I pulled a rose out of my bouquet. "This is for you," I told Dr. Hallam, putting it in his buttonhole and feeling suddenly shy. "A thank you for all the calculus lessons, and the music, and everything else." I'm not usually the soppy type, but I forced myself to add, "Thank you from the bottom of my heart." I'm sure the doctor was as embarrassed to hear it as I was to say it, but words were all I had to repay him with, so I tried to make them good ones.

Ma bridled, visibly jealous. "How do you expect that to work, Thea?" she said crossly. "For heaven's sake put a pin through that flower, or it'll fall right out."

"There's one in the library," Dr. Hallam said. "Let me get it." He took his time getting the pin, and by the time he came back, Ma'd calmed down.

Later, when she was out of the room, the doctor said he had something for me, too. "It's just a token, really," he explained, handing me a small brown-paper-wrapped package. "But I think it might be better if you told your mother it was from someone else."

I took his advice. "Look, Mother," I said, showing her the gift later. "Homer gave me an autograph album!"

*

Graduations at Central always began (late) with the graduating seniors entering from the back of the auditorium and marching by twos down the center aisle and up onto the stage. The order of the marchers was alphabetical except for the six highest-ranked students, who led the way. As valedictorian and salutatorian, Homer and Lydia should have walked side by side, with me and the fourth-place student, another girl, behind them. But Lydia, as I mentioned, was engaged to be married, and her pastor, father, and fiancé—and possibly also Lydia herself, although I don't know that anybody asked her—felt that, being engaged, she could not possibly walk beside any man other than her pastor, her father, or her fiancé. Lydia's family suggested I should be moved up in the procession to walk beside Lydia, while the Escoes insisted Homer should keep his place, and Lydia be moved back to walk beside the fourth-place girl. The Escoes were richer and more socially prominent, so they won. I didn't know about the change until we were getting in line, but from the minute I heard I was going to walk onto the stage to be graduated as I'd always wanted to, at the head of my class, I didn't care anymore that I hadn't been named salutatorian. I hated giving speeches anyway. As the orchestra struck up the processional, and ignoring the fiercely-whispered reminders of the crabby P.E. teacher that graduates must not touch each other, I took Homer's arm. We marched into the auditorium like that—first in the line, arms linked, our backs straight and our heads high.

The ceremony was opened with a prayer by one of the three preachers in attendance, and afterward Central High's principal delivered what I heard was pretty much the same address he gave every year. Homer was next on the program, and if it's not immodest of me to say so, since I helped him write it, his speech was pretty good. After Lydia and the other two preachers had taken their turns, the school band murdered a medley of patriotic songs, ending with the Star-Spangled Banner to get us all on our feet for the presentation of the diplomas. By the time all the graduates had collected theirs, most of the audience had their wraps and hats on, and some had already slipped away.

The parents and audience members who hadn't left early followed the senior class to the school cafeteria, where punch and cookies were laid out. Since we were first in the procession, Homer and I were first to get there, of course. Homer went to get me a cup of punch and himself a cookie from every plate he passed while we waited for our families to come.

As soon as Homer wandered off, Mr. Mack walked up to me. "Here you go," he said, offering me an envelope. "You didn't ask for it, but here you are anyway." I guess I looked blank, because he added, "It's a recommendation to college. I'm sure you must be going."

Stupid with surprise, I nodded.

"Well, all right, then," Mr. Mack said with a grin. "I don't know how much use it'll be to you, but take it with my best regards anyway. You earned it."

I accepted the envelope with a weak, "Thanks." After my meeting with Mr. Brody, I'd lost all confidence any teacher would give me a good letter, and had never tried to get another.

"I wish you all the luck in the world, Miss Carter," Mr. Mack said, holding out his hand to shake mine. "I don't doubt for a minute you'll do well in life."

Then he excused himself and walked away to talk to another student before I had time to thank him again more forcefully. Letters of recommendation were supposed to be submitted sealed and unread by the person they recommended, but Mr. Mack had done nothing more than tuck the envelope flap in. Curious, I peeked first—then took the letter out and openly read the whole thing. Miss Thea Carter, the letter said, though not the best speaker the undersigned had ever taught, was unquestionably among the brightest and most determined. "Given the chance," Mr. Mack had written, "she will enhance the reputation of any university she attends."

Only the thought of what it would do to my mascara stopped me from bawling my eyes out right then and there.

As Homer was handing me a cup of punch, Ma rushed up and hugged me. She was so excited I only managed to stop her from hugging Homer too by handing her my punch. While Dr. Hallam was shaking my hand, Homer said suddenly, "Stay here, okay, Thea? I'll be right back," and disappeared into the crowd. I gave Mr. Mack's letter to Dr. Hallam, along with permission to read it.

For the better part of a year, I'd been simultaneously looking forward to and dreading having to meet Homer's family, and now, suddenly, it was happening. Homer walked back toward me with his parents and sister in tow. It might have been my imagination, but I thought the look on Mrs. Escoe's face suggested she'd caught a whiff of something unappetizing and thought it might be me.

I knew Homer's sister Meggie slightly already, since she was a Central High sophomore, and when I looked closer I realized I'd seen his mother before, too. She sat on the school board I'd repeatedly pled with for permission to take advanced classes. I promised myself I wouldn't hold it against her. Attorney Escoe was an older, bulker version of Homer.

Homer made the introductions, and hands were shaken all around. As Ma met the Escoes, she turned up the volume all the way on her Old Southern Charm. Dr. Hallam and Mr. Escoe were already somewhat acquainted—lawyers get sick like everybody else, I guess—and the two of them kindly kept up a friendly conversation between them while my ma and Homer's sized each other up. Ma'd been ready to approve of the Escoes since the first minute she'd known they existed, and after the two ladies chatted for ten or fifteen minutes, Mrs. Escoe seemed cautiously satisfied with Ma, too. Me she appraised like a piece of merchandise, but when she didn't reject me outright, Homer caught my eye, and we heaved mutual silent sighs of relief.

Mr. Escoe was the first to notice the families and teachers in the cafeteria were beginning to drift away. Leaving the new graduates for an hour or two to pass and sign each other's albums and yearbooks was another school tradition.

"Time for us old folks to push off, I guess," Mr. Escoe said heartily, pulling his wife's hand through his arm. Giving Homer a sharp look, he added, "Nine-thirty on the dot, son. Not a minute later. You understand me?" His tone was probably the same one he used in the courtroom, because Homer nodded meekly.

Meggie produced her own autograph album and begged to be allowed to stay, too (Mr. Escoe said no), while Mrs. Escoe and Ma wondered aloud to each other whether it was quite safe for anybody to be out "so late" as nine-thirty. Since Homer and I had been out after ten and even eleven o'clock plenty of times already, I assumed the demurrals were mere motherly *pro formas*. Dr. Hallam made it easy for Ma to relent by offering to return for me when the signing party broke up at nine o'clock, but the plan finally agreed upon was the one Homer and I had made a week before, which was for Homer to bring me home in the jalopy. We said our goodnights and Ma kissed me again—also *pro forma*, I think, because Ma wasn't generally a kisser. Dr. Hallam had read Mr. Mack's letter by now, and before he turned to go he tapped the pocket he'd put it in and murmured, "This goes straight to Chicago." I couldn't imagine anyone in Chicago being impressed by a letter from an Oklahoma high school teacher, but the doctor seemed to be taking it very seriously.

Homer handed his yearbook off to the first person who asked for it, and it went around the room so many times before it got back to him that some people ended up signing it twice, but I carried my album from friend to friend myself. The girls exclaimed over its flower-embellished green plush cover and signed with verses, while the boys mostly just scrawled their names. I didn't care what anybody wrote as much as I cared about the brief, intense conversations I had along the way. Everybody in the room, including the chaperones (who were all teachers), had been used to seeing each other every school day for years. Now, it was possible some of us would never see each other again. That made me sad.

Homer caught the mood, too.

"Makes you think, doesn't it, Thea?" he said as he climbed into his side of the jalopy. "Everything in life has a beginning and an end, and a big thing in our lives just ended and will never come back."

"School?"

"Childhood."

I felt like my childhood had ended a long time before, but didn't say so.

I tried to be comforting. "It's all right, though. We'll be too busy being adults to miss childhood. Anyway, old things will be always be ending and new things beginning. Might as well get used to it."

"Until we die," Homer said solemnly.

"Yeah, our lives will end, too. Someday."

"Death's the last ending, and it'll be followed by the last ever beginning, which will be—heaven." Homer turned to grin at me. "I hope."

I'll say it right out. Not much of what I'd ever heard about heaven appealed to me, and least of all the idea it was infinite and unchanging.

"I hope heaven won't be all the same forever," I said. "Eternal bliss? All play and no work makes Thea a dull girl."

Homer whistled and shook his head. "I never know what to think when you say things like that, Doll."

We parked in the dark awhile—but not long, because Homer had to be home by nine-thirty. He kept checking his watch, explaining that, although his dad wasn't particularly strict with him (it was another story with Meggie, apparently), when he did issue an order, he expected to be obeyed.

"It'll be different once we're in Stillwater. We'll be able to do anything we want," Homer murmured between kisses, apparently forgetting that college dorms had rules and curfews, too. "Stillwater's going to be great." Then, since it was late enough there'd be no one to see, he let me drive the jalopy home. He'd put in a self-starter, a pedal on the floor, and wanted me to try it.

*

Ma'd already gone up to bed by the time I came in, but Dr. Hallam had left a light on in the living room for me. When I turned it off, I noticed a light was still on in the library, too, and the library door was open. The doctor was apparently still awake. I was glad about this, partly because it gave me a chance to thank him properly for my bouquet and album, and partly because I was too keyed up to go straight to bed.

Though he was writing when I tapped on the doorframe, the doctor greeted me as graciously as ever. "Did you have a good time? You look like you did."

I said I had, and thanked him for his gifts, as I'd planned. Unplanned, I also said, "I kind of wanted a cup of tea or something. I'd be happy to make you one too, if you'd like it."

Dr. Hallam agreed that a cup of tea would be nice, got up, and followed me into the kitchen. "I'll help, if you show me how this works," he said, eyeing the stove.

So I showed him how to light his own stove, then filled the kettle for him and put it on. "Haven't you ever cooked anything before?" I asked, as I got out the kitchen teapot and cups.

"Over a campfire. Once. The result was uneatable, and I was forbidden to repeat the experiment."

"Was that when you were in the army?"

"That's right."

"Where you met Mr. Dennis?"

The doctor didn't answer this.

"To be honest," I said, determinedly overriding the voice in my head advising me to leave Mr. Dennis out of the conversation, "a minute ago, when I saw you were writing something, I was kind of hoping it was a letter to him."

Dr. Hallam didn't answer.

"Do you ever write to him? I mean, it's not my business, but I know he writes to you, so I thought you might."

"I was writing a cover for the letter from your speech teacher," the doctor said, very curt.

"Oh."

The kettle started whistling, and the doctor reached for it.

"Use this," I advised, quickly giving him a folded towel. "That handle's hot. Do you know Mr. Dennis's address?"

Ignoring me, the doctor asked, "How much tea does one put in the pot for two people? I wasn't watching when you did it."

I told him. "I don't think we have any lemons," I added. "Is sugar and milk all right?"

"Just sugar, please."

I turned off the stove (the doctor'd forgotten) and poured for us. Dr. Hallam didn't sit down at the table to drink with me, which seemed like a clear signal I should drink up my own tea and leave quick. I disregarded it.

Instead, I continued, "I think you should write to him. I think you should invite him to visit."

No answer.

Maybe the boys who claimed before every school dance that they were absolutely going to spike the punch for *sure* this time had finally carried through with their plan. Whatever the reason, I found myself saying, "In fact, I think you should ask him to move here."

The doctor turned to set his cup and saucer in the sink, though I hadn't seen him drink from it. His back to me, he said, "It's late. You need to get to bed."

"It's okay. I don't have school anymore, so I can sleep in tomorrow. I don't know what you and Mr. Dennis quarreled about, and maybe it was something that can't be patched up. But if it can be, I think you should apologize to each other and forget about…whatever it was, because you were happy when he was here and you're not happy now and I'm guessing he's not happy now either. And that's what life's for. Being happy. I just figured that out tonight, by the way."

"It's not that simple." Dr. Hallam turned my way again. "It's not as simple as being happy or not."

"Okay, I know it's not simple, but it's important." When the doctor didn't say anything, I added, "Are you afraid because of that job in Chicago?"

He started. "Pardon?"

"I think you might have left a job there because of a scandal. Is that right? Are you afraid another scandal will stop you getting the new one you want at Cook County?"

The doctor studied me for about an hour, it seemed like, and then asked, "Where on earth did you hear that?"

I figured he deserved to know. "Madame Bailey," I admitted. "She told me you left Chicago and moved here because there was some kind of scandal about you and Mr. Dennis being homosexuals."

When I said the word "homosexual," Dr. Hallam visibly flinched.

"I see," he said after a minute, very coldly; then asked, "Do you have any idea what you're talking about? Do you know what that word *means*?"

"I think I do. I read about it in your books. It means you and Mr. Dennis love each other."

"It means a great deal more than that! I don't mean to impugn your intelligence, Thea, but whatever it was you read, I believe you may have missed the point of it."

"The point about homosexuality being 'deviant' and all? No, I got it."

I stared into my teacup and thought for a minute. If what I'd been thinking was wrong—if I'd been wrong to believe Madame Bailey—then I'd just for sure thumped a hornet's nest.

Only I was pretty sure I wasn't wrong.

"Look," I said, raising my head. "I know I shouldn't argue with medical books, because the people who write them know a lot more than I do, but honestly, I don't think they should have used that word. 'Deviant' *sounds* medical, but there's nothing medical about poking around in other people's business."

"It's not a case of 'other people's business,'" Dr. Hallam said stiffly. "What you're accusing me of is a very serious matter!"

"I'm sorry if I'm wrong. I didn't mean to upset you."

The doctor stared at me for another little while, and then suddenly sagged back against the drainboard and crossed his arms. "I didn't say you were…wrong." He stared at the floor and didn't talk for a minute. "You're not wrong," he said finally. "You just don't fully understand what you're saying. The seriousness of it. The societal implications. And so forth."

"Well, if society would keep its nose to itself, it wouldn't be implicated," I answered. "What's the 'and so forth'?"

The doctor uncrossed his arms then crossed them again, tighter. "Surely you know homosexuality is immoral. That means people like me have a profoundly degrading influence on society."

I shook my head. "Don't take this wrong," I said. "But as far as I can see, you don't have a lot of any kind of influence on society. You mostly just keep to yourself. You have a big influence on me, but it's a good one. What makes you think you're degraded?"

Dr. Hallam said bitterly, "I was born degraded."

"Is that why your parents don't speak to you?"

The doctor didn't answer this, but I could tell by the look on his face what the answer was. "My parents tried every way they could to… to elevate me, if I may put it that way. They thought if they could make me walk and talk like a real man, I'd become one. I had diction lessons, physical training… Every advantage you can think of. My grandfather even insisted I change piano teachers to one who'd make me play in a more 'masculine' style. If it had been left to him, I wouldn't have played at all, in fact. Need I say that nothing worked?"

"It did in a way. I haven't heard you play the piano, but you walk and talk very manly. More than most men, even. Is that why you joined the army?"

"It's one of the reasons. Look, Thea, somehow or other, I'm not reaching you. Let me put this in another way. Do you know what the Bible says about men like me?"

"Sure." I finished my tea then quoted, "It says, 'You shall not lie with mankind as with womankind; it is an abomination.' Leviticus, chapter eighteen. I don't remember the verse number."

"*So…?*" Dr. Hallam prodded.

"So what? The Bible also says insects have four legs and pi equals three. And if it can be wrong in one place, it can be wrong in another."

The doctor started to say something else but curiosity got the better of him. "Does it really say pi equals three?"

"Kings," I informed him, pouring myself another cup of tea. "Also Chronicles. There's a description of the basin in front of the Temple in Jerusalem, and both those books say it measured ten cubits from rim to rim and took a line of thirty cubits to measure around it."

"Interesting," Dr. Hallam said thoughtfully. "That would seem to indicate—" His tone turned stern again. "But of course, the Bible was never intended to be a mathematics textbook!"

"Fair enough, but how about this?" I countered. "In Hebrews it says a new covenant *will* succeed the old, and in Luke it says the new covenant *has* succeeded the old, and in Romans—I think chapter seven—the Bible says flat out that we've been *released* from the old covenant and laws, and it *doesn't* say 'except for Leviticus.'"

The doctor uncrossed one arm and rubbed his forehead wearily. "I sense there's no point in my continuing this line of argument."

"You're right," I agreed.

I hadn't always been able to afford to get library books because there was usually trolley-fare to pay to get to the library to check them out, trolley-fare to pay to get back to the library to return them, plus a two cent per day fine for every book I didn't have trolley-fare enough to return on time. But Ma owned a Bible, so I could always read that, and I had. Many, many times.

"Anyway, what's the point of Bible quotes?" I asked. "Even Ma will tell you God didn't write the Bible with His own hand. He has to inspire people to do His writing for Him, and if you consider what poor material that means He has to work with, it's no wonder if some of what He says gets written down wrong."

"Good God, Thea!" the doctor burst out, looking shocked, but half laughing, too. "Surely your mother didn't raise you to be so cynical!"

"My mother didn't raise me at all. I raised myself. I'm sorry if I didn't do a good job."

"No, no," Dr. Hallam said quickly. "You're fine. You did a fine job. I didn't mean it that way."

He finally came to the table and sat down.

After a minute, he explained quietly, "It's not just the Bible. The trouble is that most people believe I am...depraved."

"No," I contradicted. "The *trouble* is that you agree with them. Anyway, why do most people even have to know? It's wrong for you to *have* to hide how you feel, but it's not wrong for you to *do* it. People hide things about themselves all the time. You can bet I don't tell anybody about Ma!"

The doctor thought about this for a minute. "Well, there's another problem," he said. "Dennis."

"You mean because he's mad at you?"

"As a matter of fact, he's not. He should be angry with me, of course, but for some reason, he isn't. I'm talking about the fact that Dennis finds it very hard to hide anything. He isn't as careful as he should be, and he takes risks. One risk he took got him sent to Joliet for three years."

"He got arrested at a dance club or something, didn't he? Wasn't that it?"

"You are depressingly well-informed," the doctor said gloomily. "Yes. Denny loves to dance."

"But you weren't at the club yourself, right?"

"No. I should have been. I'd have gotten Dennis out in time. I know a raid when I see one coming."

"You can't be sure of that," I objected. "If you'd been there, maybe all that would have happened is that you'd have done time, too. Anyway, you're not giving Mr. Dennis enough credit. He's smart enough to learn his lesson. Did he ever disarm another artillery shell after that one he gave you?"

"No, but he didn't stop taking chances. He was decorated for it, in fact."

"Well, okay," I conceded. "But he was supposed to be brave. The officers told him to be. Anyway, you must have taken a few chances yourself. Mr. Dennis said you were almost court martialed once."

"Dennis was exaggerating. I was reprimanded. *Slightly* reprimanded."

"What for?"

"I believe I mentioned it took me eight months to get home after the armistice?"

"Yes."

"In fact, I could have come home much sooner. I was *supposed* to come home sooner. Instead, I took Dennis traveling. He'd never seen Europe, and I wanted to show it to him."

"All right, but if you knew you might get reprimanded if you didn't go home when you were supposed to, then you were taking a risk. You just thought the risk was worth it, the same as Mr. Dennis thought the risk was worth it when he went to that club."

Since the conversation seemed to be going pretty well, I sat back in my chair and got comfortable. "I think Mr. Dennis made the best he could of going to prison because even if being sent up wasn't fair, it was just." Before the doctor could object to this, which he looked like he was about to do, I added, "What I mean is, the law he broke is stupid, but it's the law, and he broke it. But I think the reason he isn't mad at you is because his conscience isn't clear about the way he hurt you, and I think he'll be a lot more careful now that he's seen that even if you don't go to prison, you can lose jobs and what-not if he gets himself in trouble. I'll bet he knows to watch out for raids now, and you should give him a chance to prove it."

I got the impression the doctor almost didn't want to be persuaded. "It would be selfish of me to restrain him," he said, turning stiff again. "Dennis likes to do quite a *lot* of things that aren't what I'd call prudent, but he deserves to live as he sees fit."

"Well, maybe he'd see fit to be prudent if it meant he could be with you. Maybe if you were together, he'd be so happy he wouldn't feel like he was being restrained if you told him he had to dance at home instead of in a club. And maybe you'd be so happy you'd dance with him. That's the point of life, like I said. To be happy."

"So long as our happiness doesn't ruin other people's. You're forgetting that part."

"People who stick their noses in other people's business and then complain about what they find are making their *own* unhappiness," I declared.

Dr. Hallam, still a little stiff, agreed to consider what I'd said, and then changed the topic. I think we were both ready for a new one.

He started by talking about Europe, probably because he knew I never got tired of hearing about Europe. The doctor'd spent a lot of time there as a young man, sometimes touring around with tutors his parents thought would "straighten him out," and once with his younger brother. I hadn't known before Dr. Hallam had a brother. When I asked what his brother did, the doctor first said, "As little as possible;" and then that he was a lawyer in a firm founded by their grandfather.

"Let's just say Paul's in no danger of being either overworked or underpaid there," he told me wryly. He added that his brother despised him, but said the feeling was mutual so I shouldn't worry about it.

He mentioned the letter from Mr. Mack, saying it would do me a world of good in Chicago. "Your test scores will prove your intelligence, but the admitting committee also wants to know you're motivated and diligent." Then he remembered how I wouldn't say why Mr. Brody hadn't given me a letter, and asked me to tell him. It turned out to be a relief to get the story off my chest, and I wished I'd done it sooner. Dr. Hallam called Mr. Brody a fossil.

Although he still seemed reluctant to talk about Mr. Dennis, when I asked, the doctor told me he had three younger brothers and a little sister who he loved and got along fine with, only his parents hadn't let him see them for several years for fear they might catch Mr. Dennis's homosexuality.

"See? You two need to be together so you can be family for each other," I advised; then I wondered out loud if Ma didn't want me to see Tom and Janie because she was afraid I might catch their independence.

"I suspect you're on to something there, Thea," the doctor replied.

We talked about some other things—nothing important. Just this and that—until Dr. Hallam finally said, "Disconcertingly forthright as you sometimes are, Thea, I always enjoy our conversations. However, it is now two o'clock in the morning, and time you were in bed."

I had to turn around and look at the clock myself before I could believe him.

Smiling and not stiff anymore, the doctor emptied the teapot and helped me wash the dishes. "Was your graduation all you hoped it would be?" he asked me.

"Better, even," I assured him. "Except the speeches were too long. Also, the music was bad, and there were too many prayers. But the rest of it was lovely. Thank you again for the album and flowers. I know the flowers were from you because they're not the kind of thing Ma would think of."

The doctor admitted he hadn't thought of them, either. "Fran told me they were customary." Since it was so late, he walked me up the stairs to the apartment but didn't come in.

Ma was asleep and snoring in a way that meant she'd had more than a few. I was angry—and disgusted—until I saw her Bible was out, and when I looked in it, that she'd pressed the corsage I'd given her between its pages. That softened me enough to recall what Dr. Hallam said, that she was doing the best she could. Some people's best is still bad.

The pressed flowers gave me an idea.

After rolling Ma onto her side so she could breathe better, I stood where a shaft of moonlight gave me light to see by and slipped a rose from my bouquet into my album on the page Homer had signed.

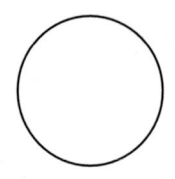

Chapter Twenty-One

I woke up so late on Sunday it was almost time for Homer to come pick me up. Ma was already dressed and downstairs. I could see her from our front window, sitting at the kitchen table. I guessed from the slump of her shoulders she had a pretty bad hangover, and when she was hungover, Ma tended not to eat unless somebody else made food and put it in front of her. Even though I knew this, I went ahead and treated myself to a warm bath before getting into my nicest school-clothes and making up my face. I'd turned eighteen, so Ma couldn't stop me from doing it.

"Want an egg, Ma? Or just toast?" I asked as I walked in the kitchen door. "You remember today's my day to go driving with Homer, right?"

She didn't look at me. "I remember."

"So— egg?"

"No, thank you."

I lit the broiler and slid some bread slices under it. Dr. Hallam had bought a toaster and made his own toast at the breakfast table now, but the toaster could only toast one piece of bread at a time, whereas the broiler could fit several, so I never used it.

"I'm making you a sandwich, too," I told Ma. "That's for lunch. I should be home in time to make dinner."

Ma made some grumbly answer I couldn't interpret.

"And I found your bottle, so don't bother to look for it." I pulled the toast out and started buttering it. "Honestly, Ma, I don't know how you drink that stuff. It smelled like gasoline."

"I was lonely. I'd never touch liquor if I had someone to talk to," Ma said, for once not avoiding saying the word "liquor" or that she drank it.

I put our toast on the table and sat down across from her. "Eat that," I ordered her like a child, then said, as I usually did when she made me not talking to her the excuse for her drinking, "Well, we're talking now, aren't we? Would you like to go to church on Sundays instead of just listening to services on the radio? You could make friends with other church people."

Ma sniffed. "Who'd want to make friends with me? I keep somebody's house."

When I referenced "publicans and sinners," Mother told me not to get smart with her. "There aren't many people in this world Christian enough to be friends with somebody's servant and not make them feel like dirt all the time," she muttered.

"Come on: Take another bite. That's it," I urged. "Ma, other 'servants,' if you insist on calling yourself that, have friends. There's no shame in being a servant."

Another sniff. "They're friends with other servants, maybe. I'm used to something better."

"Ladies, you mean? Well, how about joining a club or something, then? What about Eastern Star? Lots of 'ladies' belong to that."

"They'd never take me."

"Have you tried?"

No answer.

"Okay, what about the Ladies Music Club? That one's got 'ladies' right in its name."

"I used to play the piano, you know."

"I do know. That's what made me think of the Music Club. So how about it?"

No answer but a shrug.

I coaxed and argued with Ma through two slices of toast and a cup of coffee, but she wouldn't budge, insisting no club or society she could possibly want to belong to would have her.

Finally she burst out, "If my own daughter doesn't want to talk to me, why would anybody else?"

"Ma…" I sighed, shaking my head. I glanced at the clock. "Time for me to go. Your sandwich is in the icebox, at the top. Remember to eat it, okay?" I came over and put my arm around her shoulders. "Look, I love you, Ma," I said, squeezing gently, "but Homer's waiting, so I've got to go. You want me to marry him, right? Before I can marry him, I've got to keep company with him first. That's how courting works."

Mother clutched at my hand. "You don't have to marry him." She looked up at me hopefully. "Now that you've graduated from high school, you could get a good job and we could stay together." I probably made a face, because she added quickly, "What I mean is, we could stay together for a little while and live cheap while you saved up money to get married on later. It's good for a girl to bring money to her marriage."

She was back to pretending I'd never mentioned going to college.

"We'll talk about this later," I said, mentally planning how to avoid ever talking about "this" again. "There's some roast beef left. How about beef hash for dinner? You like my hash. And don't forget to eat lunch, okay?"

I kissed her cheek and left.

Another couple we'd gone driving with before, Carl and Ruth, were waiting in the flivver with Homer.

"Say, Doll," Homer greeted me. "There's a carnival out near Edmond. What do you say? Want to go?"

"Oh, honey, I'd love to, but I can't! I'm broke," I cried. It was the literal truth. Aside from my emergency carfare—itself down to one nickel from my preferred two—I didn't have a penny in my pocketbook.

I was surprised to find the other three all assumed I meant I'd left my "graduation money" in the house or that it had already been banked. Everybody else in the car had gotten money gifts for graduation—in Homer's case, substantial ones, he hinted.

"My treat, then," he grinned. "In fact, I would have treated you anyhow because you're my girl, but you also deserve to be treated for being too smart to blow all your money on carnivals." Then he added, "Hey, want to drive? Who wants Thea to drive us to Edmond?"

The vote was three against my one. "What if I get caught?" I protested. "I don't have a license!"

"Doll, my dad's a *lawyer*, remember?" Homer drawled.

So I drove the jalopy to Edmond, which if you add in the detour the boys made me take so they could stare at some new oil derricks going up just outside the city limits, was the longest distance I'd ever driven. After that, I spent the next four hours having the time of my life riding carnival rides—creaky and somewhat scary—and eating carnival food, which I found delicious. My standards were low. Anything I didn't have to cook myself seemed delicious to me. In late afternoon, Ruth and I watched as Carl spent three times and Homer twice what a celluloid Kewpie-doll was worth, shooting at tin targets to win a "free" one. My doll was cheaper than Ruth's because, recalling what Homer had said earlier, I "happened" to mention to the carnie reloading the guns that Homer's dad was a lawyer. The carnie immediately diagnosed Homer's gun with some problem that necessitated replacing it with another gun he pulled out from under the counter, and with the new gun, Homer easily made five shots in a row, and I got my Kewpie. The carnie claimed prizes were one to a customer, so we wandered off.

Later, while the boys were buying near-beer (Homer'd heard the secret word "Wilson" would get them served real beer instead), Ruth asked me who "that good-looking older man" was who'd come to see me graduate.

"That was Dr. Hallam," I told her. "He's a…neighbor."

"Lucky you!" Ruth laughed. "Our neighbor's a witch. What kind of doctor is he? A minister? He dresses like one."

Now that I thought about it, the doctor's clothes, though high quality, *were* kind of sober. Mr. Dennis had ragged on him about it. "A medical doctor," I said as Homer and Carl walked up. Turning to them, I asked, "Well, what about it? Did it work?"

Homer took a cautious sip. "It's so bad I can't tell," he said with a grimace. "What do you think, Car?"

Carl couldn't tell either.

I took Homer's cup from him and sniffed it. "It's just near-beer," I said, handing it back. I naturally didn't mention how I knew what ethyl alcohol smelled like.

Meanwhile, Carl was asking Ruth who we'd been talking about.

"Thea's neighbor," she explained. "The man who came with her mother to graduation, remember? Turns out he's a doctor."

Wanting to give Dr. Hallam all due credit, I put in, "He taught me calculus."

"What'd you say his name was?"

"Hallam. H-A-L-L-A-M. His office is in that new building next to the hospital."

Carl wrinkled his nose. "Hallam," he repeated. "Didn't I hear something about him?"

I held my breath.

Homer spoke up, waving the question away. "Forget it," he said. "My dad'll vouch for him. He looked into the story, and it didn't turn out to be true; just a rumor started by some other doctor who didn't like a better-trained man moving into his territory."

"What *was* the story?" Ruth asked eagerly.

Homer and Carl looked at each other, but evidently neither of them had heard exactly *what* wrong thing the doctor was suspected of having done.

"It was malarkey anyway." Homer shrugged. "Come on. Let's get something fit to drink, because this stuff isn't, and I'm thirsty."

We stayed at the carnival for another hour, then started for home when Homer mentioned his dad expected him to be at his summer job in the Escoe law office bright and early next morning. Carl said he needed to get home, too. His father, who was an accountant for an oil company, had gotten him on at the firm as an office boy. A soupy look passed between him and Ruth as he told Homer and me we could expect wedding invitations to arrive as soon as he had gotten himself promoted to clerk. Homer drove this time, and we were all too tired to talk much. Homer was probably thinking about college, and Carl about one day being an oil broker—his stated ambition. I don't know what Ruth was thinking about. Wedding dresses, maybe.

I spent most of the drive thinking about the talk I'd had with Dr. Hallam.

What I thought was that I'd done the wrong thing by encouraging the doctor to invite Mr. Dennis to come live with him in Oklahoma City. In fact, I'd done the wrong thing by encouraging the doctor to stay in Oklahoma City himself. Personal reserve was not considered a virtue in Oklahoma. Though Oklahoma City had a population of around a hundred thousand people, the atmosphere of the place was small-town "frindly," as we Okies say it. Everybody knew, or knew of, each other and each other's business, and liked it that way. Chicago—with almost three million busy, bustling city-folks who from what I'd heard couldn't have told you their nearest neighbor's names—would be a safer choice of a place to live for a man who had something he wanted kept quiet. I promised myself that as soon as I saw him I'd tell the doctor that, much as I'd miss him if he left, I thought if the job at Cook County didn't work out he should keep looking for one in Chicago, or maybe even New York.

"You're awfully quiet, Doll," Homer said, reaching over to take my hand as we reached the outskirts of the city. "Whatcha thinking about?"

"Nothing much," I lied.

"Sixty-nine days to Freshman Week. I'm counting them down. You sent in your letter yet?"

Homer meant a letter accepting Oklahoma A&M's offer to me. "Stamped and ready," I replied. "It'll go out tomorrow." Dr. Hallam assured me I had a good chance at Illinois if I got a seven hundred on my College Boards, but I hadn't received my score yet (it was due any day) and I was sure I'd never get a seven hundred.

He thought the University of Chicago would probably want a seven-fifty.

With Carl and Ruth in the jalopy's back seat, Homer and I couldn't park, but as we parted at the doctor's door I said, "Thank you for giving me a wonderful day, Homie," in a way I hoped would let him know what I really meant, which was that I loved him.

He must have understood me. As he kissed me, he whispered, "Love you, Doll. See you next Sunday."

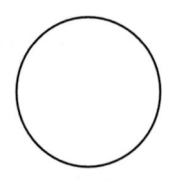

Chapter Twenty-Two

I expected to find Ma in the doctor's kitchen, and possibly even starting to make our dinner. I knew she'd be cold sober by now. When I took away her half-empty bottle, I also checked her purse to make sure she didn't have enough money to replace it. Being Sunday, there were no delivery men to slip her any, either, and the dry cleaning shop where she could have got a snort for a quarter was closed. She was still in the apartment, though. From the kitchen window I could see the bathroom light on upstairs. I started getting out the hash ingredients, telling myself if she hadn't come down by the time I got the potatoes parboiled, I'd go up and get her.

Dr. Hallam came home while I was mincing the beef. As he usually did, he stuck his head in at the kitchen door to say hello, and as he also usually did, when he saw I was alone he stepped in for a minute to ask if I'd had a good day.

I didn't need any more invitation than that to immediately blurt, "Okay, I want to take back something I said to you last night."

Dr. Hallam's face instantly took on the stony, far-off look I'd seen on it before. I knew what it meant now, so before he could get the idea I was about to tell him I'd decided he was an abomination after all, I quickly explained I only meant to say I thought he should go live in

Chicago.

"I hope you get that job you want," I babbled, "but if you don't, I think you should try to get a different one there. You're always going to be a fish out of water in Oklahoma, and people look closer at strange fish than they do at ordinary ones, so they'll notice you too much."

Before I could unmix my metaphors, Dr. Hallam's expression relaxed. "I've been called an odd fish before," he said, smiling, "but never in precisely that way." Indicating the hash ingredients spread out on the table, he asked, "Do you think you have enough there to feed three? I got a phone call earlier that lasted so long I missed dinner."

"I absolutely do," I said. "It's just going to be hash, though. Is that all right?"

"Hash would be wonderful. And afterward, let's talk more about Chicago, shall we? Just the two of us."

"Should I go up and get Ma now, or would you rather I waited until closer to the time to eat?"

"Whenever you think," Dr. Hallam said, and then went upstairs to wash and change, which he always did as soon as he got home from his office or a hospital.

I decided to get Ma right away, and hurried up to the apartment. I took my Kewpie-doll with me to show her, because Ma loved Kewpies.

I don't know how to describe what I found when I got upstairs. I haven't had practice describing it. I've never been able to talk about it before.

When I opened the apartment door, a smell like bad plumbing hit me. I muttered something like, "Oh, lordy," then called out, "Did the toilet back up, Ma?" and waited for a few seconds for her to answer.

I think that's what I did. I don't remember for sure.

Whatever I did—or said—Ma didn't answer, so I went in, leaving the door open behind me to air the place out. I tossed the Kewpie onto the chair and went toward the front window to open it, too, and called, "Ma?" a few more times on the way.

Halfway to the window, a noise made me look toward the bathroom. Ma was on the floor, half-sitting and half-lying down, hanging onto the side of the tub. Her face was horrible—blotchy and grayish-blue—and her breaths were shallow gasps.

As I ran to her, I slipped in something. Vomit. There was more in the toilet, and more down the front of Ma's dress. She'd soiled herself, too. When I got to her, I pulled her away from the tub and helped her to lay all the way down, but on her side, like I always laid her when she'd been drinking. I talked to her the whole time. I told her she'd be all right. Her arms and legs flailed like she couldn't control them.

My heart pounding, I said, "I've got to leave you for a minute, but I'll be right back, okay, Ma? I've got to get Dr. Hallam. Okay, Mama? I promise I'll be right back."

I think she answered me. I think she said my name. "Thea. Thea." But I'm not sure.

I ran to the bed and got a pillow for Ma's head and the bedspread to put over her, and then I ran for the house. The doctor was just coming downstairs. He heard me shouting—I don't know what I shouted—and called that he'd get his bag, so I turned around and ran back up to the apartment again. I was sitting on the floor next to Ma, talking to her and trying to wake her up, when he got to us.

He told me to go find what she'd had, if I could, and went to work on Ma. As I left the bathroom he was pulling up her eyelids and feeling her pulse. I brought what I found—a fruit jar—and knelt beside him.

It didn't take the doctor even a second sniff of the jar to know what was in it was bad. He got a bottle from his bag, sat Ma up and tried to make her drink from it. Ma's eyes were open, but she was only partly conscious, and I don't think he was able to get much into her.

"Call an ambulance, will you, Thea?" he said quietly. "We'll get her to the hospital."

I started up, but before I'd taken two steps, the doctor stopped me. "Let's take my car," he said. "It's faster. Do you think you could get the keys? They're on my dresser." As he spoke, Dr. Hallam lifted Ma off the floor and carried her to our bed. She'd lost more weight, and he didn't need any help from me to pick her up. I left him bending over her as I ran for the house again.

I went fast, but by the time I got the keys, the doctor was already coming downstairs with Ma in his arms. He'd wrapped her in the wool blanket we kept folded over the back of a chair in the summer. Ma was moving and mumbling, which reassured me. With the doctor instructing me, I managed to start his car and back it out of the garage. Then I got in the back seat and the doctor laid Ma down with her head in my lap.

"It'll be all right," he kept saying to me, along with similar things. "We'll take care of her."

He drove very fast and ran stop signs.

"Something's happening!" I cried. "Ma's shaking! Real hard! She's shaking all over!" My mother's mouth moved spasmodically, spit running from the corners of it.

Dr. Hallam glanced back. "Just hold onto her. Don't let her hurt herself. You don't have to do anything else."

"But what's wrong with her? Ma! Mama!"

"It's a seizure. She'll come out of it in a minute. Just keep holding her the way you are. That's exactly right."

He spoke as calmly as ever, but he drove even faster.

At the hospital, Dr. Hallam pulled up to the ambulance entrance, and as he jumped out of the car, he threw the Plymouth's keys to a man who looked like he was about to challenge him about it. Then he ran into the hospital and came back with a nurse, and an orderly pushing a gurney. The orderly took my ma from my lap, and he and Dr. Hallam together put her on the gurney and covered her with more blankets, and then the nurse came and helped me out of the car. She led me in a different direction from the way Dr. Hallam and the gurney were headed. She said some things to me, but I don't remember what. When I craned my head to see where Ma was going, the nurse let me stop and look. She repeated the same things the doctor had said: Ma'd be well taken care of. Everything would be all right. Her way of saying them wasn't as convincing as the doctor's, but I tried to believe her.

As the orderly wheeled Ma through some swinging doors, I saw her start to shake again, harder than before. Dr. Hallam put his arms over her to hold her down.

When the doors shut, the nurse led me by my arm to a washroom to help me clean myself and my clothes as far as they could be cleaned, which wasn't far. They were sticky with vomit and stank of pee. I asked the nurse again and again about my ma, but couldn't make out what she answered.

When I was as clean as the nurse could get me, she led me to the hospital waiting room and left me. There were some other people there. A woman was crying in the corner.

After a while, Dr. Hallam came.

"Is Ma okay?" I begged him. "Will she be okay?"

He said he didn't know, but hoped she would.

"When will you know?"

He didn't know that either. He asked me if I was cold.

I hadn't noticed I was shivering. "Can I see her?"

Instead of answering my question, the doctor said he'd get me a blanket.

He left for a minute—or an hour, or a week—and came back with one. As he helped me put it around my shoulders, he said, "I found a quieter place you can wait. Would you like that?"

I nodded, so Dr. Hallam led me back the way the nurse and I had come to a small room near the ambulance entrance. As we walked past the doors, for some reason it seemed important to me to look to see if his car was still there, but it wasn't. The small room had a desk and a couple of chairs in it. Dr. Hallam moved the chairs so they were side by side and helped me wrap the blanket around myself so more of me was covered. It was a hot June night, but I was still shivering. I sat down, and the doctor sat beside me, and as he told me for the hundredth or so time everything would be all right, he laid his hand on my shoulder.

Aside from a few handshakes, the doctor'd never touched me before. I'd pegged him from the first as not a touchy kind of man. But he rested his hand on my shoulder for the whole time we sat in that room, which like everything else that night was some indeterminable amount of time. An orderly stuck his head in once to ask if we wanted coffee. I said no, but the doctor said yes, with cream and sugar. When the coffee came, he made me drink it.

Eventually a nurse came to the door and said if I wanted to, I could see my mother. I jumped up so fast I got dizzy. I was all right again in a minute, but Dr. Hallam took my arm on one side and the nurse on the other, and they walked me together to a long room with six beds. Only two of the beds had people in them, the one nearest the door and the one farthest from it. My mother's bed was the far one, and had screens set up around it.

I knew as soon as I saw her that my mother was going to die. The doctors had done what they could for her, but now they were letting her go. That's why they brought me to her. They were letting her go. Strangely, I wasn't angry about this. There was a chair near the bed, and I sat on it. Dr. Hallam and the nurse stepped away to talk. I couldn't hear what they said. While they were gone, I moved my chair close enough to the bed that I could reach my mother's hand and take it. It was cold, and from time to time it gripped mine feebly. Each time she clutched at me, I told Ma I was there and wouldn't leave her. The doctor came back with a chair for himself and sat close beside me again. This time, he put his arm around my shoulders.

Ma's face was dark—blackish—when I first sat down, but as time passed—hours of time, I think—it turned pale. Her hand relaxed. At one point I sat forward and rubbed it between both of mine, repeating that I was with her, but I could see she didn't hear me. When I sat back, the doctor put his arm around me again. I turned toward him and rested my head against his shoulder. I didn't cry or feel like crying. I was numb.

Ma's slow, shallow breaths stopped. I jerked away from the doctor and shook her hand hard. I think I called to her. She started breathing again. I did that twice, but then the third time I didn't do more than squeeze Ma's hand a little tighter in mine. She gasped and took another few breaths, and then her face changed in some way I can't describe. Her body seemed to sink into the bed. Ma didn't look like herself anymore. The hand I let go of was a stranger's.

The nurse came—a different one from before. Dr. Hallam had probably called her, but I didn't hear him. The nurse didn't do any of the things I thought nurses did when someone died. She didn't check to see if Ma had a pulse, or pull the sheet over her face. She came in and looked and then left again. As Dr. Hallam was leading me away, we passed the nurse and a man who was maybe a doctor returning to Ma's bed. The patient from the bed near the door was gone, and the bed had been stripped. It was day now, late morning; sun streamed in from the windows.

Dr. Hallam took me to a nurse's station, where at a word from him, one of the nurses found me a place to sit and offered me water. I said I wasn't thirsty, but she brought me water anyway, and I drank it. I watched the doctor as he went here and there and talked to this person and that, including a policeman who was carrying what appeared to be the fruit jar Ma'd taken her last drink from. I wondered how he'd gotten it. As far as I knew, the doctor and I left the jar sitting on the apartment's bathroom floor.

Another man, this one in the white coat that identified him positively as a doctor, came toward me with papers in his hand. Dr. Hallam stopped him, and the two of them talked for a minute. In the midst of their talking I heard Dr. Hallam say, very clearly, "My goddaughter." As soon as he said this, the other doctor gave the papers to him, and Dr. Hallam read and then signed them.

A few minutes afterward, he came and took my arm to help me up. The same nurse who'd brought me water took my other arm, and once I was steady on my feet, she walked with the doctor and me to a side door and unlocked it so we could get out. I thought she would want the blanket I was wearing back, but she didn't ask for it. Dr. Hallam's car had been parked not far away, and his car keys left on the seat. The doctor helped me in, and we started for home.

As we pulled away from the hospital, he told me quietly, "I called

Fran. She's going to stay with us for a few days to help out."

Mechanically, I said, "I'm all right."

"I'm sure you are," Dr. Hallam agreed. "But please do us the favor of letting us help you if we can. I know you'd want to help us, if our situations were reversed."

I understood what he was saying, and he was right. I would have wanted to help the doctor, or Francie, or anybody who needed help. It was just that there was nothing anybody could do for me.

I said as much, but Dr. Hallam asked me to let them try.

He parked the car in front of his house instead of going up the drive to the garage, and walked me to the front door the same way he had at the hospital, holding my arm. The door was unlocked, but as we entered, he rang the bell—probably to let Francie know we'd arrived. She came running from the back of the house to meet us, wearing my apron and drying her hands on a dishtowel. I guessed she had been cleaning up the food I'd left spread all over the kitchen table that I'd been going to make into beef hash. Francie didn't say anything—or maybe she did, and I didn't hear her. All I know for sure is that when she got to me, she put her arms around me and held on tight. I closed my eyes and tried to pretend for a minute it was my mother who was hugging me, but Ma had never been a hugger, so it didn't work.

"How about something to eat?" Francie asked when she finally let me go. "You two hungry?"

The doctor didn't answer. I said I wasn't.

"How about a bath, then?"

I almost agreed before I remembered the state we'd left the apartment's bathroom in. I looked toward the garage and shuddered, then shook my head no.

Francie carried right on as if I'd said yes. "We're going to put you in the guest bedroom, all right?" she said, leading me toward the stairs. "It's got its own bathroom, so you won't have to share." Aside to Dr. Hallam, she added, "Help Thea with that blanket, okay, Dr. Hal? I'm afraid she'll trip on the stairs."

The two of them got me upstairs to the guest room, where I stood like a stone with Dr. Hallam's hand on my shoulder while Francie bustled around getting a bath running and bringing me a pair of her own pajamas to put on when I got out.

"I made it a good, hot one," she said, taking me from the doctor and guiding me toward the tub. "Have a nice, long soak, and then come down and we'll all have lunch. I'll rustle up a dressing-gown for you and leave it on the bed, okay?"

I sat in the bathtub without remembering to wash for the first ten minutes or so. Then I let myself slide all the way down under the water, and pretended for a minute I was miserable enough to let myself drown. I sat up again because I wasn't. I didn't feel happy, but I didn't feel miserable, either. I felt nothing. I washed myself all over, including my hair, and then I got out and dried myself. Dr. Hallam's bath-towels were twice the size of Ma's and mine, and twice as thick. His laundry service scented them with lavender. I put on Francie's pajamas and combed my hair back.

In the bedroom, a dressing-gown Francie'd gotten from the apartment was waiting for me, as she'd promised it would be. But it was the wrong one. The system my mother and I had for clothes was that when Ma got a new thing, her old one became mine. The dressing-gown Francie'd brought down was too new. It wasn't mine; it was Ma's. I walked to the bed without knowing I was doing it, sat down, and put the dressing-gown up to my face.

It smelled like my mother.

Until that moment, I hadn't cried a single tear. Now I cried and couldn't stop. Whether Francie heard me from the kitchen or whether she was coming up right then anyway to check on me, I don't know, but a minute later she was there. Sitting beside me on the bed, she held and rocked me while I cried into my mother's dressing-gown. Dr. Hallam came up too and stood in the doorway looking sad. The two of them let me cry without trying to stop me until I finally stopped by myself. At some point they either guessed or I told them what had set me off, and while I was calming down Francie sent the doctor into the spare room to get her own dressing-gown. She held it for me to put on, and then the two of them took me downstairs to the kitchen and gave me soup in a cup to drink.

As soon as I'd swallowed a little, my eyes went shut by themselves, and my head dropped forward. The doctor helped me get upstairs again while Francie went ahead of us and opened the guest-room bed. I fell into it and was asleep before my head was on the pillow. It was one o'clock or so in the afternoon, and I slept until six.

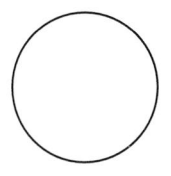

Chapter Twenty-Three

Dr. Hallam and Francie were in the kitchen when I came down again, along with Alice. Francie said Alice had come to cook us dinner.

"Alice does all the cooking around our place," she explained. "I'm hopeless in the kitchen."

I offered to help, but nobody'd let me.

Alice went back to making chicken and dumplings, and Dr. Hallam asked me if I felt up to talking.

"You mean about Ma?"

"Yes. There are some decisions that need to be made. They can wait a few days if you need them to, though. Don't rush."

I said I was all right.

Dr. Hallam studied me like he was trying to decide whether I was or not, and I guess he decided I was, because he went on, "I was able to get in touch with your sister."

"Jane?" I sat up and tried to concentrate better.

"Yes. I thought you'd want her to hear the news as soon as possible."

"Is she all right?"

The doctor smiled. "That was her first question about you, too," he said. "Yes, she and her family are all well. Mrs. Harvey"—Jane's married name was Harvey—"made a suggestion. I told her I'd relay it to you, but we agreed you should have the final say on anything to do with your mother. Would you like to hear what she said?"

Jane's idea was that I should bring Ma's body back to the little town I was born in, and bury her there beside our dad, near Ma's own mother.

I had to think about this for a minute. Ma'd hated that town. She'd never called it anything better than "pokey," and sometimes when she'd been drinking, she'd called it something worse.

But at least that way she'd rest with family, and anyway, the burial ground wasn't in the town proper. "I don't know how to get her there."

"By train is usual," Dr. Hallam said. He said he'd "taken the liberty" of looking into the situation, by which he meant he'd saved me the trouble of looking into anything myself, and Ma—Ma's coffin—could travel in the baggage car of the Dallas train most of the way. "A local mortuary will pick it up at the station in Durant and bring it on from there," he explained.

"How much will it cost?"

"Your sister offered to make the funeral arrangements."

I recognized this as an evasion, but decided on second thought to let the matter go for now. What would be the point of knowing the exact amount of my debt to Dr. Hallam when I was flat broke anyway?

"I'm afraid I'll have to trouble you to come with me when I make the arrangements with the mortuary here," the doctor went on. "I don't have the legal standing to do anything without your authorization."

The "mortuary here" turned out to be the best one in Oklahoma City; the one that buried all the rich people. Ma was leaving the world in the style she'd always wanted to live in.

"Can I go on the same train as she does?"

"You could," the doctor said. "But what if we drive down instead? I think we'll be much more comfortable that way."

"You're coming?" I asked, surprised.

"Of course."

I stayed up long enough to have a few bites of Alice's chicken and dumplings then said I was tired again and went back upstairs to the guest room.

When I got there, I lay down on the bed but didn't sleep. I didn't cry, either. I'd passed the place of tears and fallen into some deeper pit of grief. A weight in my chest made it hard to breathe, and the effort of lifting the weight when I inhaled and letting it down gently again when I exhaled didn't leave me enough energy to cry if I'd wanted to. I'd never spent a day of my life away from Ma. I'd never lived an hour in a world Ma didn't live in, too. She'd made me what I was, which was the exact opposite of herself: responsible, where she was unreliable; active, where she was passive; pragmatic, where she was impractical; relentlessly, insistently realistic, where Ma liked to dream. If I only existed as Ma's inverse, did I exist at all now that she was gone? And if I did exist, how would I manage to live? The path I'd set my heart on walking required, if not help, at least company on the way. Dr. Hallam had gotten me as far as the trailhead, so to speak, but if things worked out the way he wanted them to, he'd soon be leaving me for Chicago.

Anyway, the doctor had a life—and problems—of his own to deal with.

Francie was warm and kind, but I had no claim on her, or Alice, either.

Which left Homer. I loved Homer, and I believed he loved me, but he was an eighteen-year-old male and wanted what every young male wanted, including a home of his own to head and a wife to cater to his needs and whims. Ma's death was the death of a lot of things—most of all my certainty that if my choice came down to a safe life with Homer or a university education, I'd choose the education.

At some point I fell asleep, and when I woke up it was Tuesday.

Dr. Hallam had to work in the morning, but after lunch we went together to arrange to have Ma's body shipped "home"—if she ever thought of the place that way, which I doubted. A woman at the mortuary took down the information the doctor gave her, and later a man asked me if I wanted to see Ma and seemed disappointed when I said I didn't. After that, the doctor went to the hospital to see patients while at home Alice made a late dinner for us. She let me help this time. I still couldn't eat much.

As soon as dinner was over, I packed a suitcase the doctor lent me with clothes Francie brought down from the apartment, but I didn't own a black dress, and Dr. Hallam had sent the one of Ma's I'd ordinarily have borrowed to the mortuary so she could be buried in it. Luckily, Francie had a black dress and black gloves she was willing—she went so far as to say "happy"—to let me wear for the funeral, and Alice lent me a black cloche hat. A cloche was meant to go on over bobbed hair and mine was long, but it was the only black hat we had among the three of us, so I'd have to make it fit somehow. Dr. Hallam packed a suitcase, too, and put a black armband on his coat-sleeve.

Ma's train left the Oklahoma City station at nine fifty-eight that night, and on Wednesday morning, the doctor and I got in his car and started south ourselves.

As we passed the last familiar Oklahoma City landmark, I emerged from the grief-pit a little and suddenly found I had a lot of questions I wanted to ask.

The first one was, "Did you quit taking the newspapers, or just hide them from me?"

Dr. Hallam didn't say anything for so long I knew he must be trying to decide whether to lie or not, so I added, "I'm guessing you hid them."

The doctor cleared his throat. "Prohibition is a political issue, and politicians are prone to exploit anything they think might advance their agenda."

"Which agenda is Ma… Is Ma's…" I didn't want to finish.

"Both," said Dr. Hallam. "Your mother was the victim of a crime. Whether the crime would have been committed if the sale of alcohol were legal is a point of contention." When I didn't answer this, he added, "I'm afraid you'll have to speak to the police at some point."

"Me?"

"I'm afraid so."

I stopped staring out the window and sat up indignantly. "Do they think *I* got her that— that— *stuff*?"

"Good God, no. They just want to know if you have any information that might lead them to the person who did. Several other recent fatalities from methyl alcohol poisoning may be linked to your mother's, which means, essentially, that someone has committed several murders. The authorities would like to know who it is. If you want me to, I'll see to it you're questioned in the presence of an attorney."

I shook my head. "If I show up with a lawyer, the police'll think I'm guilty of something. I'll talk to them. I don't care. I've got nothing to hide."

The doctor looked over at me and smiled.

I went back to staring out of the window for another hour or so.

Ma'd always wanted to make the papers, I thought as I stared, only of course she'd wanted it to be for something nice, like growing roses or writing poetry. Ma'd never actually grown any roses or written any poems that I knew about, but she'd always hinted to me that if she did, her roses and poems would be good enough to land her picture in the newspaper because she'd been born for something special like that. If there was a heaven and Ma had made it there, I hoped it was far enough away from Oklahoma City (likely) that she'd never know she finally *had* made the papers, both the morning and evening editions, for dying from drinking bad hooch.

I didn't realize I was crying until Dr. Hallam nudged me to offer his handkerchief. I shook my head "no," and pulled out my own.

"Who's your goddaughter?" I asked abruptly.

The doctor didn't try to pretend he didn't know what I was talking about. "I'm sorry," he said immediately, talking fast. "That was presumptuous. The signature of an interested party was necessary to release your mother's body to a mortuary. I meant to spare you…that, but of course I should have talked to you first. Please—"

I didn't let him get any farther. "Did you mean me by it?"

"I— Yes."

"Okay. But now you're taking it back?"

"I'm taking back my presumption. If you'll let me."

I started crying again, harder. "Take it back later, then, would you? Telling somebody I was your goddaughter was the nicest thing anybody ever did for me, and I'm not ready to give it up yet."

While I was talking, Dr. Hallam pulled the car over to the side of the road. When he put his hand on my shoulder again like he had at the hospital, I took advantage of it to slide across the front seat and rest my head on his shoulder to cry there. As I've said before, the doctor was very un-touchy, but this time he put his arm all the way around me, and after waving his other hand around for a minute like he didn't know what to do with it, he awkwardly used it to pat my hair. His gestures were kind and comforting but lacked the eagerness of Homer's caresses, which made me feel safe.

I got hold of myself pretty quickly.

"Okay. Finished," I said, wiping my eyes and sliding back away. "I'm sorry." I blew my nose. "I didn't mean to get all weepy on you. I'm all right now. You don't have to pretend to be my godfather anymore."

Dr. Hallam surprised me by saying, "Good, because I'd rather not pretend. I'd rather make it official. May I?"

"What?"

"May I be your godfather? I know there are usually religious formalities associated with taking the position, but maybe we can defer those for now. God and I aren't currently on speaking terms."

I couldn't help but laugh a little. "You don't have to."

"I know that. I'm asking it as a favor."

Lordy, I was crying again. "Okay, but you don't have to," I said—no, sobbed. "I want you to, but you don't have to."

"Godfather it is then," the doctor said.

*

A spur off the highway deposited Dr. Hallam and me on the main street of the town I was born in, directly in front of the slightly nicer of the town's two hotels. I had an impression the town had grown since I'd last seen it (I only remembered it having one hotel, for instance), but it was still a "pokey little place" by anybody's measure, and I was the opposite of sorry to have left it.

When he saw me hesitate to get out of the car, the doctor asked,

"Do you want me to drive you around before we check in? I could take you to see your old house, if you remember where it was."

I didn't remember, exactly, and I didn't want to see the house anyway. I was fighting a strange feeling that *Ma* was nearby. And if she was anywhere, the likeliest place to find her would surely be her old house.

I shook my head. "Let's just go in," I begged.

As Dr. Hallam was getting our bags out of the back of the car, the hotel door opened and a woman leaned out to call, "Dorrie? Dorrie, honey?"

The name meant nothing to the doctor, and he didn't turn. I did.

A younger, plumper, more cheerful-looking version of my mother was behind us.

As soon as she saw my face and knew for sure it was me, my sister Jane called "Dorrie?" again, ran to me and grabbed me in her arms. "Dorrie!" she said, over and over. "Oh, Dorrie, I am so glad to see you-all!"

My body remembered the hug she gave me, one arm around my back and the other arm holding my head to her shoulder, her own head bent over mine. It was the one I'd been craving for years without knowing it. For a moment, I was seven years old again. "Janie, Janie," I murmured, nestling close.

When Jane released me, I saw the doctor had taken a couple of steps back and was watching us—well, me, mainly—and looking quizzical.

"I forgot you used to call me that," I told Janie, wiping my eyes. I repeated to the doctor, "I forgot she used to call me 'Dorrie.' Here's my sister, Dr. Hallam. I've talked about her."

The doctor put down the bags and came forward, extending his hand when he saw Jane intended to offer hers. Jane wasn't reaching for the doctor's hand, though. She dodged it, in fact, and slipped her arm around him without letting go of me, and gave us simultaneous half-hugs. "We spoke on the telephone, remember, Doctor?" she said warmly. "You seem like family already."

When she planted a kiss on his cheek, I said to myself, mentally grinning, "Welcome to southern Oklahoma, Dr. Hallam."

Finally releasing us, Jane looked me up and down again. "Oh my, just look at you!" she said then. "You're all grown up! Now, have you-all had supper? No? Come right in, then. I was just telling Ida Mae when you pulled up that she should hold back some chicken for you. She'll have it on the table in two shakes."

Unlike the one in Dallas, there were no formalities connected with check-in at this hotel. As we entered the lobby, an elderly man was already shuffling forward with our room keys, and although the doctor insisted on carrying the bags himself, the old man led the way upstairs anyway, to "see you-all get settled in right."

In the years I'd been away, I'd forgotten about the local accent, which was generally more Arkansan than Texan in flavor except for the use of "you-all" instead of "y'all" for both the singular and plural of the second person, which is pure Oklahoman. Five minutes of Jane's company found me right back to saying "you-all" myself, plus a few other things outsiders generally characterize as "colorful." I even slipped and said "ain't" once. I'm not proud of that.

By the time the doctor got back from putting our suitcases in our rooms, Ida Mae had opened up the dining room and was loading a table with cold fried chicken and slaw and apologizing that biscuits and gravy would take time to make. When the doctor and I said we didn't want any biscuits and gravy, she brought us homemade bread and watermelon pickles instead. At sight of the spread, I got a little of my appetite back.

Jane had already eaten, but she sat at the table with us to talk.

I knew he was curious, so as soon as Dr. Hallam sat down, I explained, "I was 'Dorothea' originally. That's why Jane calls me 'Dorrie.' Ma named me after her sister, who died when she was a baby."

Then I asked, "What's the matter?" because Jane's mouth was hanging open.

"Is that what Ma told you? That Aunt Dorrie died when she was a *baby*?"

"Yes, why? What's wrong?"

"What's wrong is that it's not true! Aunt Dorrie didn't die young! She died last year! She and Ma were real close until around the time Dad died, and then they had a big fall-out of some kind that made Ma so mad she up and changed your name over it!"

"*Ma* changed it? She said it was my idea!"

"No such thing," Jane declared. "Now mind, I can't tell you what it was Auntie and Ma fell out about because Auntie would never say, but I'm sure it was Ma's fault. Ma fell out with everybody. Aunt Dorrie was the nicest lady in the world, and everybody loved her."

Ma lied to me about my *name*?

I processed this in silence for some time. We all did.

When Jane could finally talk again, she said, "Now, just in case you-all are wondering, Jim and the kids are coming down from Ardmore tomorrow for the funeral, but I wanted to get here before the service in case there was anything special you wanted done for it. Was Ma's favorite hymn still 'Rise Up, Rise Up,' Dorrie, or should we pick something else?"

I guessed "Jim" must be Jane's husband but had to ask if "the kids" she mentioned were hers.

Janie stared at me. "Of course they are! Who else's would I be talking about?"

"And you live in Ardmore now?"

Seeming confused, Jane asked Dr. Hallam, "Is she all right?" Turning back to me, she said, "Now, honey, you know we live in Ardmore. We've been there for years."

"No, I didn't know. I thought you lived in Pauls Valley. I guess Ma didn't know you moved."

Jane leaned across the table to squeeze my hand. "Of course she knew! I wrote her about it! Jim works in a bank there. Didn't Ma tell you about that?"

I shook my head.

"Well, what about the letters I sent to *you*, then? Didn't you read your birthday letters?"

"I never got any birthday letters."

Jane dropped my hand and fell back in her chair. "Sweet Jesus," she said, and stared at me.

"Did you get the address wrong? I bring in the doctor's mail most days, but I've never seen a letter from you in it."

"I didn't send them to any address," Jane said tightly. "Ma never gave me any address. I sent them General Delivery, and I registered the ones I put money in so I know Ma was picking them up. She didn't let you read them?"

"She showed me Christmas cards from you. They just had your signature on them."

Jane's eyes flashed angrily, making her look more like our mother than ever. "Well, when I *sent* those cards, they had letters and five dollars in them! I sent five dollars at Christmas, and another five to each of you every year for your birthdays. I suspected Ma'd try to get your money away from you, but I never dreamed she'd keep back the letters!" Then she repeated, "Sweet Jesus!" which to a Baptist counts as strong language.

Dr. Hallam said quickly, "I found your telephone number in your mother's purse, Mrs. Harvey. Thea had no idea how to get in touch with you."

It took him a few minutes to calm Janie down, but once he had, Janie told us about how a year after Ma sold the house, she married Jim Harvey, a friend of our brother's, in Pauls Valley, and started having kids.

"Two boys and a girl," she announced proudly. "Frank is ten—we named him for Dad, of course—little Jim is seven, and Sarah's four. Big Sarah's my ma-in-law. She's a fine woman; nothing like Ma!"

While the doctor and I finished eating, Jane talked about other relatives I'd forgotten I ever had, as well as a few I did remember who Ma had only mentioned over the years to remind me how badly they'd treated "us," by which she meant her. It must have been a boring conversation for the doctor to listen to, but he was very nice about it.

"Oh, lordy, just look at the time!" Jane said finally, glancing at the clock on the dining room wall. "Time to let you-all get to bed. Don't get up early, Dor—" Jane had evidently noticed Dr. Hallam always called me Thea, because she corrected herself. "*Thea*, I mean. The service isn't until eleven, and I know you-all are tired." As I stood up, my sister came around the table to hug me again. "Oh, honey," she sighed, her cheek resting against the top of my head. I was as tall as Jane now, so I had to bend my knees to make the posture work. "I missed you so much! Ma said you didn't miss me, but she was lying again, wasn't she?

Please say she was lying! You did miss me sometimes, didn't you?"

As I had the first time, I melted into my sister's hug. "I missed you a lot, every day," I murmured, choking on tears. "Ma said *you* were the one who didn't miss *me*."

Jane cried when I said this. So did Ida Mae, who'd listened to our whole conversation without even trying to pretend she wasn't.

"Well, I just wish one of us had known enough to tell Ma to go straight to—"

Being a good Baptist (or as she'd have pronounced it, "Babdis"), my sister didn't finish this sentence.

I didn't lie awake long after I got into my bed at the hotel. I was so tired even the lumpy mattress couldn't keep me from falling asleep. But I did a lot of thinking in the quarter hour or so it took me to doze off, and every thought was unflattering to Ma's memory. The fact that she'd stolen money Janie'd meant for me didn't surprise me, but Ma'd stolen people and memories from me, too, and that made me angry. She'd even stolen my name.

I didn't cry myself to sleep like I had every other night since Ma'd died, but if I had, I wouldn't have been crying for my mother. I'd have been crying for me.

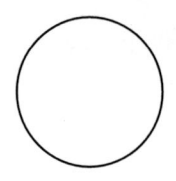

Chapter Twenty-Four

The church where Ma's funeral was held was far from full, but as the principal mourners, my sister Jane and I were required to sit in a front pew and be stared at, while Dr. Hallam and Jim got to be farther back. One of the church ladies tried to put Jane's children into the front pew with us, since Ma was their grandmother, but some other church ladies took her aside, and after they all whispered together for a minute, the first lady took the kids down to the basement to play instead. A card identified a large arrangement of yellow roses I knew nothing about as being from me. I was touched that Dr. Hallam remembered my mother loved yellow roses.

The preacher was the one from my childhood, now very old. He described Ma as "God-fearing," which was probably true, and a devoted mother, which, depending on how you define "devoted," probably wasn't. There was no choir, and the piano was out of tune.

By tradition, at the end of the service everybody filed slowly past Ma's coffin, with Jane and me walking last in the line. The Spanish Flu had thankfully put an end to the custom of kissing the corpse even in southern Oklahoma, but people still expected Jane and me, as Ma's daughters, to linger beside her a minute. Jane didn't, but I did. Since arriving in the town, I'd seemed to hear

Ma's voice and sense her presence all around me, in every building she'd hated and every dusty street she'd scorned, but the figure in the coffin was only a mute effigy. The high-class Oklahoma City mortuary had done a good job; the effigy's face showed no sign of what Ma'd been through. She looked the way she'd have wanted to look, in fact, which was just how I wanted to remember her. I stared until I memorized the serene, dignified version of my mother that lay in the coffin, then stepped away, and Dr. Hallam came to stand with me while I watched as the lid was closed and screwed down. Jane had already left the church.

When my father was buried, his body was carried the mile to the cemetery in a mule-drawn wagon and his mourners walked, but times had changed, and we rode in cars behind a motor hearse instead. The service at the graveside was short. Since most of Ma's mourners were old, Dr. Hallam had been drafted as a pallbearer, and after the Lord's Prayer had been duly recited, he and the other pallbearers lowered her coffin, my roses atop it, into the ground. After Janie and I each dropped in the customary handful of earth, the preacher stepped forward again to issue a general call for sinners to repent, led us in a straggling chorus of "Blessed Redeemer," and then everybody turned—likely with relief—and headed for the cemetery gates.

My sister and I stopped for a minute at Dad's grave. "I really hoped Tommy would come," she said sadly, staring at the headstone.

"I hoped he would, too. He was always Ma's favorite."

"That was like being a mosquito's favorite," Jane snorted. "Made him likely to be sucked dry. Truth to tell, I'm a little worried about Tom. I think he might have inherited Ma's weakness."

"For liquor, you mean?"

Jane nodded. "You take my advice and stay away from that stuff, honey. It's the devil's invention. Well, time we got ourselves over to the lunch, I guess. Nobody can eat until we come, and the kids must be starved by now."

The funeral lunch was held at the home of a former neighbor, two doors down from the house where I was born, which had been painted and added onto so much I couldn't recognize it. I didn't recollect that Ma and the neighbor had been close, but she was good friends with Janie. I sat at a long table with my sister's family and Dr. Hallam and twenty people I didn't know and tried to eat while I watched with a degree of jealousy I'm ashamed to confess as Jane mothered her brood. She was everything a mother—a parent—ought to be: loving, patient, and happy with herself and her world. Until I was seven, my sister had been more of a mother to me than my own was, and I remembered that back then I'd prayed to God every day to make Jane my mother for real. In some ways, I'd never stopped wanting that. Poor Ma could never compete.

After we ate, Jane and I sat in the house's porch swing and talked. Jane spent two hours or so telling me all about her life, and Jim's, and her kids'—especially her kids'—and I had about five minute's worth of news about myself to report.

"I graduated from high school this year," I ventured.

Jane said she wasn't a bit surprised to hear this. "You were always the smartest little girl in the world!" she exclaimed. "I told Doctor the first time we talked on the telephone that he just wouldn't believe what a bright little thing my sister always was. Do you know what he said to me? He said, 'I'd believe it.' Wasn't that nice?"

"He's always nice. I think I might go to college, too."

Jane reacted to this revelation with a "Gracious me!" that recalled our mother. "Well, you know it used to be kind of rough out in

Weatherford," she said, "but I hear it's gotten to be a real nice little town."

She assumed I meant the two-year state teacher's college in Weatherford. I didn't bother to correct her.

I'd begun to realize that aside from a few years' shared memories, my sister and I didn't have much in common. Maybe we could make new memories together. I hoped we could. But for the time being our lives were so different that even the thought of attempting to bridge the gap between us made me tired.

When she saw I had nothing more to say, Jane resumed telling me cute stories about her children, while I watched out of the corner of my eye where, ten feet away, Dr. Hallam and Jim were sitting with coats off, vests unbuttoned, and feet comfortably elevated on a stump, drinking something that was almost certainly moonshine.

Eventually, Jane's children came back tired from playing and climbed wearily onto the swing to sit with us, and shortly afterward Jane said it was time they started for home.

"We need to get to Ardmore before dark," she told me, getting up. "One of the headlamps in the Essex is about out of kerosene."

My sister and I cried as we said our goodbyes—the only time either of us cried all day. Jane had never had any tears for Ma, I think, and I was about cried out of mine. At parting, Jim told me not to be a stranger, and Frank and little Jimmy kissed me and remembered to call me "Aunt Thea." Little Sarah was already asleep on her father's shoulder.

"Come see us soon, now," Jane called from the car window. "You too, Doctor. You-all are family now, and the latchstring's always out for family at our house."

I believed my sister about the latchstring. I wasn't quite as confident that the time together she and I had lost could be made up enough for us to truly be "family" again.

*

Next morning, as we pulled onto the highway, Dr. Hallam asked me how I was feeling.

I said I was okay. "Better than you, maybe. How's your head?"

It took him a minute to get what I meant. "Oh, that… Well, I didn't have much." He smiled. "I wouldn't have minded having a shot or two more, in fact. It reminded me of grappa."

"It's the devil's invention, you know."

"All my favorite things are. But you're all right, you said?"

"I'm fine. A little mad, maybe."

"I think anger is appropriate. I'm angry, too."

I thought he'd misunderstood. "I meant at my ma," I clarified.

"So did I."

"You're angry at my mother?"

"Very angry. She took advantage of you."

I didn't think I should agree with this, given that Ma was hardly cold. "I'm sad too, though," I said quickly.

"That is also appropriate. I wish I'd intervened more. I should have."

"No, you shouldn't. If you had, Ma'd have packed us up and moved us."

"That's what I was always afraid of."

We drove without talking for a while, and then Dr. Hallam said, "There's something in the glove box for you. It came the day before we left, but I didn't think you were ready to see it then."

The "something" was an envelope, and the return address on it was the University of Illinois at Urbana.

Inside was a single-sheet letter.

"It's a 'no,'" I said, crumpling it.

"That's fine. Illinois was something of a long shot anyway," the doctor answered calmly.

"It was a no-shot, you mean," I retorted. The weight in my chest was back, even though I would have sworn I hadn't wanted to go to the University of Illinois anyhow. "I could never have gotten in there. I would've needed at least a seven hundred to even be considered."

"Rejection always hurts," the doctor said. "But you're jumping to a conclusion. This has nothing at all to do with your College Board score. Illinois is a state school. They're mandated to admit Illinois state residents preferentially. They simply met their enrollment quota before they got to your application, that's all."

I said "Ha!" Not very respectful, I know.

"You should ask me how I know this," Dr. Hallam nudged, like I was his student again.

"Fine," I grumped. "How do you— No, come to think of it, I *shouldn't* ask you how you know because I don't care how you know. I'm going to Stillwater, remember?"

"You aren't curious?"

Okay, I was.

"Go ahead," I sighed. "Tell me."

"I know you weren't rejected on the basis of your College Board scores because you haven't gotten your College Board scores yet. I called Fran this morning. They still haven't arrived at the house. Since the College Board releases scores to the test-takers and their preferred schools simultaneously, if you don't have your scores, the University of Illinois doesn't have them either. Therefore, you could not have been rejected on the basis of a low score. All right?"

"All right," I conceded. "Okay. I feel better."

"Good. Part of my job as a doctor is to make people feel better if I can." Then he said, as he always did when I mentioned Stillwater, "I hope you'll wait to make a final decision until you see what Chicago says." This time, he also added, "Please?"

Since it meant so much to him, and since Dr. Hallam was the reason I was going to college at all, I agreed to wait.

*

Francie wasn't staying at Dr. Hallam's anymore, but I slept in his house the night we came home anyway, partly because I couldn't face the apartment yet and partly because I'd told the doctor he should go ahead and risk gossip about him and Mr. Dennis, so I didn't feel like I could do anything that made it look like I was worried about gossip myself.

The next day was Saturday, and although the doctor usually had Saturdays off, he went to work to make up for a day he'd taken off because of Ma. He was gone by the time I got up but left a stack of letters addressed to me on the kitchen table where I'd see them. Three were from old teachers, including Mr. Mack; two were from neighbors; and one was from the Escoes.

I opened that one first.

On one side of a correspondence card, Mrs. Escoe had expressed her "deepest condolences" in the usual set phrases and signed it, "Sincerely yours, Mr. and Mrs. Virgil Escoe." Under that, Homer and Meggie had signed their own names, but not added any condolences of their own.

I sorted through the stack again. There was no separate note from Homer.

I told myself boys never liked writing letters, and especially not sympathy letters. Once he could figure I was home, Homer would probably telephone. In fact, since tomorrow was Sunday, he might even just show up as usual to take me driving. I'd throw myself on his chest and he'd comfort me. I was relieved to think that from now on I could pretend to Homer that my ma'd been normal and not have to tell him any of the bad things about her.

Of the other letters, Mr. Mack's was the nicest. He wrote that he'd always remember my funny speech, and that if life was fair, nothing but good things would ever happen to people like me. The other teachers (literature and biology) just said they were sorry.

After I read the letters, I looked for the morning paper, but it was missing. I guessed Dr. Hallam had taken it with him to work. I cleaned the doctor's house the way Ma'd been hired to do but hardly ever did, then made a pot of the tomato soup he liked and put it in the icebox to warm up later for his dinner. After that I called in an order to the grocery for lamb chops and green peas to be delivered to make up the rest of the meal.

The afternoon edition of the paper arrived before the doctor got home. There was nothing in it about what had happened to Ma, but I could easily guess that a letter to the editor expressing the view that people who drank bootleg and died only got what they deserved was in reference to it. Feeling sick, I stopped reading and refolded the paper carefully to put back on the front porch for the doctor to find. Since he was obviously trying to protect my feelings, I felt the only decent thing for me to do was to allow him to think he'd been successful. Then, since my mood was already rotten, I decided I might as well stop stalling and get on up to the apartment and clean it fit to be lived in again. I wondered whether the police just took the fruit jar Dr. Hallam and I left in plain sight on the bathroom floor, or if they searched the place. I'd heard when the police did a search, they generally left a mess. As I'd told the doctor, I didn't have anything to hide, but judging by all the surprising things Janie'd told me, I couldn't be entirely certain Ma hadn't. With dread in my heart and a mop and bucket in my hand, I unlocked the apartment door and stepped in.

Stepped in—and stepped straight back out again, looking around myself in confusion.

The first thing I thought was that in a daze—I'd spent most of the last week in and out of one—I'd wandered past Dr. Hallam's garage to the neighbor's and opened the wrong apartment door. Then I remembered the neighbors didn't have a garage apartment, so I cautiously stuck my head back in to have another look around.

It was Ma's and my apartment, all right. Or at least it was the twin of ours in size and shape and placement of windows and doors. But it smelled of new paint, and the walls were creamy white instead of olive. In place of the old brown roller shades, the windows were hung with pink-and-green curtains. Not olive green, either, but a prettier shade, like a spring leaf. The bed was brand new. Smaller than the one Ma and I shared, it had a wooden head and footboard in the latest "Moorish" fashion instead of chipped, painted iron, and a rose-colored bedspread with green trim. There was a Moorish-style dresser, too, with my Kewpie atop it, her fat cheeks a perfect match for the curtains. Under the window, where the light was good, was a darling little painted desk, and a proper bracket on the wall held my mother's fancy clock. For a long time, I'd hated that clock. I discovered I loved it now. The bathroom was green with white trim, and instead of Ma's and my old thin ones, there were new towels on the rack that were like the doctor's—big and soft with fancy knotted fringes. A long mirror hung on the back of the door, and a potted begonia sat on the windowsill.

I hadn't cried for my ma for two days, but lordy, how I cried over that apartment! It was the room of my own I'd always dreamed of, only better.

*

When Dr. Hallam came home, he sat in the kitchen while I cooked dinner and talked with me about how I should spend my summer. The doctor's idea for it was that a lovely apartment of my own, access to his house at any time, and an "allowance" from him to buy whatever I needed came free with being his goddaughter. A daily cook-housekeeper would do all his housekeeping—mine, too, if I wanted—and cook all the meals, which I would eat with him in the dining room.

My idea was that I'd take over my mother's job.

"Where I come from, all anybody does for a goddaughter is to give her a cup when she's born and a Testament when she joins a church. If you won't let me work for you, I'll get a job somewhere else. I'm not going to sit around for a whole summer and live off you."

"Really? That's all?" the doctor asked, seeming genuinely interested. "My godparents gave me a stock portfolio. As for 'sitting around for a whole summer'—well, why not? Leisure would certainly make a change for you. Or you could study. You *should* study, in fact. During Freshman Week, you'll take placement exams, and if you don't score high enough in any required subject, you'll have to make up the deficiency by taking elementary level courses that won't count toward graduation. I know you're worried about your French, and your Latin could probably use work. I've been asking around. There are other native French speakers in town. Let's get you another tutor."

"I can study and keep your house, too. I've been doing it for years."

I didn't add that since he was pretty certain to move back to Chicago, I was afraid to get used to a better style of life than I'd have once he was gone.

We went back and forth for a while until I happened to use the word "dignity" (as in "leave me my dignity, dammit!"—my first post-Ma swear), which made the doctor immediately relent. He agreed to hire me as his cook-housekeeper at the same rate he'd paid Ma, less the part he'd paid to me. I insisted on that point. The one thing Dr. Hallam wouldn't bend on was that I had to eat at the dining table with him, beginning five minutes after we reached our agreement, because the lamb chops were done. We shook hands on the deal, and he carried in the soup.

At the end of the meal, I asked the doctor if it'd be all right if I was gone for most of the next day, without letting on I expected to be out driving with Homer.

"Of course not," he said. "I'll be at work anyway. Enjoy yourself."

*

But Homer didn't come to take me driving, and he didn't call me, either.

I didn't want to believe a name scribbled on the bottom of a letter written by his mother was the last I was ever going to hear from someone who'd claimed to love me, so I decided not to give up on Homer until Monday's mail delivery—changing that on second thought to Tuesday's, in case he'd waited for the weekend to write. As a working man, it would be reasonable for Homer to take care of his personal business on the weekends, and it could easily take two days for even an in-town letter to arrive. I spent most of the day reading the doctor's French version of *Les Misérables* aloud to brush up my accent.

On Monday, I didn't get a letter from Homer, but in the afternoon Dr. Hallam telephoned from work to tell me the police wanted me to come down to the station to be interviewed.

"I'll take you this evening, unless you'd rather go with Fran. She offered."

I said I'd rather have him, which seemed to please the doctor.

Walking into the police station, I was so scared my teeth chattered, but the interview itself turned out to be nothing. Everybody I spoke to was kind and respectful. I'd been dreading having to talk about the night Ma died, but the police didn't want to know about it, so I didn't have to. All the police wanted to know was where my mother'd gotten the stuff that killed her, and I didn't have any idea about that. I was pretty sure it wasn't the shady dry cleaner. He'd sold Ma plenty, but nothing that had ever made her sick. I mentioned him anyway, just to get him back for making it so easy for her to get cheap hooch by the jigger. Judging by the reaction of the officer questioning me, the police already knew about the dry cleaner.

Afterward, Dr. Hallam took me out to eat. We went to a place near the stockyards reputed to have very good beef—which it did, but it also reeked of the stockyards. Being from Chicago, the doctor probably didn't notice it.

I'd found out a few things from the police. "I guess what happened was in all the papers," I said midway through the meal, meanwhile rearranging the string beans on my plate with my fork. "What happened to Ma, I mean."

"There was some press coverage."

I nodded. "They told her name and her. . . job, and so forth."

"Neither your mother's name nor the work she did is any cause for shame, Thea."

"What about my name? Did they print my name?"

"Absolutely not," the doctor said firmly.

I wondered if he'd somehow seen to that.

"Still," I continued, "anybody who knows my mother just died could figure out she was the 'Mrs. Frank Carter' who was a cook-housekeeper who drank herself to death at an address in your neighborhood. I can't blame anybody for not wanting to have anything to do with me after that." By "anybody," I meant Homer, of course.

I wasn't hungry, but until I said this, Dr. Hallam had seemed to be enjoying his meal. Now his fork went down with a bang. "Because to be a constant friend to someone in difficulties would reflect badly on them?"

The way he spoke made me look up. The doctor was scowling at me. I'd never seen him scowl before.

Startled, I said, "No, just— Oh, you know what I mean!"

"I don't. Explain it to me."

I knew any explanation I gave might only make the situation worse, but stupidly, I explained anyway. "Well, because having a mother like Ma sort of makes me look bad, too," I said nervously. "I mean, she raised me and all."

"I see. Just as having a son like me makes my parents look bad. It's interesting you should say that, because until now I was under the impression you felt it was wrong of them to disown me."

Well, I'd walked straight into that one.

I'd have claimed he'd misunderstood me, except we both knew he hadn't. I'd said exactly what Dr. Hallam was accusing me of saying.

I couldn't take it back, so instead, I apologized. Humbly. "It *was* wrong of them. It was completely wrong of them. I'm sorry I said what I did. I'm just feeling sorry for myself."

Even before all the words were out of my mouth, the doctor stopped scowling.

"I just—miss Ma," I confessed, beginning to mess glumly with my beans again. "I know she was kind of terrible in some ways, but I can't help it. I loved her, and I miss her."

The doctor surprised me by saying, "I miss my mother, too."

"You do?"

"Oh, yes. Quite sharply, at times. Mine's 'kind of terrible in some ways' too, but she's still my mother. No birthday goes by—hers, or mine—that I don't think of her. No Christmas." He picked up his fork again. "It's gotten easier over time. It'll get easier for you too, I promise."

"What about your dad? Do you miss him?"

Dr. Hallam answered this with a shrug that said he either didn't or didn't want to talk about it.

"Okay. And you miss Mr. Dennis, too. Did you apologize to him yet?"

Down went the fork again. "Thea…"

"All I mean is that if you have words with somebody, it's good manners to apologize after."

"There would be no point." The doctor stared at his plate. "I know Dennis. I'm sure he's moved on by now."

*

I didn't get a letter from Homer on Tuesday, either.

Dr. Hallam got one, though (not from Homer, of course). He came home from work almost dancing with it in his hand.

"I got it," he exulted. "I got the job."

For a minute, I didn't know how to feel—happy for the doctor or unhappy for me. "At Cook County? Congratulations."

"Thank you. Here: Here's the offer. Have a look."

I did and said, "Lordy," when I got to the place where the letter stated what the doctor's salary would be.

"Don't feel shy about buying yourself whatever you want," the doctor told me dryly. He looked around the kitchen. "This room needs repainting. How long do you think it will take to sell this house? The job doesn't start until October. Will that be enough time?"

Numbly, I said, "Well, the apartment doesn't need any work, anyway. That'll save you some trouble." I tried not to sound sad, but the fact was I'd miss my pretty little room. A lot.

Dr. Hallam turned around so fast I almost didn't have time to get a big congratulatory smile back on my face before he looked at me.

"I hope I didn't do the wrong thing by waiting to tell you," he said quickly. "I thought it would be better to wait to mention making a move until it was certain. You've had so much on your mind."

I assured him he'd done the right thing. "It's not like I didn't guess anyhow."

"I take it your letter still hasn't arrived?" the doctor asked.

I shook my head.

"All right. Maybe tomorrow."

"Tomorrow for sure," I agreed.

Dr. Hallam was talking about my College Board scores. I was talking about Homer.

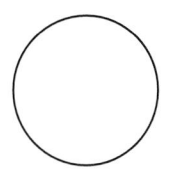

Chapter Twenty-Five

On Thursday, the mailman delivered an extra-big stack of mail that did not include any letter from Homer but did include my College Board scores. I stood in the open front doorway of Dr. Hallam's house staring at the envelope for three or four minutes before I could make my shaking legs work well enough to carry me back inside and my trembling hands close the door behind me.

I put the doctor's mail on his desk where it belonged, laid my College Board scores—unopened—on the kitchen table, walked out the kitchen door and up to my apartment, and lay down on my bed.

Nobody'd ever told me a broken heart could feel like cold fury. After staring at the ceiling for ten minutes, rage steadily building, I got up again. My autograph album lay on my desk. I went to it and moved the rose I'd pressed on Homer's page to the one the doctor'd signed. Then I took the Kewpie off my dresser, went outside, and chucked it as hard as I could into the next-door neighbor's garden. The neighbors had a little girl I'd minded a few times—bratty in some ways, especially to "the help," but mostly cute—who I figured would love to have a Kewpie. I'd have thrown the lavaliere, too, but if Homer did the decent thing and sent me back the pen and handkerchiefs I'd given him, I'd owe him the necklace in return.

The Kewpie disposed of, I headed out for a walk.

There was a lot I needed to figure out, but two things were already clear to me. The first was that whatever had been between Homer and me was now over. My mother's ugly death had either destroyed his love for me or his parents' tolerance for our relationship. I didn't care which, since a man would need both stronger affections and a stronger character for me to respect him anyway. The second thing I knew was how much I'd counted on Homer's desire to marry me to be my safety net if for some reason college didn't work out.

Well, college hadn't worked out. Not the way I'd planned it, anyway. Not only was my safety net gone, but there was no way I could stomach going to a school where I'd run into Homer every day. My safety net had failed me, the doctor was leaving, and my kin were virtual strangers. If I still intended to get to college—and I absolutely still did—I needed a new plan.

I thought it was possible that I could still get myself admitted for the fall term at the state college in Norman, but the deadline to apply for a scholarship there had passed. I did some mental calculations and reckoned I could save enough money over the summer to get me through the first semester, but at the end of it I'd have to leave, broke and with no documented job experience beyond part of a summer of delivering groceries. I was afraid leaving mid-year might count against me later when I tried for readmittance and a scholarship, too.

An alternative plan would be for me to rely on my high school diploma to get me a well-enough paying job that if I worked at it for a year or two and lived frugally—I knew how to live frugally—I could save enough to pay for a full four years at Norman, assuming that while I was in college, I also worked summers. I knew most people who tried to do that never went back to college. They got to like their jobs (or at least their salaries), or fell in love and got married and had babies. But I wouldn't be like that. I wouldn't. I'd save up, and I'd go back.

The only other potential plans I could come up with required night work (hard to get and dangerous for a girl), an unusually understanding daytime employer, or a moderately-sized miracle to work, so I decided to start looking for a job. I won't deny I cried a little inside when I thought of having to wait a year or more to start college, but not many tears made it all the way to my cheeks. A college degree would still be mine one day. It was only a matter of waiting longer than I'd planned on to get it.

I cried over Homer, too. I loved him.

I didn't get back to the house until Dr. Hallam had been home for half an hour. When I walked in, he was coming down the stairs.

He greeted me cheerfully. "Well, what about it?" he asked, smiling. "Was today finally the day?"

"Yes."

One look at my face and the doctor's expression changed instantly from happy to grim. "I don't believe it," he said flatly, stopping where he was and staring at me. "Good God. All right. These things happen. May I see?"

I gestured mutely toward the kitchen.

"In there? Fine. Let's go have a look." The doctor kept repeating, "Everything's fine," as he walked me to the kitchen door and gently guided me through it. "A single exam means nothing. It's insignificant."

He sat down at the table and pulled out the chair next to him for me. Once I was sitting too, Dr. Hallam picked up the College Board envelope, turned it over—and stared at it blankly.

"It hasn't been opened," he said, pointing at the flap.

"No."

"*No?*"

"I couldn't."

The doctor rested his elbows on the table and his head in both hands, and laughed for five straight minutes.

"Thea, you scared the— the *life* out of me," he finally managed to gasp, still laughing. "I thought either I'd gone crazy, or the College Board had." He offered me the envelope. "Will you please open this, for God's sake? I've been on pins and needles since May."

"I made a plan," I blurted. I was eighteen now, fully grown, so apparently I was never going to grow out of blurting. "I want to tell you my plan first."

The doctor leaned back in his chair. "You made a plan," he repeated, still smiling. "A plan about what? Never mind. Let's just hear it."

"A plan for what I'm going to do next year. I'm a person who always has to have a plan, okay? And my old one didn't work out, so I had to make a new one."

Dr. Hallam fanned himself with the College Board envelope. "I hope the new plan involves opening this," he sighed.

"It does, but my scores are irrelevant. I can't go to Stillwater next year. I don't want to say why, but I can't. And it's too late to get a scholarship anyplace else, so what I'm going to do instead is get a job and save up, and if I can get into Norman next year with a scholarship, I'll do that, but if I can't get a scholarship, I'll keep my job until I've saved up enough for four years, and then I'll go."

"To Norman?" the doctor asked. I'd never mentioned going to Norman before.

"Someplace like Norman, anyway. A state school, where the tuition isn't too high."

Dr. Hallam straightened up. "What about Chicago? Don't tell me they turned you down!" He looked around like he expected to see a letter from Chicago crumpled the way I'd crumpled my letter from Illinois. "Because I spoke to—"

He'd spoken to…whom? I wanted to know, but didn't give him a chance to tell me. "I haven't heard from Chicago," I said quickly. "But that doesn't matter, because I don't think I'll get in there, and even if I did, I can't afford to go."

"I think—"

"Not even with a scholarship. Chicago's expensive."

"That's not—"

"*I can't go*," I repeated firmly. "I need— I need to be safe. I need to do things in a safe way. I'm not a person who can just go out and do things and trust to luck to make them work. I can *make* going to Norman work. *I* can make it work. So that's my plan. Norman."

I guess Dr. Hallam was tired of me interrupting him, because this time he didn't say anything until he was sure I was finished.

When he finally spoke, it was in his kindest "doctor" voice. "That's a very good plan, Thea. You've made a good plan. Very solid."

Getting up, he went on, "I'm not much of a planner, myself. That's what comes of having money, I guess. I could always buy my way out of bad planning. Would you like to have a cup of tea with me? I'd offer coffee, but it seems too late in the day for coffee."

"I'll get it." I started to rise.

"No, no. Let me. I think I remember how. No, wait: Should I fill the kettle first or light the burner? Doesn't a stove need to heat up before you can cook on it?"

"That's just the oven. Fill the kettle first."

"Just the oven. All right."

Neither of us said anything more until the tea was made and in front of us. The doctor remembered to turn off the stove this time.

Sitting down opposite me, he said, "Thea, I think the University of Chicago would challenge you in ways not many colleges could, but I understand if you prefer the safety of familiar surroundings. You've just lost your mother. It stands to reason you're disoriented. A state university is a perfectly reasonable choice in the circumstances, and if that's what you want, that's fine. What is *not* fine is the idea of you putting off your enrollment for a year."

"I have to," I said tightly.

"Not necessarily. You—"

"I *have* to."

The doctor sipped his tea before saying, "You know you're very stubborn, don't you? People must have told you that before."

"I have to be stubborn, too."

"All right, there's something in that." The doctor set his cup down and put his fingertips together. "If I understood you," he said then, "for some reason, you want your College Board scores to be irrelevant. Is that right? Well, as a matter of fact, they *are* irrelevant. Your scores were always irrelevant. It was always my intention pay for your education—the whole of it, not just your tuition. I only suggested you apply for bursaries because I thought being awarded one would bolster your self-confidence."

I studied him for a minute.

"Okay. I think that kind of worked," I admitted. "But I don't have one now because I'm not going to Stillwater, and I can't take your money. It wouldn't be right."

"Why not? I'm your godfather. It's traditional for people to take money from their godfathers. I certainly took plenty from mine. Are you saying that was wrong?"

"No, but yours was your real godfather."

"And I'm your real godfather. I thought we agreed on that. Do you need me to say it officially in a church? Fine. We'll go to church. Mine or yours?"

I couldn't help but laugh. "You'd hate mine."

"I'd hate mine, too." Dr. Hallam picked up his cup again and swirled the dregs of his tea. "Either one would put God to the trouble of adding 'hypocrisy' to His list of my other sins. Thea, you're the closest I will ever come to having a child of my own. Indulge me in this. Let me be a little fatherly."

We talked a while longer—it doesn't matter what we said—until the doctor pointed to the College Board envelope again and asked, smiling, "Now?"

I twisted my hands together. "I can't. You do it."

With aggravating slowness (or maybe it just seemed that way), the doctor got up, got a paring knife from a drawer, and slit open the envelope.

He offered it to me. "Last chance!"

I shook my head.

Dr. Hallam peeked first, looked at me and smiled, peeked again, and then pulled out my score sheet. "Seven hundred and seventy," he announced, turning it for me to see. "According to my source, that rates a full tuition-waiver at Chicago. I think it would probably get you a red carpet and rose petals strewn in your path at Norman, and since no university is ever too full to take an applicant with a score of seven-seventy, we could probably get Illinois to reconsider if you wanted to. The choice is entirely open, Miss Carter. Where would you like to go?"

I was so shocked by what I'd scored it took me more than a minute, I think, to get enough of my breath back to ask, "If I pick Chicago, will you come see me sometimes?"

"I will come see you if you go to the moon," Dr. Hallam said firmly. "Probably more often than you want me to."

"Not possible," I said, smiling now, too. "Chicago, then."

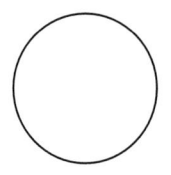

Chapter Twenty-Six

Dr. Hallam teased me later that instead of his money making my College Board scores irrelevant, my College Board scores made his money irrelevant—but he went ahead and spent a bunch of it on me anyway.

After getting me a trunk to take to college, he drafted Francie to help me fill it with everything I might want for the school year. He was winding down his medical practice in preparation for moving to Chicago and didn't need her at the office most days, so Francie had plenty of time to shop.

Having worn my mother's made-over castoffs for most of my life, anything new and picked just for me was all the luxury I needed, and Francie and I put together a modest wardrobe of moderately-priced skirts and blouses and sweaters—sweaters were very "collegiate," Francie informed me—that would give good service. I never wanted to so much as look at my dancing dress again, so I gave it back to Francie, who knew another nurse she said would love to have it. I was going to give her back my graduation dress, too, but on her suggestion we dyed it Nile green, and then both decided it looked so good I should take it with me to wear for "best."

One thing the doctor didn't pay for was my bob. That was Homer's treat.

I waited six weeks, and when a parcel containing a pen and monogrammed handkerchiefs still hadn't shown up at my door, I sold my lavaliere necklace at a second-hand jewelry shop. The jeweler gave me three-fifty for it—exactly half, he said, what it cost new. Three-fifty was just what I needed for a bob (including tip) at a good barber, so that's what I spent it on. It seemed appropriate. Homer'd nagged me to get my hair bobbed the whole time I was "his girl." Cut short, my wavy hair turned so curly both Francie and Alice swore that from the back I was a dead-ringer for Clara Bow. From the front I wasn't as pretty as Clara Bow, but with my hair bobbed I felt like I was just as stylish as she was, and I loved it.

The doctor's house sold quickly, and in the first week of September, movers arrived to undo all the work my mother'd done arranging his furniture and I'd done unpacking his books. Watching the rooms gradually empty didn't make me as sad as I expected it to. The soft furnishings from the garage apartment were boxed separately and shipped to my dorm, while my bed, desk, and dresser went into the moving van.

"My home will always be a home to you, too," Dr. Hallam said, and to my mind, none of the books in his library contained a prettier sentence than that one.

When the movers drove away, the doctor and I took one last look around before locking up the place and leaving it for what was likely to be forever.

After checking all the drawers and closets—twice—the doctor stood at the bottom of the staircase looking silently up toward his old bedroom.

I let him look for a while, then said, "I found the box of Mother's things in the basement. Thank you."

"I didn't know what you'd want, so I saved everything."

I told him I appreciated it without mentioning that, except for Ma's wedding ring and Bible, I'd transferred the contents of the box directly into a barrel that now sat behind the house waiting to be picked up by the rag-and-bone man. Jane had asked for the ring, which I guessed she wanted more for its association with Dad, who'd bought it, than Ma, who'd worn it for forty years; and suggested the Bible go to Tom. The only memento of Ma I wanted was the walnut bracket clock, whose face I had looked at so often growing up that it was inseparable in my mind from my mother's, and almost seemed to resemble it.

"I took your advice and wrote to Dennis," Dr. Hallam said suddenly, breaking in on my memories. "You were right that I owed him an apology. I wish I'd done it months ago."

I pretended to be surprised, but I wasn't. I knew he'd written. I saw the letter in the outgoing mail when I was putting out one to my brother Tom. Mr. Dennis currently lived in a place called "Cicero," it seemed. I didn't know where Cicero was in relation to Chicago, but I hoped it was near.

"Are you ready to go?" the doctor asked.

"I guess I am."

Dr. Hallam's agent in Chicago had called earlier to say he'd found just the house the doctor ought to buy, so he was taking that night's train up to see it. I had a driver's license now, so I drove him to the station. He'd invited Francie to move to Chicago too, saying he didn't expect to ever find a better nurse, but when she said she couldn't because of Alice's job, the doctor gave her the Plymouth as a parting gift. After I dropped him off, I was going to take it to her and spend a last couple of days at her house before heading to Chicago myself.

Francie gave a farewell gift to Dr. Hallam, too: A picture of her and Alice. In the picture, Alice was wearing a wedding gown trimmed with the same lace that was on my graduation dress, with Francie standing where the groom would ordinarily have been, holding Alice's arm. I wondered how I'd missed guessing for so long.

The train was boarding when we arrived at the station, so the doctor and I only had a few minutes to talk.

"When you get to Chicago, I'll pick you up at Union Station and take you straight to the campus," Dr. Hallam told me, over the noise of other people's goodbyes and the conductor shouting for the passengers to board. "That won't give us much time together before you have to check in for Freshman Week, but at the end of it I'll come take you out to dinner and show you the house. How will that be?" Only the freshman class was on campus for Freshman Week, and no family visits were allowed during it as a means of encouraging the new students to get to know each other.

I said I liked the plan, then risked making the doctor uncomfortable by adding that he was the best godfather anybody could ever ask for and I loved him.

Actually, I wasn't risking anything. I knew for certain he'd be uncomfortable.

Although the conductor was becoming insistent, I put my hand on the doctor's arm to stop him from going. "Why don't you write a letter to yourself?" I suggested. "An apology, like you wrote to Mr. Dennis."

"Beg pardon?" he asked, startled.

"I said, *write yourself a letter*. You apologized to Mr. Dennis. Now you need to apologize to yourself for acting like your parents and not appreciating what a good man you are."

Standing directly behind him, the conductor shouted, "'Board!" so loudly the doctor jumped.

"Think about it," I urged. "Okay, I know you have to go, but promise me you'll think about it." I planted a firm, goddaughterly kiss on his cheek. We southern Oklahomans—I'd always be one—did that kind of thing.

The doctor was too surprised by what I'd said to return my kiss or even wish me a last goodbye. He stared at me until the conductor finally used the old trick of snatching his bag from his hand and throwing it into the coach vestibule to get him onto the train. Instinctively, Dr. Hallam followed his bag, which was what the conductor counted on.

*

As he'd promised he would, late the next Sunday afternoon, Dr. Hallam met my train in Chicago.

"Have a good trip up?" he asked, holding my arm and guiding me through the crowd.

"Lordy, how do you stand having so many people around?" I muttered—then remembered I lived in Chicago now, so I'd better start getting used to lots of people myself. "Yes, it was fine. What about the house? Did you buy it?"

"Not yet. I'm waiting until you can see it."

I'd noticed before Dr. Hallam didn't trust his own taste.

"Does it have room for a piano?"

"A what? Oh. I don't know, really. I wasn't thinking of a piano when I looked at it. Is this your only bag?"

"Yes. I shipped everything else to my dorm. Well, any house you buy has to have room in it for a piano, because you're getting one."

"Am I?"

"Yep. No more punishing yourself."

As we emerged from the terminal, I craned my neck to look first one way and then the other.

I saw what I was hoping to see.

Ninety-nine out of every hundred men who insist on wearing their hats on the backs of their heads look terrible that way. Homer Escoe, for example. Dennis Diedrich was an exception. On Dennis Diedrich, a pushed-back hat looked *good*.

We reached the taxi-stand. I fumbled in my purse and pulled out a paper. "Quick," I demanded. "Tell me how to do this."

"Do what?"

"Take a cab in Chicago. How much should I tip?"

"I'll take care of it."

"You can't. You're not coming with me." Pointing, I said, "Mr. Dennis is standing right over there, and you're going to go say hello to him."

Dr. Hallam looked but didn't answer me.

A cab pulled forward, and the cabbie approached us to ask, "Where to?"

Before the doctor could speak, I showed the cabbie my paper. "I want to go to this address. How much will that be, please?"

"This your only bag? Two bucks."

"Thank you."

The doctor tore his eyes away from Dennis and reached for the cab's passenger door. "He's waiting for someone else," he said firmly. "It stands to reason. There's no possible way he could have known I'd be here today."

No way at all.

"Maybe," I acknowledged, "but there's no law that says two people who meet by accident in a train station can't talk to each other. Go on, and I'll see you next Friday, the way we planned." I gave him a shove in Mr. Dennis's direction. "Quick, now, before he gives up and leaves. And tell him hello for me, will you? In fact, give him my love."

"Thea—" Dr. Hallam began.

Then he stopped himself from finishing whatever he'd been about to say, and instead muttered something under his breath that was unintelligible except that it definitely contained the word "hell." Pulling a five-dollar bill out of his pocket, he shoved it into the cabbie's hand. "Get her there safely," he ordered him. "Carry her bag to the dormitory, do whatever else she needs you to do, and keep the change."

Since the "change" would be more than the actual fare, the cabbie's, "Yes, *sir!*" was very enthusiastic. He held the door for me, and then asked as he slid into the front seat himself, "That your dad, Miss?"

"Almost. My godfather."

Other cabs and milling pedestrians blocked us from leaving immediately, so I had time to see Dr. Hallam begin walking, slowly and uncertainly, in Mr. Dennis's direction.

"You a college girl?"

"Yes. First year."

"Yeah, I get lots of college kids in my cab. I guess that means you're real smart, then."

"I hope I am. I'll need to be to graduate."

We pulled away from the curb. The doctor was walking faster, and before traffic blocked my view, I thought I saw Mr. Dennis's right hand already reaching for the doctor's.

As I settled back in my seat, the cabbie caught my eye in the rear-view mirror. "Hey, you want me to drive you in the long way, so you can see more of the school?"

"Oh, I'd love that!" I cried. "But how long will it take? I have to be checked in at my dorm by six o'clock sharp."

"You'll make it," the cabbie assured me. "You got plenty of time."

Time? I had my whole life ahead of me.

"Sure," I agreed. "I've got plenty of time."

By The Same Author

The *Antlands* series:
Book 1: Antlands
Book 2: Annasland
Book 3: Farlands

Historical novels:
Marriage and Hanging

Other writing:
The Complete Raffles (Annotated & Illustrated)

Available now via your local Amazon store

About The Author

Genevieve Morrissey is a passionate student of British and American social history, but through one of those strange little quirks of fate she spends most of her days talking with scientists.

Thea is her second work of historical fiction.

She enjoys reading obscure books, travel, good cooking, and solitude.

Stay up to date with Genevieve and her writing via her web site:

antlands.com

Made in United States
Cleveland, OH
28 April 2025